S is
for
STRANGER

Louise Stone

worked as a teacher before turning her hand to fiction. She was brought up in Africa and the Middle East and then 'as an adult' travelled extensively before moving to London and finally settling in the Cotswolds with her partner, and now baby. When she's not writing, you will find her scouring interior design magazines and shops, striving toward the distant dream of being a domestic goddess or having a glass of wine with country music turned up loud. As a child, she always had her nose in a book and, in particular, Nancy Drew. *S is for Stranger* is her first psychological suspense thriller and it was shortlisted for the Harry Bowling Prize. She also writes women's fiction under the pseudonym Lottie Phillips. Readers can find Louise Stone, otherwise known as Charlotte Phillips, on Twitter @writercharlie or at www.writercharlie.com

LOUISE STONE

S is for STRANGER

CARINA

Carina UK
An imprint of HarperCollinsPublishers
1 London Bridge Street
London SE1 9GF

This paperback edition 2016
1

First published in Great Britain by
Carina an imprint of HarperCollins*Publishers* 2016

A catalogue record for this book is
available from the British Library

ISBN: 9780008205744

Set by CPI - Group(UK) Limited,

Printed and bound in Great Britain by
RR Donnelley

To my wonderful parents.

Fracture for fracture, eye for eye, tooth for tooth.
As he has injured the other, so he is to be injured.

Leviticus *chapter 24: verse 20*

CHAPTER 1

September 2011

I tapped the rim of the table with my right forefinger: one, two, three. Bad things didn't happen when I counted to three.

'Don't you like strawberry?' I asked, twiddling my straw with my other hand. 'You can have mine.' I pushed the chocolate milkshake in her direction and she shook her head. I gave in and took it back. 'So, how's school?'

'OK.'

We had been playing this game for over an hour now: I asked the questions and she offered one-word answers. Licking my lips, I went in for another drag of the sweet, sickly chocolate drink. I turned to look out the window and pulled a face. Milkshakes were not my thing. I had thought it was what all eight-year-old girls liked doing – eating junk food and visiting Claire's jewellery shop.

'You don't like it, do you, Mummy?' Amy asked me and nodded toward the milkshake.

I smiled – caught out. 'Not really. What about you?'

Amy revealed the first small smile of the day. 'No.' She looked down at her lap. 'I don't like milkshakes. Daddy knows I don't like milkshakes.'

'I just thought –'

Amy looked up. 'It's OK, Mummy. You don't live with me so only Daddy knows.'

I felt the familiar stab of guilt. 'Right, yes.' I picked up the menu. 'What would you prefer?' I needed to face it; I was out of touch.

'I'm not hungry. Daddy made me pancakes for breakfast.' She slid down further in her seat. 'When did Daddy say we should go home? To Daddy's home.'

My face fell. 'Um, he said four o'clock.' I looked at my watch, tapped its face three times. I hoped Amy hadn't noticed. 'It's only two-thirty. Do you want to head back?' I said cheerily; too cheerily. I mean, was the day going so badly that my daughter wanted to return home to her father already?

'No…' She fought tears. 'I wish we were a family again, like my friends at school have.'

'I know, but you're no different to anyone else. You know that, right?'

She gave a small nod. 'I guess. My bestest friend said she wanted her parents to split up.'

'Really?' I said, raising my eyebrows.

'Yeah, because she thinks it's nice to get two of everything.' She paused. 'I told her it's not nice.'

I frowned and, desperate to keep her happy, I offered, 'Shall we play I-spy?'

She pulled a face. 'Mummy, you're not very good at this game.'

'Shame.' I shrugged my shoulders and looked away. 'Because I've already come up with one.'

She rolled her eyes. 'Okkaaay.'

I grinned. 'I spy something beginning with B.'

Amy looked behind her, swivelling in her seat. 'Burger?'

I shook my head.

She furrowed her brows. 'Book?'

I shook my head again.

'Are you playing it right?'

I nodded.

She scanned the restaurant another time, spotting a young girl playing with a doll. 'Barbie!'

'Nope.'

She giggled. 'Mummy, are you sure you're playing properly?'

'Uh-huh.' I smiled. 'Shall I tell you?'

'OK.'

'Big nose.'

'Mummy!' She squealed with laughter. 'That's silly.'

'Oh, really?' I played innocent. 'Your turn.'

She giggled. 'OK.' Her eyes flicked around the room and she twisted in her seat, looked behind her, and then she said, 'S.'

'S?'

'Yup.' She nodded happily. 'Go quicker. It moves.'

'Uh-oh.' I looked around the restaurant, my eyes skimming the counter. 'Sugar?'

'Sugar!' She shook her head firmly. 'No.'

'Skirt.'

'It's not moving!'

'It does if the person who's wearing it moves.'

'No.'

'Hmm.' I shrugged. 'Give in.'

She pointed outside. 'Stranger. That lady's been staring at us for ages.'

'You never told me we could name things *outside* too!'

Amy dropped her head into her arms on the table, in fits of giggles. 'My rules.' She looked up, laughing. 'The lady's gone now.'

I shook my head. 'Stranger, huh?' I smiled. 'That was too good.'

'Yeah,' Amy nodded, 'she was looking at you.'

'Really?' I turned my head and looked up and down the high street. 'She was probably just waiting for someone, or thought I was somebody else.'

I sat forward again, tapped the edge of the table three times, as Amy started scrabbling around in her Peppa Pig canvas bag. 'I made something for you.' She drew out a piece of A4 card folded in two and handed it to me. The front was covered in glitter and beads.

I opened it, my hands trembling slightly. Inside it read: *I love you, Mummy.* My vision blurred over with tears and I brushed them away with the back of my hand. 'Ames, it's beautiful. Thank you so much.' I pushed down the lump in my throat. 'Did you make it at school?'

She shook her head. 'No, last Tuesday. With Daddy.'

'Really? With Daddy?'

'I felt sad and Daddy said we could play art time.' She stumbled over her next words. 'S-so, I made you a card.'

I sighed and put my hand out across the table. 'Ames.'

She didn't give me hers and instead traced the outline of Peppa Pig with her forefinger.

'Well,' I said, changing the subject and withdrawing my hand, 'are you looking forward to October? Going to the fair? For my birthday?' I smiled. 'That's only a month away.'

She nodded glumly. 'I want to go to Claire's now.'

I put my hand up and signalled to the waitress for the bill. 'Do you know what you want?'

Amy smiled. 'A pink bracelet with a star on it. Frannie from school says it makes dreams come true.'

'That does sound good.' I leant in and put my card on the table. 'Are you allowed to tell me your dreams? I know I'm not meant to ask.'

'That you and Daddy aren't cross at each other,' she said simply.

I took the card machine from the hovering waitress and typed in my number, grateful for an excuse to busy myself with something else. I could have seen that one coming and I walked right in – now I was stuck for words. One thing I knew was that there were some things in life that a charm bracelet or any amount of dreaming couldn't make happen.

I'd have loved to tell her my own dream: I wanted to take her home with me. Run away, if necessary. I knew that Amy might never understand how her father had controlled everything in my life: how I felt trapped and how one glass of wine in the evening quickly led to a bottle, and how I eventually yearned for the bitter hit of vodka in the mornings too.

Amy stood up and shrugged on her pink duffel coat.

'That's nice. Is it new?' I pointed at the coat.

'Yeah.'

'Did Daddy buy it for you?'

'Yeah. Well, it came from Sarah.' She looked at the ground. 'I still like the one you bought me, though.'

Sarah. I knew very little about her but I did know that Amy appeared to adore Paul's new woman. Once, and only once, I had sat outside the school gates in my car waiting for Sarah to appear and pick up Amy. She was disappointingly slim and good-looking, maybe a bit obviously so, and my guts twisted when I saw how Amy bounded up to her and hugged her with the kind of affection I hadn't seen or felt from Amy in a long time.

'I'm sure you've grown out of that one by now. Besides,' I smiled, 'it's very nice. Pink is much better.'

She walked in front of me and I thought: I could do it now. Take her away from here. We could set up a new life elsewhere. I knew that I could find a job – my career was the one thing I had focused on over the last few years – and Amy would soon adapt to a new school, new friends.

Once outside, she turned, took my hand and, as if reading my mind, said, 'You know that thing where I have to tell the people who I want to live with?' She scuffed the toe of her black patent shoe on the ground. 'I don't really want to choose between you and Daddy.'

'I know, sweetheart. No one's really asking you to do that.' I straightened her coat collar. 'Anyway, they'll be really nice and easy to talk to, I'm sure.'

'I think I want to live with you, Mummy.'

My heart skipped a beat. 'Really?' I asked as evenly as I could. 'Well, you know how much I'd love that but it's always your choice. Remember that.' I drew her into me and kissed the top of her head. 'Ames, you mean the world to me. It's all going to be OK. I'll make sure of it. I cross my heart.'

'Mummy?'

'Hmm?' I mumbled into her full head of auburn curls, inhaling the glorious smell of Timotei shampoo.

'The stranger's there.'

My head shot up and I followed Amy's gaze.

'What's she wearing, Ames?'

'A blue jacket.' She pointed.

My eyes moved fast over the pedestrians opposite: shoppers, a young couple stopping briefly to kiss, an old man with his head bent in concentration, a street seller flogging pashminas. Of all the roads in London, Oxford Street was a minefield when it came to spotting a person you recognise, let alone a stranger. I focused on the scene again, my eyes filtering the fast flow of pedestrians. That's when I saw her, but I didn't recognise her.

She stood up against a wall, stock-still. The woman did appear to be staring our way. I grabbed Amy's hand and moved toward her, my eyes never leaving her. A taxi honked his horn as we made our way across the street.

'Careful, love,' the driver shouted out the window.

'Mummy? Slow down.' Amy clung onto my hand more tightly.

Just as we reached the other side of the road, the woman turned and walked fast past Boots and headed down Stratford Place. I started after her, my hand firm around Amy's.

'Mummy?' Amy's voice quivered ever so slightly with fear. 'Mummy, you're holding me too tight.'

I had come to a halt – she was moving too fast – and Amy buried her head in my jumper.

'Mummy? You're scaring me. Who are you following?'

'That woman you saw. I don't know who she is. No one, I expect. No one,' I murmured, but there was something about her. Was it her hair or something about her face that made my skin prickle? Unease washed over me as I tried to push away the fleeting images of Bethany skipping through my mind. 'I just wanted to find out if the woman you saw thought she knew us,' I said, aware of Amy's frightened eyes on me.

'But the woman I was talking about headed down to the Tube.' She looked momentarily perplexed, but then, and not for the first time, gave me an encouraging smile; my daughter had taken on the role of mother. 'Can we go to Claire's now?'

'Of course,' I agreed, but I was distracted, because I thought I had seen the woman walking fast along the street. I shook my head, gave a small shrug of my shoulders and smiled. 'Come on then. Let's get that charm bracelet, shall we?'

She nodded and we moved off, me inwardly counting the cracks in the pavement: three, six, nine. I looked over my shoulder just as we went to round the corner and gasped aloud as I stepped on the tenth crack. Amy hadn't noticed as she hurtled toward the shops, but I looked behind me once more. The woman had most definitely gone, but the knot in the pit of my stomach hadn't.

CHAPTER 2

One month later

The twenty yards or so separating us gave me time to put my sunglasses on and take a deep, cleansing breath. I hadn't slept for more than a couple of hours, worried about spending a day with Paul. I couldn't remember the last time we had been together, the three of us. Perhaps this was the first time in three years. Sure, he was there when I picked Amy up on a Saturday but, otherwise, we kept our distance.

Soon, my anxiety was quashed by children's squeals of delight, the smell of candyfloss and the warm, comforting heat of October sunshine and, I thought, how bad could it be? I spotted Paul and Amy stood on the corner of Acton Green and quickened my pace. Despite setting out early, the Tube had been on go-slow.

'Sophie, nice of you to make it.' Paul looked at his watch.

'The Tube. Signalling problems.'

'You should've set out earlier.'

I turned to Amy. 'Hello, darling.'

'Hi.' She smiled up at me. 'Happy birthday.'

'Thank you. Getting pretty old, huh?' She laughed momentarily before running off. 'Even in a month she changes, doesn't she?'

'Children do that.'

'Here are the tickets.' I opened my wallet and handed the small pink slips to Paul. 'I bought them online to save queuing.'

We walked in silence and joined Amy at the entrance. Paul handed the tickets to the official before Amy ran off again.

'Ames, wait up,' I called out.

'Amy!' Paul tried this time, jogging after her.

Amy turned around. 'Yeah?' she shouted.

'Slow down there, cowgirl,' he said breathlessly and hugged her close, kissing the top of her head. The gesture made me tense; my stomach churned up.

I walked fast to catch up.

'Come on, let's go!' Amy skipped about in front of us, eager to explore.

'What do you want to go on first?' Paul asked.

'The rollercoaster,' she said, without pause for thought.

'OK, you're going to have to count me out.' I put my hands in the air in mock-surrender. 'Unless you want a very ill Mummy on your hands.'

'I'll take her then,' Paul said, shooting me a look. 'One of us has to be with her.'

'How about I take you on the teacup ride later, Amy?'

'OK, but the rollercoaster first.' She rolled her eyes.

'Right.' I cleared my throat. 'I'll go and get a bottle of water then. You guys want anything?'

They shook their heads and started toward the rollercoaster. I spent the next ten minutes wandering through the crowds before I stopped to buy a bottle of Evian. The rollercoaster stood some way off in the distance and I could just about make out Paul and Amy taking off their belts and dismounting the ride, chatting happily. To my alarm, Paul pointed to the ground and walked off. Amy stood obediently next to the ride and I tried to catch her attention with a wave but she didn't see me.

I dodged a pram as it mowed its way across my path and walked straight through a gaggle of teenagers shouting over the top of my head. The fairground was swollen with people moving in all directions and the air was thick with the smell of fast food. I looked in Amy's direction again, now having to stand on tiptoes to see over the crowds.

My heart started to beat faster; panic flooding my body. A stranger, a woman in a black coat approached Amy and started chatting to her. It was the woman, the woman from outside the hamburger joint last month. Walking faster now, I had her in my eye line but I was still too far away. My breath caught as I watched her stoop down to Amy's eye level and unfurl her hand. I couldn't see her face but she appeared to hand something to Amy and Amy giggled with delight. A cold sweat engulfed me and I wanted to scream for everyone to get out of my way. My daughter was in trouble and I needed to get to her. I had told Amy never to talk to strangers but she was such a trusting child. I watched the woman stand upright and ruffle Amy's auburn curls. I didn't know who the woman was, and I ran faster.

'Amy!' I shouted, my words swallowed whole by the milling crowds. 'Amy!'

A young woman stepped in front of me and I tripped, falling to the ground. Without hesitation, I picked myself up and wiped my dirty hands on the back of my jeans, ignoring the throbbing pain in my left wrist. I looked from side to side, desperate to regain my bearings.

'Excuse me,' I said more loudly now. 'Can you get out of the way?' I put out my arm and started shoving people. A woman to my right tutted and a balding man shouted 'Oi' in my ear. But it worked and a gap slowly opened up. Once I had managed to escape the main avenue of stalls, I cut a left and ran to the rollercoaster ride. Amy was nowhere to be seen.

'Amy,' I hollered, moving from left to right and back again. 'Amy, where are you?'

People were staring but I didn't care.

'Amy!'

A tap on my shoulder.

I spun around. They were stood in front of me: Paul holding Amy's hand.

'Amy.' I couldn't disguise the anger in my voice. 'Who were you talking to?'

'When?' Her gaze tipped downwards.

'Back there, next to the ride. I was trying to get your attention.' I pointed to the rollercoaster.

'No one.' Amy shook her head.

'What do you mean *no one*? I saw you.'

She shook her head again and pushed her fisted hands into her coat pockets, like she was trying to hide something.

'What have you got there?' I grabbed her hand and prised her fist open. A red lolly fell to the ground. 'Where did you get this, then?'

'For God's sake, Sophie, leave her alone. It's just a lolly,' Paul said, taking my arm and jamming his fingers firmly into my coat and skin. 'She's here, I'm here, and that's all that matters now.'

I let go of her and Paul continued to hang onto me, his fingers hot on my chilled skin.

Through clenched teeth, I said, 'Do you mind?'

Paul released my sleeve and gave me a withering look. My head pounded with the onset of a headache.

'Sorry, Amy.' I hugged her close. 'I didn't mean to shout. You just gave me a scare, that's all.' I turned my attention to Paul who was looking at me like I had lost it.

'And where were you? Where did you go?'

'To the toilet,' he said, unflinching.

'To the toilet,' I repeated, 'to the toilet. You call that good parenting?'

'I was only a few minutes.'

I inhaled deeply.

'Sophie, maybe you're tired. You look tired, if you don't mind me saying.'

He was trying to undermine me but I was familiar with his tactics and I didn't rise to the bait.

'Amy, how about you and I go get some candyfloss or something,' I suggested, my voice calm except for a slight tell-tale waver. 'How does that sound?'

Amy looked to Paul before answering. He started to protest but surprised me. 'Go on, Amy, it'll be nice to spend some time with Mummy.'

'OK,' she agreed quietly.

I took her hand and gave it a squeeze.

'Meet me here in twenty, OK?' Paul said, and pointed to the information booth sign. I nodded. 'And I mean twenty. No later.'

Amy led me from one stall to another and we finally stopped to watch a young boy focused on winning a Winnie-the-Pooh-Bear at the coconut shy. We stood in silence for a few moments before Amy's face took on a weighted seriousness.

'Mummy, why do you get so angry with Daddy?'

'Because we don't always see eye to eye. But it's not you. You do know that?' I put my arm around her. 'I'm sorry about shouting at you earlier. I was just worried.'

She paused. 'I didn't do anything wrong.' She pulled the cuffs of her coat further down.

'I know that.' I studied Amy's face. 'Were you talking to someone back there?'

Her lower lip started to tremble. 'No. You told me not to talk to strangers.'

'I know,' I said, more gently now, 'but did a woman talk to you? I know you wouldn't approach a stranger yourself.'

She shook her head furiously from side to side and hugged me, burying her head in my coat. 'Don't worry, Ames. It doesn't matter anyway, does it? You're safe now. That's the most important thing.'

'Mummy?'

'Yep?'

I didn't expect it. Her words knocked me for six. 'Daddy says we shouldn't talk about you any more.'

There it was; like a knife in my heart. No warning. 'He does, does he? And why's that?' My voice was pitched high, unnaturally high.

'Because he says that, when you left, we had to make our own world and, so, if we talk about you, it's...' She stopped.

'It's what?'

'It's like you're still my mummy.'

I looked away, tears threatening to overspill onto my cheeks. 'I *am* still your mummy and I've wanted more than anything to see more of you.'

'Daddy says you don't really want to see me any more and that's why you didn't come over on Saturdays.'

'No, not at all,' I started and stopped. 'I wanted to see you, Amy. You need to trust me.' I knew it was inadequate and, yet, I knew she'd never accept the truth or want to hear it: how could an eight-year-old girl understand her father hadn't allowed me to see her? I also didn't want to admit that I had had no control over the situation. That if I turned up and caused a scene, it would only upset her and Paul would make me out to be the bad guy. I knew that the least I could do was to protect her from arguments. 'Anyway, Ames, let's get that candyfloss and head back to Daddy, yeah?' I was desperate to change the subject.

She nodded, hurt etched across her tiny features.

I gave her a few pound coins and watched her walk confidently up to the candyfloss seller. She asked for two sticks and turned around to check if that was OK. I put my hand up and indicated three. She changed the order. I couldn't believe how she had grown up, the same little girl who at one time preferred to remain wrapped around my legs, her small pudgy hand in mine.

My phone vibrated in my bag, cutting through my thoughts. Paul, no doubt. We had been over twenty minutes. I rummaged around in the tote, found the phone and hurriedly tried to flip it open before the third ring ended. I got it on the fourth.

'We're just coming back.'

A rough, low, muffled female voice filled the phone.

'Happy birthday, Sophie.' A pause. 'Your turn.'

'Who is this?' I managed to blurt out, my heart pounding furiously. I could hear someone else calling out my name and then, the call went dead.

The voice. So familiar.

Blood rushed to my ears, my heart hammering my chest.

I looked over to the stall to check on Amy and dropped my mobile to the ground, my eyes fixed on the spot where she had just been standing.

She was gone.

A deathly chill passed over my body, my heart dropped into my stomach. Half a beat later, I snapped out of it and quickly retrieved my phone off the ground. I moved erratically from one side of the stalls to the other, my eyes desperately scanning the crowds.

'Did you see where that little girl went?' I asked the candyfloss seller.

'Huh?' The overweight man squinted at me through his spectacles.

'The little girl who just asked you for candyfloss. Did you just sell candyfloss to a girl about this high?' I showed him. 'Auburn hair?'

He shrugged his shoulders and called over me to the next customer. I whipped around. Droplets of sweat formed on my upper lip. I clasped my throat; dry as parchment paper.

'Amy!' I called out, my voice drowning in the hubbub of the fair.

I attempted to control my shaking hand as I scrolled through the phone menu looking for Paul's name. It went straight through to voicemail. I tried again. My eyes darted left and right searching for any sign of Amy's pink duffle coat or strawberry blonde hair. She had vanished. I prayed to god she had found her way back to her father. It didn't seem possible: I had taken my eyes off her for less than thirty seconds. I wanted to scream at the woman staring at me as she passed by with a pushchair and her young son hanging onto the handle, I wanted to shout at the man who had just dug his elbow into his friend's side and nodded in my direction. They both walked off laughing. Thirty seconds. Where had she gone in thirty seconds?

Paul eventually picked up.

'Sophie?'

'I can't find her, I can't find Amy,' I shouted over the mounting noise. 'Is she with you?' A moan escaped my throat. I pushed the phone up against my ear in an effort to drown out the arcade games and music.

'What do you mean you can't find her?'

'She was here,' I said. 'Oh god, oh god…' My face crumpled. Large tears landed on my lips, I licked them away and wiped my nose on the back of my sleeve. 'Where are you?'

'At home,' he answered.

'Home?' I shouted. *How much time had passed? My mind felt a familiar fuzziness, the same sensation warning me of the onset of a panic attack. My body telling me I was in danger.* 'What are you doing there?'

'Where are you?'

'What do you mean, where am I?' I shouted, throwing my free arm into the air. 'I thought I was with you! At the fairground!'

The phone line went silent.

'Sophie, I don't know what you're talking about. I wasn't at a fairground with you today.'

CHAPTER 3

I felt cold, shaking furiously; DI Ward said it was the shock and advised me to do my coat up, wrap my scarf tightly around my neck. But I couldn't warm up. An icy, hard dread sat in the pit of my stomach and I knew that, until I found Amy, it wouldn't go away. I dabbed pointlessly at my eyes with tissues but they were disintegrating after two hours of constant use; white bits fell to the floor. I wondered if tears could run out. At this point, it didn't seem that they could. Whenever I managed to slow my breathing and try to focus on what was being asked of me, I thought the tears might have stopped but then, in a heartbeat, I'd remember and fresh tears would spring up.

'Here.' DI Ward handed me a new one. 'It's clean,' she assured me.

'What happens now?'

The detective surveyed the scene, taking in the chaos of the fairground. I was trying not to get my hopes up but, surely, with an active search party on the lookout, our chances of finding Amy had just gone up ten-fold?

DI Ward gazed at me, her brown eyes steady. She put a hand on my arm. The gesture lacked warmth and made my skin crawl with goose bumps. 'We start at the beginning. Tell me what happened.'

'I should've, you know. I should've kept a closer eye on her.' My words were coming out all garbled and I stopped, took a deep breath, and started again. 'When I couldn't see her, I thought maybe she had just wandered off. But, I knew in my heart, she doesn't do that. She's such a good child.' I blew my nose. 'We had just been chatting, you know?'

'Have you told the missing persons tent?'

I shook my head, my gaze shifted downward. She quickly removed her arm and started walking in that direction. I got the impression the no-nonsense detective was finding it hard to deal with my tears.

'No,' I said lamely, jogging to catch up with her. It hadn't even entered my head.

'Well, Ms Fraiser, it's always a good place to start. Amy might have headed there herself.'

'Right,' I said, a woman reprimanded.

DI Ward led me over to the marquee and addressed the nearest official, a tall girl of no more than nineteen kitted out in jeans and trainers.

She flashed her ID. 'This lady's little girl is missing. Can you put a call out?' She looked at me. 'Ms Fraiser, tell her what you know. Where you last saw her.'

'So how old is your daughter?' the girl prompted me. 'Why don't you tell me what she was wearing?'

'Ms Fraiser, the quicker we act, often the better the result,' DI Ward urged.

I went to speak but my body had shut down. Inside I was screaming: I shouldn't be having this conversation. This kind of thing happens on film sets, not in real life. Why was everyone acting so goddamn calm and rational? They wanted me to think straight; but my brain was a fug of emotions and every fibre of my being so taut, I thought I might snap right in half.

The tears had started to flow again and the detective spoke more softly this time. 'Ms Fraiser, we all want to find your daughter. You're going to have to help us out here. What was Amy wearing?'

I dabbed my nose and eyes before filling the girl in on the details. DI Ward thanked the girl and took me to one side.

'So, I need to ask, your daughter, Amy, is she at risk? For example, does she suffer from any medical conditions?'

'No, she hasn't got any medical conditions.' I leant heavily against one of the marquee's poles and just as quickly straightened up. 'Course she's at bloody risk, she's missing!' I shoved my shoulders back. 'I saw someone talking to Amy earlier. A woman.' She nodded. 'She was wearing a black coat and I think she might have bribed her with a lolly.'

'How do you know she gave her a lolly?'

'She had one in her hand.'

'So you spoke to Amy after her meeting with this woman?'

'Yes, I saw her talking to her and ran in Amy's direction. When I did find Amy, the woman had gone.' I paused. 'But…'

'But what?' She shifted her weight from one foot to the other.

'Amy told me she hadn't spoken to anyone.'

'And you're sure she had definitely spoken with a woman?'

I squinted at her. 'Yes, I'm not delusional.' But even as I spoke, the fuzziness started up, the tingling at my temples. *Had I imagined it?* 'I have this feeling I know this woman.' I looked up. 'I think she's come back for me.'

I held my head in my hands, willing the tingling to go away. I couldn't have a panic attack now and not after all this time; what if the court found out? Why would they hand me my child if the attacks were back?

'Who, Ms Fraiser?' When I didn't answer she said, 'Are you feeling OK?'

I looked at her, terrified that the attack would get worse. My hands were trembling, the grass was shifting in front of me. I rammed my hands into my hair and dug my nails into my scalp, willing myself not to black out. The ringing was intensifying in my ears and I could hear my shallow breathing. *I needed to control it.*

The detective was behind me now, her hand on my back. 'I'll get help.'

'No,' I whispered. 'I'll be fine. Can you just get me a glass of water?'

She looked at me intently for a moment and nodded before walking off. As soon as she had left I forced my shoulders back and exhaled and inhaled loudly until the ground started to come into focus, the ringing had dimmed and as the DI reappeared, a gust of air cooled the sweat on my face.

'OK?' She shoved the glass in my direction.

I nodded.

'OK, what were you saying about the woman?'

'When I was at university,' I started. My lower lip trembled. 'I witnessed my friend die. Cold-blooded murder. I think the woman was there but I don't know, I blacked out at the time. The whole thing was like a dream.' I paused. 'A nightmare.' I shook my head, tried to physically remove the fog that descended every time I thought of that night. A coping mechanism, the Priory therapist Dr Hurst, had said: a way of protecting myself.

The DI clenched her jaw, started scribbling madly again in her notebook. 'Why are you relating the two?' Her eyes bored into me. I could tell her mind was already running my profile through the system: she wouldn't find anything.

I leant against the pole again. 'I don't know. The woman's voice was so familiar.'

'You heard her voice?'

'She rang me just before Amy disappeared.' I bit my lip. 'Although, why the woman would know my number...' My voice trailed off. *Maybe I was imagining things, maybe it was another trick of my imagination. It wasn't feasible, was it?* 'No, I don't know what I'm talking about.' I paused. 'But there was something about her voice.'

The DI's shoulders visibly tensed. 'Why do you think Amy said she didn't speak to a woman?'

'I guess she didn't want to get into trouble.'

'Maybe she genuinely didn't?'

She didn't have to say it: she thought I was delusional. *Maybe I hadn't seen the woman. Maybe because it's my birthday, I'm remembering... She died on your birthday twenty years ago.* I shook my head hard; I didn't want to remember. Amy was missing but it has nothing to do with the night Bethany died.

My heart twisted when I thought how angrily I'd spoken to Amy only a couple of hours ago: I had been worried about her talking to a stranger. I hoped that wherever she was she realised I wasn't cross with her. Had she run away because she thought I was angry? Had she run away because, as her gaze often told me, she was scared of me? *What if there had been no woman and I had accused Amy of talking to thin air? She would think her mother was mad: again.* That thought caught me unawares and I stifled a sob.

DI Ward nodded. 'OK, I just need to be clear on everything. When Amy went missing, what were you doing?'

'Buying candyfloss. Over there.' I pointed to the stallholder at the far side of the green. 'I gave her money and she went up to order it. Next thing I know, I get a phone call. It was an unknown number and this woman's muffled voice said, "Happy birthday" and "Your turn". I looked over again and Amy was gone.' I gave a small shake to my head. 'Just like that. Gone.'

'This caller said "your turn"? and what on earth does that mean? Are you sure?'

I wasn't sure of anything any more.

'I presume it was a withheld number?'

'I didn't check that,' I admitted, searching my bag now and scrolling through the recent call list. 'No number. See here.' I showed the display to the DI, she nodded.

'Hmm, OK.' She withdrew her notebook and scribbled a quick note. 'First, let's go and talk to the guy who sold Amy the candyfloss.'

'There's something I should tell you. It's about my ex-husb…' I walked fast to catch up with the detective but I stopped talking when I realised she was now on her phone. It had been ringing non-stop.

She spoke hurriedly. 'Thank you, DS Franklin,' the DI finished and flipped her phone shut.

I was almost running now. 'I've already asked him, Detective, the man who sold us the candyfloss. He doesn't remember Amy.'

'We'll try him again. You'd be amazed how often the presence of a police officer jogs their memory.'

'I promise you he doesn't know,' I reiterated, but she still wasn't listening.

'OK, here we are.' She turned on a smile for the ruddy-faced man sat behind the glass counter. He shot up, clearly not immune to the detective's female charm and, I hated to admit it, Hispanic good looks. Pity her personality wasn't as appealing.

Without a trace of obvious emotion in her voice, DI Ward brought the man up to speed. 'Sir, we have a woman here whose daughter is missing. Can you tell me, did you sell candyfloss to a girl about so high?' She held her hand up and looked to me for confirmation. I nodded. 'Do you want to tell him exactly what she was wearing?'

I did and he showed no signs of recognition.

'She bought three candyfloss sticks.' I knew we were raking over old ground.

'I told you before, love. I don't remember her,' he said through gritted teeth.

The detective looked at me.

'She was here,' I stated flatly.

'To be fair to the lady, I don't remember many people I serve what with being here all day and so many people passing through. This isn't one of them country fairs. London is full of strange faces.'

DI Ward thanked him for his time and we made our way back to the tent. I spoke a silent prayer as we entered. But Amy was nowhere to be seen. The detective chatted briefly to the same girl before turning back to me. 'You had something you wanted to tell me?'

The tension that had enveloped me for the last hour gave way to heaving sobs. The DI put her hand tentatively on mine and gave a reassuring squeeze.

'Come on, you can tell me,' she encouraged.

I tried to explain the call to Paul, stopping every few seconds to take a deep breath.

'Wait a second, Ms Fraiser,' she said, quickly removing her hand from my arm. 'Are you trying to tell me you spoke to your ex-husband? Mr Mitchell, was it? And he denies ever being here? And you're absolutely sure he was?' DI Ward frowned and shook her head. 'Is that what you're saying?'

I wiped my eyes with the back of my sleeve. 'That's correct.'

She scratched her head. 'Are you sure that Amy isn't with your ex-husband?'

I recoiled. 'Detective, what are you suggesting?' She glanced at me. 'My daughter is missing. M-I-S-S-I-N-G.' I spelt it out for her. She shot me a disparaging look. 'If we were to go to Paul's house now, and Amy isn't there, does anyone mind explaining to me where my daughter is?'

'Do you have any proof that Mr Mitchell and Amy were here with you? A photo on your phone?'

I didn't like where this was going. 'No. Nothing,' I said flatly; there hadn't been any time to take photos.

'In which case, I think we'd better go and talk to your ex-husband.' I noted the weariness in her voice.

My mind was spinning with questions, doubts. I couldn't understand it. I rubbed my stinging eyes.

'We definitely came here together.' I felt defeated. A voice at the back of my head was taunting me: *it's not real. None of it's real.* 'But I suppose Paul could've taken Amy home,' I finally conceded. I pinched myself to confirm I could in fact feel pain, that I did exist.

'How about I drive you over there and we'll get this all sorted out?'

I nodded and obediently followed DI Ward to her car. It was late afternoon now, the midday warmth replaced by a cool autumnal breeze. I climbed onto the rear seat and shut the door, then I remembered and took out my wallet. At the back, behind my credit cards, I kept a small passport photo of Amy. I looked at it, caressing the glossy picture with my thumb.

'I do have a photo. This is Amy.' I showed the photo to the detective as she started up the car.

DI Ward pressed her lips together. 'Is this a recent photo?'

I nodded.

'We'll find her, Ms Fraiser. Don't worry. It'll all be fine. I'm sure it's just a misunderstanding.'

I stuffed the photo back inside my wallet and looked out the window. Bethany's face stared back at my reflection. I let out a sob, squeezed my eyes shut and when I looked once more, I just saw myself: a haggard and frayed version of my young self.

CHAPTER 4

Detective Ward eyed me in the rear-view mirror. The whole trip was made without a word – small talk felt inappropriate. Why did she keep looking at me like that? I'm not sure what she expected me to do.

Anyway, I was glad we weren't talking. Hysteria was building inside me, I could feel it was at the point of bursting and, if I had been asked to speak, it would've torn through me like a river breaking its banks. My hands gripped the fabric seat edge and I kept my eyes locked on the slow-moving London traffic and changing scenery. Luckily, the detective had displayed no sign of wanting to get emotionally involved; it was easier this way – for both of us.

She finally spoke. 'It's not far is it?'

'No, just down here,' I confirmed. 'His house is just along this road. There it is.' I pointed at the familiar Victorian red brick. She murmured acknowledgement and looked up and down the road for a space. Unable to find one, the detective parked on a double yellow.

DI Ward started to climb out of the car. 'Right, come on then. Let's talk to Mr Mitchell.' She hopped out and waited for me to do the same. I didn't move; my limbs refused to cooperate, as if they too were in fear of what the next few moments held.

The DI opened the passenger door. I got out slowly, every movement jerky. The detective's hand brushed my arm as she went to close the door. Her touch caused me to jump.

'Sorry,' she said, scrutinising my face. 'OK?'

I nodded my head tiredly. We walked to the front door and DI Ward pressed the bell. I could hear Paul shuffling about inside. Just as she was about to ring again, Paul flung the door open.

'Sophie,' he said, his eyes questioning, 'what are you doing here? And who's this?' He smiled tentatively at the detective. 'Where's Amy?'

'Paul!' I shouted, re-finding my strength as adrenaline shot through me. I bolted through the door, knocking Paul to one side, and moved toward the back of the house. 'What do you mean, where's Amy? Is she here?'

'What are you talking about?' he called to me down the hall. 'She's with you. It's Saturday, you always take her on a Saturday.'

'I beg your pardon? She's with me?' I was hurrying back toward him, my face flushed with colour. A swathe of red moved rapidly up my neck.

'You collected her this morning, Sophie. Where *is* Amy?' He looked furtively behind DI Ward. 'Is this some kind of joke?'

The detective moved forward to introduce herself. 'Mr Mitchell, I'm DI Ward. Your ex-wife reported your little girl missing. You were at the fairground with them, to celebrate Ms Fraiser's birthday?' Her tone sought affirmation.

His eyes widened and he paled. 'Missing!' He took a deep breath and turned to me. 'Sophie?'

DI Ward cleared her throat. 'The fairground, Mr Mitchell, were you at the fairground?'

'Um, I'm afraid, Officer,' Paul said, his eyes moving from DI Ward to me, 'I wasn't at any fairground. Sophie did ring me a couple of hours ago asking where I was. I told her I was at home.' He ran his hand across his forehead. 'You had better come in.' Paul frowned at me and nodded for the detective to go through to the living room.

She made her way through but remained standing. Paul stood on one side of the room, me on the other.

'OK, do you think Amy might have run away?' the DI asked.

I looked at Paul. 'Do you think she might have run from the fairground?'

Paul glanced at me, rage causing his face to twist. 'What fairground, Sophie?'

I turned to the detective. 'Do you see what I mean?'

She gave a slight nod. 'Mr Mitchell, you weren't at the fairground today?'

'No. I don't know what she's talking about.'

'OK, do either of you think Amy might have run away?'

We both shook our heads.

'She –' Paul started.

'She,' I cut in, 'was fine when we were together.' I looked hard at him. 'We were together.' *Weren't we?*

'Nothing happened that might have upset her?'

I looked at the floor. 'Like I told you, when I saw her speaking to a woman, I did get a bit cross.' I nibbled my lip. 'But only because I was worried.'

'OK.' The DI's eyebrows furrowed. 'And, Mr Mitchell, where were you?'

'Out and about.' He glanced at me. 'I went into town for some food, that kind of thing.'

I gasped. 'Out and about?' Spittle covered my lip. 'What are you doing here?'

The DI ploughed on. 'Could Amy be with friends, relatives?'

'Of course, she could be,' I said, 'but she was with me.'

Paul turned to me now. 'Yes, she was with you. Where is she now?' He ran his hand through his hair and clenched his fist as he did so. 'It doesn't make sense.'

'OK, Mr Mitchell,' DI Ward said, 'can you phone around her friends, close relatives, and check she isn't with them?' She thought for a second. 'Does she have a favourite place she might go to?' She looked at us in turn.

Paul was staring at me. 'I don't think so.' He paused. 'Sophie, what the fuck is going on here?'

'I can't think of one now,' I said quietly.

'OK, Ms Fraiser, can I have that photo you showed me earlier? You said it was taken recently?'

'Yeah, it's a month old. We went to a passport booth together.'

I searched my wallet and handed it to her and with relief saw that it was one of two copies. Amy's face stared up at me and I traced the outline of her face with my forefinger. I wanted to reach into the photo, grab her, hug her, never let her go.

'Right, I just need to make a quick call.' The DI backed out of the living room and stepped outside.

'Paul, where's Amy?' I said, my voice a hot whisper as I dropped my bag to the floor. 'Don't do this to me! Why are you lying?'

'I have no idea what you're talking about. I'm not lying.' He seemed furtive. 'Are you having a you-know?'

I waited, let him explain, even though I knew what he was implying. 'A you-know?'

'An episode. When you,' he pursed his lips, 'make stuff up. Imagine things.'

I stared at him in stunned silence, tapped the sofa three times. 'You won't get away with this.'

Paul didn't say anything and left the room. I could hear him addressing family members, parents of Amy's friends.

'Mr Mitchell? Ms Fraiser?' Ten minutes later, DI Ward stepped back into the hallway and made her way to the living room. 'DCS Fields is on his way over. I just need to ask a few more questions.' She looked at us. 'Right, then. Mind if I sit down?' She gestured to the sofa before sitting down on the paisley-covered cushions. The fabric was a remnant of our failed marriage. I had always hated it. Paul's choice. Not mine. I sat myself at the other end.

'Right, so let me get this straight, Mr Mitchell,' she started to say.

'You can call me Paul,' he interrupted.

'Right, OK, Paul,' she tried again. 'Can you confirm that you were not at the fairground today, on Acton Green, with Ms Fraiser? That you have no knowledge of a day out?' She jotted something down in her notebook.

'That's correct.' He wrung his hands.

'And that you believe that Amy was meant to be in your ex-wife's care today?'

'Again correct.' He cleared his throat, started pacing. 'I'm not sure I get what's going on here.' The blue vein on the side of his neck was pulsating. He looked at me. 'What's going on, Sophie? If anything's happened to her…' He tightened and released his fists like he was readying himself for a fight. 'I shouldn't have let her go. You've been acting strangely lately and my gut instinct said it was wrong. But I didn't listen, did I? I didn't think to myself: Sophie is just not well enough to look after our daughter with,' he looked at me, 'your drink problems, the delusions, the OCD.' He slammed his fist on the wall. 'No, and now our daughter is missing.'

'Do you see what he's doing?' I asked.

DI Ward flicked her ballpoint open and closed. I wished she would've done it twice more, just to be sure that no harm was going to come to Amy.

She looked at us in turn. 'What's he doing?'

'He's having you believe I'm unable to look after Amy.' I started picking at the skin around my fingers. 'Like I'm mad.' I paused and looked at Paul. 'Isn't that right, Paul? Is this all for the court's benefit? Because all that's going to happen is, you're going to be arrested for hiding away your daughter!' Even as I said it though, I realised how irrational I sounded. Why would Amy's own father put her in danger? It made no sense. My eyes prickled with exhaustion.

'I have no flaming idea what you're going on about, woman! But yes, in my opinion, you are mad. Though I didn't have to do anything to convince the detective here!' He was up now, circling the room. Unexpectedly, he jabbed his finger in DI Ward's face. 'I'm right, aren't I? You didn't need any convincing?'

I had never seen him like this: quite so wired, quite so panicky. Or maybe I didn't know Paul as well as I thought.

'Do you mind?' DI Ward looked at him and he placed his hand by his side. 'Ms Fraiser, do you know where Amy might be?' She glanced at me; because even she must have realised how ridiculous that sounded. Though, it didn't stop me from wishing I could get my diary out and check I hadn't delivered her at a friend's house. Hadn't Elsie from school wanted to go to the pool one Saturday? My diary was just inside my bag, if I could just get it out and check. But I couldn't because I needed to look like I was sure, be convincing, even though now I wondered if I really had forgotten what I had done today.

'No, I don't know where she is.' It was honest.

'Are you sure you didn't arrange for her to go to a friend's house or perhaps she went out and returned to your house in Richmond?'

'Why wouldn't I remember something like that?' I said, affecting total disbelief.

'I tried a few numbers whilst you were outside, Detective,' Paul interrupted. 'No one's seen her.' A moment's silence before he spoke again. 'Are you sure she's not at Frannie's house? I couldn't get through to her parents.'

'Paul,' I warned, 'you know she's not at Frannie's house.' *Frannie?* Panic rose in my throat: why had I thought her name was Elsie? Then I had the sickening realisation that Elsie had been *my* best friend at school. Amy had wanted to go swimming with Frannie, *her* best friend. I momentarily wondered what other fragments of my past my mind could weave into the present day.

I clamped my hands together. 'He is lying. I left my house this morning to meet Paul and Amy at the fairground. We were all there. At the fairground.' It felt as if the walls were closing in on me.

'OK. Let's just wait for DCS Fields. He'll be here shortly,' DI Ward said, sitting back in the sofa. I nodded and stared ahead, continuing to peel the skin around my nails, counted the bricks around the fireplace. A photo of Paul holding a newborn Amy sat in view. I don't remember ever having one taken of Amy and myself. I suddenly realised that there was no evidence that I was Amy's mother: no photos of us together, no drawings we had coloured in, nothing. Paul left the room. I could hear him pacing in the kitchen, muttering under his breath.

After a few minutes, the doorbell rang and the DI Ward let out an audible sigh of relief. Paul rushed down the hall to the door and showed DCS Fields into the living room. The detectives exchanged fleeting glances. He was an overweight stern-looking man. But I knew that he had authority. Maybe he was enough to get Paul to admit he was lying. The Detective Chief Superintendent smiled at his expectant audience. Paul and I looked at him like children eager for the magician to pull the rabbit out of the hat. DCS Fields rubbed his hands over his eyes and fished around in his front pocket for his spectacles.

'Mr Mitchell, Ms Fraiser,' DI Ward addressed us.

Paul sat on the edge of the sofa as if ready to pounce. I couldn't read his body language at all: one minute he was furious, the next, he appeared fidgety and anxious.

'One of you needs to tell me the truth,' DI Ward continued smoothly. 'Am I going to have to haul you both in for questioning?'

I looked back at the photo. 'I don't know where Amy is.'

'She has Amy, or she did have as of this morning,' Paul said, his eyes not leaving mine. 'You do know she's an alcoholic? That she attends AA?'

'That's probably not relevant, Paul,' DI Ward replied slowly.

'Did you ask if she's been drinking today?' He focused on DI Ward now.

'I haven't!' I sat bolt upright and massaged my neck with my hand. 'I haven't had a drink. You have to believe me.'

I started to cry, at first only a few tears until it grew and I was sobbing, my shoulders shaking uncontrollably. A moan escaped my lips and was unlike any sound I've heard before. Its rawness shocked me. 'What are you doing, Paul? Where's our daughter? If you harm her, I swear to god, I'll…' I wiped my nose on the back of my jumper. 'I don't know what you're up to but I never knew you could sink this low. If this is for the courts, then you wait till they find out Amy's own father was willing to put her at risk.'

He flinched and for the first time today I felt I had hit on a truth.

The detectives stepped out of the room and Paul just stared at me. He kept clearing his throat but, otherwise, didn't speak.

'Where's Amy, Paul?'

He ignored me.

For a while, I sat in numb silence before standing up slowly and walking over to the ottoman by the window. I sat down again.

He watched me until I couldn't take it any more and I looked out the window at the fading light. I leant my forehead against the cool glass, weeping. Once I had started to cry, I couldn't stop but, honestly, I didn't really try. The tears gave me some sort of release. I felt powerless: all I wanted was to hold Amy in my arms, tell her it was all going to be OK. It was as though someone was wringing my heart, the pain piercing my chest. Often it was said that the loss or death of a child was the same as losing a limb. But it was more than that: it was as if your soul started to die, your reason for being had been wrenched from under your feet. Amy was my world, the glue that kept my world together. Without her, I was afraid I might break.

CHAPTER 5

The room was small with no window. A starchy white emulsion covered the walls and the radiator in the corner remained firmly off. I shivered and rubbed my arms in the hope of generating some heat. DI Ward offered me a cup of tea.

'Sugar?' she asked as she left the room. I shook my head.

She took a long time getting the tea. It was as if I were on trial but I wasn't sure why. Was I guilty? Any guilt I felt was because I had been cross with Amy when she had spoken to the woman. Instead of being angry, why hadn't I asked her about it gently? Perhaps the incident with the stranger had been coincidental but how did this person know my number? Why was Paul lying? That thought made my stomach turn: Paul, the man I had wed and lived with for eight years, would put his daughter – our daughter – at risk. He must have known something, I was sure of it. But by this late stage in the day, my body and mind felt weary, the tingling by my temples had returned: the events less than three hours ago were becoming increasingly hazy. I gripped the edge of the table as if to hold onto reality, what I felt to be true, for a moment longer.

I couldn't warm up; I pulled my coat more tightly around me and tapped the edge of the table three times, then six, then nine. My body had become a cold, lifeless shell. What was the point of living when my daughter was out there? Alone. Despite my body's inability to move, my mind conversely ran at high speed, running through the events of the day: spotting Amy and Paul on the corner of Acton Green, the woman in the black coat, the lolly, the way Paul had held my arm, Amy's innocent face staring up at me, candyfloss, the empty space where Amy had just been standing.

The woman. The woman, had she been there that night Bethany died? Had I seen more than I thought? I hadn't told anyone I was there, except the doctors at the Priory, but every time I told them, they gave me more pills, talked to me more until I eventually shut down. I mean how could I have been at a murder that doesn't exist on record?

I thought to myself: if DI Ward walks in on the twenty-first tap, it would be OK. I flicked my finger against the side. *Twenty*. DI Ward entered the room before my finger hit the side of the table again.

'I thought you could do with it,' DI Ward said as she returned and placed a mug in front of me. 'Sugary tea.'

I took a small sip and the sweet syrup burnt the back of my throat.

'Good for shock,' she explained, her eyes never leaving mine as she sat down.

My gaze flitted between the detective's mouth and the scuff-marked wall behind her; I wondered if the scuffs were the result of a high-pressure interview. I'm not sure why but I thought the suspect might be male: short-fused, not entirely dissimilar to Paul, who was undoubtedly giving them hell next door.

'Can I ask why I'm here?' I said numbly.

'Because, Sophie, I need to ask you some more questions that might help us find your daughter. But you must cooperate,' she added.

'Of course I'll cooperate. I'm just wondering if it's wasting time, that's all.'

'Well, until we clear up the misunderstanding between you and your ex-husband, I don't think it is wasting time.' She stuck her tongue into the side of her cheek.

'Is this normal treatment for a mother whose daughter has gone missing?' I indicated the room with a nod of my head. 'In films, this doesn't happen.'

'It's normal treatment for parents who appear to have communication problems and a missing child.'

I put the mug down and allowed the uncomfortable silence to settle before speaking. Silence offered me what little control I was able to muster in this situation.

'Detective, I know it's hard to believe but Paul *was* there today. He was there with me.' But even as I said it, my certainty dissipated like a wave on a beach.

She eyed me cagily, any expression of sympathy quickly fading. 'Please, tell me again why he's denying it.'

'I don't know.' I ran my hand through my hair once, twice, three times. 'We have our court case coming up.' A tear ran down my cheek. 'I mean no child should have to choose, I do see that. But, anyway, Paul's pulled every card so far to make out I'm the world's worst mother.' I thought back to my tone, the way I had talked to her on the green, then a spinning wheel of images of me drinking to block out what everyone called delusions, drinking to stop seeing Bethany's face when I slept. 'Maybe I am.'

The DI softened. 'You love Amy very much, that's the most honest thing going on here. And I'm here to figure out what's going on.'

I nodded. 'Where's Paul?'

'Next door with my colleague, DS Franklin.'

I picked up the chipped white mug once again and took a mouthful of tea.

'Sophie, I need you to convince me of what you're saying. That Paul was there.' She hesitated. 'Tell me about your marriage.'

I let out a long sigh and placed the mug back on the table. 'I met Paul at university, he wasn't at the university. He was a bit older than me. He just sort of turned up one day. I fell for his intensity. He seemed a man of the world, you know what I mean? We split up after a while but we met up again in my early thirties. I fell pregnant and he asked me to marry him.' I bit my lip. 'I'm not sure he ever wanted it.'

'What?'

'Any of it. Me or having a child. Not really. Or, at least, that's what I felt.' I gave a weary smile. 'But you know I can't deny he's always been there for Amy. Me, no. But Amy, he adores.'

'And yet you still feel he's lying about today?' DI Ward sat back. 'Paul wants to prove a point?'

I wiped my eyes. 'I don't know. Like I keep telling you, we were on the green in Chiswick together and when I phoned him, he said he didn't know anything about a fairground.' I shuddered. 'I feel like I can't be awake.'

'You mentioned being present at your friend's murder.' She shifted under my gaze. 'We've searched all our records, Sophie. There's nothing there. I mean there isn't a witness statement from you. I know you went to Aberystwyth University, you studied English. There is a record of a suicide. Bethany Saunders. Is that your friend?'

I nodded.

'You were there when she committed suicide? That would be traumatic.'

'Murdered. She was shot and I think I was there.'

'It states here that she was never found, presumed to have committed suicide because of her "state of mind".' DI Ward cleared her throat. 'Hang on, you *think* you were there?'

'I'm not sure of anything any more,' I admitted. 'I mean Bethany existed, she was my friend, she was the only person who understood me. Ever. When I woke up one morning, I remembered Bethany had been killed.' I hung my head. 'Only, my housemates at the time said I came back with Paul and then, later, Paul told me I can't have been with Bethany because I was with him at some club.' I nibbled my lip. 'Only I don't remember a bar. I only remember this house, with Bethany where she died. My therapist at the time told me that sometimes, if people we love die in a traumatic way, that we make things up; we almost want to be with them when they died. It kind of comforts the person left behind.' I felt my wet cheek. 'Does that make sense?'

The DI shifted uncomfortably, wrote something down. 'OK, let's focus on Amy once more, Sophie. First of all, the one thing we all agree on, we all want Amy back safe and sound. But, I need to be sure of Amy's whereabouts when she went missing.' She blew out her cheeks. 'I know you both agree that Amy hasn't run away today but has she ever?'

'Has she ever what?'

'Run away.'

I looked at the floor. 'I can't remember.'

DI Ward leant forward in her chair and brought her face nearer mine. I could smell stale coffee on her breath. 'You don't remember?'

I nodded. 'OK, once. Just over three years ago. I had just moved out or, more like, Paul dumped my stuff in the garage, filed for divorce and I had been forced to find a place of my own.'

'So Amy ran away because it was all too stressful? Not uncommon.'

'To look for me,' I admitted sadly, my voice trembling slightly. 'Please. I don't want to talk about it.'

'But why didn't Amy come and live with you?'

'I quickly,' I started, the lump in my throat about ready to burst, 'found out that Paul convinced Amy I had left out of choice and that I didn't love her. He likes playing mind-games.' The DI blinked. 'Look, throughout this, I've tried to make it as easy on Amy as I can. Paul keeps using his trump card, my drinking, but I haven't drunk a drop now for,' I stopped briefly, 'eighteen months, twenty-nine days and,' I looked at my watch and laughed self-consciously, 'around six hours. You become highly aware of time when you're... Well, you know.' I looked up at the detective. 'Cafcass were due to interview her next week to ask her where she wants to live. She told me she was going to tell them that she wants to live with me. And now she's gone, Detective.' I looked at the DI, my eyes blurred. 'I have to find my child. I love her so much. She's meant to be with me.'

The detective nodded, stuck out her lower lip. 'Yes, so you attend AA?'

'I'm dry, but I keep going to prove how hard I'm trying, for the courts. I thought about readmitting myself to the Priory but I'm done with therapy.'

The detective arched an eyebrow. 'Readmitting?'

I glanced at her. 'Yes, I admitted myself when I was twenty-one. I was there for three months, and then again after Bethany died.'

'Why the first time?'

'Drink.'

She raised both eyebrows this time. 'Uh-huh.'

'Yes. My parents died in June '89. I took it,' I paused, 'badly.'

The DI thought about this, scribbled something in her notebook.

'So did your drinking ever affect your ability to look after Amy? You seem to think that Paul could use it against you.'

I swallowed hard. 'I once forgot to pick her up from school.'

'Why?'

I sighed. 'Is this really relevant to finding my daughter?'

'I'm just trying to get a clear picture here, that's all.' DI Ward waited.

'I had felt stressed one morning, I often feel stressed at work. I asked my boss for an extension, went to the park and had a couple of drinks. That's it.'

'So you were drinking and you forgot to pick Amy up?'

I looked at the table. 'I fell asleep.'

'Then what happened?'

'Paul had to get her. He was angry,' my eyes smarted, 'but not as angry as I was with myself.'

DI Ward nodded and stuck her pen through the spiral of her notebook. I could see her mind at work.

'Sophie. Tell me, have you had any arguments recently? Would anyone want to hurt you or your daughter?'

'No, I don't have any friends and the only person, other than my work colleagues, left in my life is Paul.' I looked at the ground, felt my cheeks warming up, and counted the ingrained stains on the carpet, three at a time. 'Thing is, when you're an alcoholic, your friends don't stick around much. I guess, in some ways, I've distanced myself from the past. It's dangerous letting yourself get dragged back. It's like living two separate lives.' I paused, ran my tongue along my bottom lip and looked up. 'I've got Faye, though.'

'Faye?'

'She was my parents' cleaner but, really, a friend too. She was around when they died.' I nodded. 'I guess she's the only one who really gets me, knows where my mind's at.'

'OK, what about at university? As you clearly think it's relevant to this investigation, what about relationships then? Anyone who might have some sort of vendetta?'

'No.' I shook my head firmly, then I remembered. 'Well, other than Polly.'

'Polly?' The detective arched her brow.

'Bethany started getting these weird notes at university. The words were always made out of cut-up newspapers. It was obvious that she couldn't stand mine and Bethany's relationship. We were close, you know. And she wanted a part of that.'

'And her name was Polly? Polly what?'

'Actually, we never knew who it was. She always signed off "P" and because Bethany had this really weird doll that her father had given her as a child,' I pulled a face, 'it was like something from a Stephen King movie that I had called Polly, I joked that Polly the doll was behind the notes.'

DI Ward gave a small shake to her head. 'And have you heard from this person since?'

'Since Bethany died, no.'

The DI scribbled something down. 'Your parents. How did they die?'

'Car crash.' I swallowed hard. 'There one minute, gone the next. Your entire family gone in a minute, can you imagine that? How you can lose everything so quickly?'

DI Ward's lips moved almost imperceptibly at the corners, and she shook her head.

'You asked about arguments,' I continued, 'and I can't imagine anyone wanting to hurt Amy. She's eight, for god's sake. Who wants to hurt a child?' Then with a sickening realisation, I said, 'Do you think someone's hurt her?' Clutching the sides of the chair, I repeated my question. 'Do you think someone wants to hurt her? I mean, it's one thing to hurt me, but Amy...'

The DI looked apologetic. 'Sorry, I didn't mean to suggest that at all. No, for the time being, we assume that she is OK.'

'What now, Detective? This is my little girl we're talking about.' I surveyed the room and picked at a loose button on my coat. 'Look, are you going to spend your time asking me these pointless questions or find my little girl?'

'We have officers out looking,' she confirmed. 'Listen, what you said about your friend, about a murder, I want to believe you.'

I sat up.

'But your memory seems hazy, unsure?'

'Yes.'

'I wondered if you might consider therapy?'

I pursed my lips. 'I told you, I'm done with therapists.'

'No, this is a guy who works for the police, I'm not going to lie that it's a long shot but he's helped someone before, and,' she paused, 'maybe he can help you too.'

'Help me with what?'

'If you really think this woman seems familiar and you really think she may be relevant to this investigation, I need more.'

'So?'

'So, this guy is a clinical psychologist, and he specialises in using exposure therapy to provoke the trauma and bring back those crucial memories. He's cracked a case for us before, and you seem a prime candidate for him.' She hesitated. 'I know that it might seem far-fetched but let him try? If Amy has been abducted...'

'If?'

'I mean we can't rule out she may have run away, despite both your protestations.' She breathed deeply. 'Listen, our records state your friend committed suicide but some of the official documentation doesn't stack up.'

'What do you mean?'

'I mean, talk to him? His name's Darren Fletcher. He's good.' A smile crossed her lips for the first time that day. 'I think we could do this together.'

'Do you believe me, then?'

She cleared her throat. 'I would not be doing my job properly if I didn't listen to everything you've told me today.' She stood up. 'I've also arranged a liaison officer to take you back home. Her name's Fiona.'

'Why do I need a liaison officer? Is she there to keep an eye on me?'

'No, Sophie,' she said, 'she's there to look after you.'

'What about Paul? You can't let him go until you get the truth out of him. Surely, that's a quicker route than therapy?' I asked, incredulous. 'I mean he was there today.'

'Your ex-husband stands by his statement.' DI Ward hesitated. 'He says he was out shopping.' She looked at me, her gaze imploring. 'Please, try this guy. He's good.'

'Do you get something in return for a referral, is that why you're so keen?' Even as I said it, I regretted my words. 'Sorry, I don't trust therapists, they don't listen.'

'Look at it as a way of finding Amy. We can't rule anything out.'

She patted my arm awkwardly; it was quickly becoming a familiar gesture. 'We've alerted all forces and border controls.' I could sense she was struggling, again, with the intimacy of the moment. 'We'll find her. It's just up to you to help us as much as you can.' I nodded and she added, 'And Paul, of course.' She opened the door. 'Is there someone you can call? Someone to come and be with you? Other than Fiona.'

I shook my head. 'No one.'

She cocked her head to one side. 'Anyone, Sophie. You just shouldn't be by yourself right now.' She glanced at her notebook. 'What about Faye?'

'No,' I said quickly, 'she's too old and frail, I don't want to worry her.'

'But if she understands you as well as you say she does, this is probably a good time to contact her. You really need someone.'

I shook my head again, adamant. 'No, I don't want to worry her even further.'

'Even further?'

'She's always worrying about me.' I waved my hand through the air, brushing off the unease I felt in the pit of my stomach. 'I've learnt that it's easier to talk as Sophie the successful lawyer and mother to a beautiful girl, and not as,' I paused, furrowed my brow, 'not as the other side of me.'

DI Ward gave a small shrug. 'Anyone else?'

'I guess there's Oliver.' I fumbled in my bag for a tissue but the detective beat me to it and took one out of her own pocket. She appeared to have a never-ending supply.

'It's clean.'

I smiled gratefully and took it.

'Who's Oliver?'

'Oliver Dyers. He's a guy, a friend. We were reacquainted recently. I knew him at university. He looked me up a month ago. I guess I needed someone, I didn't want to be alone any more.' I blushed. 'Though, nothing's happened, so it's not like that.'

The detective nodded. I could see her mind ticking over. 'He just reappears out of the blue?'

'He wouldn't take Amy,' I said firmly. 'He barely sees his own daughter, Annabel. His ex-wife makes it difficult. He knows how hard it is to live without a child.'

'Why's he back then?'

'Because he says he thinks about me all the time.'

She nodded, stayed quiet for a moment before she said, 'I'll want to talk to him too.'

CHAPTER 6

A handful of forensics officers had been and gone. Fiona, the Family Liaison Officer, bustled in with two steaming mugs of tea.

'Here you go, Sophie,' the FLO said, handing me a mug.' 'Could be just what you need.'

I pulled a face but thanked her. She handed the other to Oliver who had made his way over to the house immediately after hearing the news.

'Do you need anything else? I'll be back in the morning, if you're OK?' The woman, a petite mousey-haired woman with speckles of grey, stood in the doorway to the living room and waited for my instructions.

'No, you've been great, Fiona. Thank you.' I smiled appreciatively. At times, in the last few hours, I had wanted to tell everyone to get out of my house and for everything to return to normal. But I knew that normal wasn't an option any more, besides which, Fiona was only doing her job.

'Right you are,' the small woman said, shrugging on a biker jacket. 'I'll be back tomorrow morning then. If not before.' She smiled at us both. 'You know, if there have been any developments. Don't forget you've got my mobile number if you need me.'

I nodded. 'Doing anything nice tonight?' I wasn't sure why I tried to make small talk.

If she was surprised by my attempt at friendliness, she didn't show it. 'I've just got to make dinner, wash Damien's football clothes. That kind of thing.' She grinned, forgetting herself. 'A mother's work is…' She stopped, flushing beetroot. 'Oh, sorry. I didn't think.'

I waved it off. 'It doesn't matter.'

She looked at me, unsure of what to say.

'Really, Fiona,' I said, 'it doesn't matter. You can't stop living your life because mine has been turned upside down.'

Fiona patted the doorjamb. 'Sorry,' she muttered again. 'See you tomorrow.'

The door slammed and the house was plunged into a thick silence. Oliver remained perched on the edge of the armchair and waited for me to talk.

'I'm sorry I called,' I stated flatly. 'I know this is all a bit out of the blue.'

'My god, Sophie. Don't ever apologise. I'm glad you called. You shouldn't be alone right now.' He gazed on me softly. 'Really.'

I sat on the sofa staring vacantly ahead. Fiona's cup of tea was quickly going cold.

'Why do we British think tea will solve everything?'

'Fiona was just trying to make you feel better. Anyway, it might warm you up.' He looked at me concerned. 'You haven't stopped shaking. I've put the heating on and you should eat something soon too.'

I mimicked the situation, 'Officer, my daughter's gone missing. Oh dear. Would you like a cup of tea?' A small giggle escaped my lips and no sooner had it made its way into the world, another one followed, until I was laughing hysterically. Only, when I held my hand up to my face, I realised I wasn't laughing any more, I was crying.

I wanted to tell Oliver to stop fussing, that he wasn't my mother. But, on the other hand, I wanted him to take me in his arms and tell me what to do. Because it felt as if my own mind had shut down, I had forgotten how to do the most mundane tasks. Forgotten, or perhaps, couldn't be bothered. I mean, what was the point in eating, drinking, sleeping when your child was missing? Amy gave me a reason to get up every morning; she made me want to be a better person. Now, she was gone.

'Do you want to lie down for a bit? Get your energy back?' He got up; put a hand on my shoulder. 'You look exhausted.'

'My daughter is missing. Why would I want a lie down?' I asked dully.

'Because you've been through a lot today.'

'I wouldn't be able to sleep.' I leant back into the cushions. 'Oli, where do you think she might be?'

'I'm not sure, Soph. But we'll find her.' Oliver dragged his hand through his hair. 'I just don't understand why Paul would lie.'

'You and me both.'

'Can you think of any reason? Anything?' He looked as desperate for answers as I was.

I put my hands over my face. 'I don't know,' I said, tears pricking the back of my eyes. 'Paul doesn't want me to get custody but would he go this far? I mean it's one thing to get at me but another to use our daughter, surely?' I sniffed. 'He started telling the detectives about the drinking, which is ridiculous because it's under control now.' I looked up. 'It is.' I gave a firm nod. 'Also, he told them that I'm not fit to be a mother. When he said that, Oli, honest to god, I was this close to…' I trailed off. Oliver sat down on the sofa, putting his arm around me. 'If he can make out I'm incapable of looking after Amy then he wins. Only, he can't go on lying forever?' Panic clamoured in my throat: was he planning to run away with our little girl? 'Can he?'

'But,' Oliver started tentatively, 'this is ridiculous. It's not human.' He tightened his hold on me. 'What kind of parent would put their own child at risk?'

'I don't know, I don't know, I don't know.' My throat was tight and dry. 'I don't know what he's capable of any more.'

'From what you've told me, Paul certainly sounds like he'd do anything to ensure he has sole custody of Amy,' Oliver agreed, 'but he loves her, doesn't he?'

'I can't imagine he would do anything to her because, as much as he hates me, he does love Amy. I know he would die if anything happened to her.'

'Has anything else happened?'

I told him about the woman outside the burger place, the same woman I thought I had seen talking to Amy.

'Who is she? A stalker?'

I shook my head. 'I don't recognise her, but her voice was so familiar. Made me think of Bethany right away.' I looked at him. 'The detective wants me to have therapy sessions, try and jog my memory as to why I know her. I told her about Bethany and the night she was murdered.' I shrugged. 'Not sure what she was thinking. Their records state Bethany committed suicide. Which is a lie.'

He studied my face. Oli had never believed me. He had agreed with the Priory doctors; I was suffering from post-traumatic stress.

'I might go and take a shower,' I said quietly.

'Good idea.' He smiled brightly, almost too brightly. 'It'll make you feel better.'

I walked slowly up the stairs and, not able to make it as far as my bedroom, I sat down on the middle stair, with a thud. I heard Oliver pad along the hall and watched him lift an envelope off the mat.

'Sophie?' he hollered and bounded up the stairs. 'Sorry, I didn't mean to shout. I thought you were in your room. You've got a letter here. Strange there's no stamp.' He touched the top of my head tenderly. 'I'll be downstairs, OK? I'm going to make you something to eat.'

'There's nothing in the fridge.'

'There will be.' He smiled and caressed my cheek between his forefinger and thumb. 'I'll go out and get something. See you in a bit.'

'Thank you.' I grabbed his hand as he turned. 'And Oli?'

'Yeah?' He looked back.

'Thank you.' I leant my forehead against his hand. 'I just want to start looking for her, you know? But I don't know where to start.'

'What did the detective say about searching?'

'She said to stay at home. There was no point in looking unless we had some idea where she could be. Also, just in case she turns up or calls the landline, I should be here.'

'You've tried her friends?'

'Paul rang around.' I sighed heavily. 'She's never had many friends. Sometimes I wonder if her not having many friends is down to the divorce, down to me and Paul.'

'No,' he said simply. 'You are a good mother and I know that you will not only have Amy back very soon but that the court will see that she really is best off living with you.' He withdrew his hand and smoothed the top of my hair. 'Just be strong. For Amy.'

He bounded down the stairs, grabbed his coat off the banister and smiled at me. 'See you in a bit.' He opened the door. 'Have that shower.'

The door shut and for the first time that day I was truly alone. I couldn't remember the last time the house had felt so empty. Strange, when I thought about it, because I lived by myself – surely, I should be used to the silence? But it was different now. The silence was filled with uncertainty, palpable fear and worry: was Amy OK? Had she come to any harm? Would I see her again?

I flipped the package over. The writing looked familiar and yet I couldn't place it. It had been hand delivered. Sliding my forefinger along the flap, I tore the end open. Inside I found what appeared to be two photos. I tipped the envelope upside down and the contents fell on the stair in front of me. Bile rose in my throat and I shoved my fist in my mouth, stifling a scream. I could feel the familiar ringing in my ears and my vision started to blur over. My breathing grew shallower and I thought I might faint, I couldn't think straight.

I picked up the photos one by one; I couldn't bear to look at them. Ripping the first photo in half, I stumbled down the stairs to the kitchen. Grabbing a lighter from the odds and ends drawer, I burnt the photo over the kitchen sink, my hands shaking. Bethany's face smouldered, her face reduced to ashes. I couldn't watch any longer; it wouldn't burn fast enough. I set fire to the second photo, watching the glossy paper curl up and shrink, when I suddenly realised I needed to keep it, keep the evidence. I blew hard on the smouldering paper and held the small remnants of the photo. My vision had started to return, the ringing in my ears subsided, and I looked in dismay at what I had done. I needed people to believe me and, yet, I was powerless in the clutches of a panic attack.

Turning on the tap I washed away any remnants of ash.

A cold sweat moved over my body, my legs buckling beneath me. I had no idea who it was from but I knew now that this wasn't a hoax. This was revenge: my past had finally caught up with me and was threatening to drag me backwards to a very dark place.

I took out my mobile and punched in the detective's number – off the back of her card – and she picked up on the first ring. 'It's me.' I told her about the photographs.

I could literally feel her perk up at the end of the phone. 'OK, great. Don't touch them any further. I need to get forensics onto them.'

I was trembling, unable to hold the phone steady. 'I've burnt them.'

'What?' DI Ward spoke sternly, disbelief flooding the line. 'Why would you do that, Sophie? I'm trying to help you here.'

'I was scared, I just wanted to be rid of them.' My voice cracked. 'I've got a piece of one though, and the envelope.'

She didn't say anything but after a pause exhaled loudly. 'Can you put it in a bag for me? Don't touch it.' She paused. 'What do you think about the therapist I told you about? Have you thought about it?'

'Yes, I've thought about it and I just think it would be a waste of precious time.'

She let out a long breath. I could sense her support for me had dramatically waned.

'I'm sorry about the photos.' A sob rose up and I cried openly now. 'But I need you believe me that it's something to do with the night Bethany was murdered.'

'Really?' She wasn't convinced. 'Actually, I think you're wasting my time. You burn the photos and you tell me you don't want to see a therapist who might be able to help you. You're not giving me much.'

'I'm telling you everything I can.'

She hesitated. 'Your friend, if you even knew her, committed suicide. I have it on record.'

'But you said, something didn't look right about it. I don't know what it is you can see that doesn't look right but I can assure you it's not right.'

'Then why not see the therapist?'

'Because therapists don't believe me.'

Her silence spoke volumes.

'The only therapist I've agreed to see since all those years ago when Bethany died is my AA counsellor, to help me get my child back. I don't need anyone prying into my past.'

She didn't say anything for a second. 'Why, Sophie? What is it we're going to find?' She cleared her throat. 'We're doing everything we can to find your daughter but are you?' Without waiting for my answer, she said, 'Bye, Sophie.'

She cut the call and I sat back on the stair, my hands still shaking, and then it began, that fuzzy feeling around my temples. I pushed my forefingers into them, squeezed my eyes shut and willed the feeling to go away. A fleeting image of Bethany snapped through my head, and then her hand with a gun in it, pulling the trigger on herself. I stood up suddenly, willing the image to disappear. How could I know what was the truth if my own mind was so unsure?

CHAPTER 7

I woke up with a start: drenched in sweat, my fingers kneading the bed sheets. I had seen Amy in my dream. She was five years old again and playing outside with her favourite teddy bear. She had invited me to a tea party. We were to have the sandwiches we had prepared earlier, lemonade and jam tarts for pudding. I was told to arrive at a certain time and to wear a hat. Amy solemnly sat me down at the child-sized table, my legs bunched up in front of me, poured the lemonade and we talked about the weather.

Daylight shone through the slit in the top of the curtain and my eyes flitted around the room. The reality of my situation hit me hard: it knocked the breath from my lungs. Silent tears gushed onto the pillow. I wanted to dream again: of Amy, of the tea party, her smile.

I stared up at the ceiling, too afraid to close my eyes should I not be able to picture Amy again.

'Sophie?' Oliver whispered in the dark.

'Oliver?' I rolled over. 'Did you get my note? I'm sorry. I went straight to bed. I was too tired to eat.'

I heard the door creak as it was pushed open further.

'I could hear you crying.' The bed sagged as he lay down next to me.

I put my hand up to my wet cheek. 'What time is it?'

'It's almost 8 am. You clearly needed the rest.'

'I didn't fall asleep until four or so this morning. I was just thinking about Amy,' I said. 'And Paul, and his lies.' He laced his fingers through mine. 'Oli, I'm scared.'

'I know.'

'I appreciate you being here but maybe it's best you leave.' I sat up, my mind thinking back to DI Ward questioning Oliver's sudden reappearance and let go of his hand. 'This,' I gestured to us, 'it's the wrong time. I mean I don't even know why you came looking for me. It feels amazing to suddenly have you back in my life, but I'm too consumed by all this.'

'That's why you need me here.' He hesitated. 'As long as you don't hold anything back from me.'

'Why did you come back?' I ignored his question, turned on the bedside lamp and noticed that he too hadn't slept.

'Because I've always loved you and I've never stopped thinking about what we could have had.' He hesitated. 'You know, if Paul hadn't come into your life.'

Oliver had told me his divorce papers had been finalised and he wanted to rewrite history; he had never got over me. I knew he had been insanely jealous of Paul and, before she died, Bethany too.

He frowned. 'I found part of a photo on the floor, by the sink. You burnt it in the sink, didn't you? I saw the lighter on the side. Was it Bethany?'

'Yes.'

He placed his hands on his thighs.

'Sophie, whatever you do, don't keep anything from me, OK? I won't be able to help you if you do.' He paused. 'Was there a photo of her in that envelope that was delivered tonight?'

'Yes.'

'Sophie...' He stopped short, clearly clamouring for an explanation. 'Damn. I shouldn't have let you open it alone.' He let out a long breath. 'You never told me what happened, after Bethany committed suicide. I remember it all being so sudden.' He looked at me, searching. 'You two had started to avoid the rest of us then, next thing we knew, Bethany was dead.' He flinched. 'I remember it painfully well because you had been out, partying with Paul. None of us knew where he came from either.' He dropped his head. 'And that was it, the end of us.'

I swallowed hard. 'I was young and stupid.'

'I've never pushed you on it before now and, I don't know for sure, but I think you're holding back on me. What did you and Bethany used to get up to?'

'Not much,' I lied.

'Sophie, I don't think you're being honest with me. Please.'

'We just went out, you know, to parties.'

'Were you at one of these parties that the rest of us were never invited to the night she killed herself?'

'She was murdered.' I clenched my jaw.

'So you keep saying, but she killed herself, Sophie. Do you really believe that after all these years?' His voice broke. 'You admitted yourself to the Priory. I visited you every Sunday, do you remember that?' He looked up, his eyes swimming. 'You often went out with Paul, when you were feeling strong, but we didn't go out. You didn't want to leave the Priory with me.' He patted the duvet. 'Paul clearly always had something I didn't.'

The memories were too painful, too raw. 'He just seemed to understand.'

'And I didn't?'

'You were like the rest of them. Telling me it was the trauma. That I had imagined it.'

'And Paul?'

'He seemed in control and I needed that, he just seemed to get it.'

'So he agreed with you, about Bethany?'

'No,' I shook my head, my voice quiet, 'the opposite. He was more sure than anyone that Bethany had committed suicide, but the way he told me…' I searched for the words. 'It's hard to explain but I felt safe.' I smiled through my tears. 'Which is ironic.'

'When I visited you, we never spoke. We would just sit there and hold hands.'

I didn't say anything.

'God, woman.' He choked back a sob. 'I wish you would talk to me. It's like there's a wall between us.'

I stifled a moan with my hand.

'I'm sorry.' He stood. 'You're probably right, you don't really need me. You never have.'

I knew he didn't mean this but I couldn't face it now. The problem was Oliver was sweet and caring, but he was as easily swayed by institution as the rest of them. The doctors in the Priory, all those years ago, had called me delusional; I was suffering from anxiety attacks and carrying guilt over my friend killing herself. I tried to tell Doctor Hurst, my consultant, but he too refused to listen and chose to side with his colleagues. He said that, if I had woken up in my own bed, it was highly unlikely, if not impossible, that I was there when Bethany died and as the police had confirmed suicide, that's all there was to it.

I was about to get up when the doorbell rang.

'Who on earth?' I shot up in bed, my stomach roiling with nerves. My first thought was that they had found Amy. I threw back the cover, quickly realising that they would have rung me. If there was an officer at the door, it could only mean that the news was bad. Even, fatal. Blood rushed in my ears.

'Wait here,' Oliver shouted from the stairs. 'It's safer if I go.'

The floorboards creaked as he made his way back down the remaining stairs. It was barely a minute before Oliver returned.

I braced myself, daring not breathe as I watched his face crumple. He couldn't bring himself to speak.

'Oh god, she's dead, isn't she?'

'No. No news.' Oliver sat down quickly and took me in his arms. 'Fiona is downstairs. She needs you to come to the station with her.'

I swung my legs off the bed and put on the same jeans and sweater as yesterday. They sat in a heap on the floor where I'd left them. I turned to him at the door. 'I'm…'

'Yes?'

'I'm…' I rapped the doorjamb. 'Never mind.'

I left, not sure of why Oliver was back in my life. He must have known that history couldn't be rewritten.

CHAPTER 8

DI Ward had got hold of CCTV footage of the street corner that faced Acton Green.

'I've been trawling this,' she said, the images running behind her. 'The whole of Saturday.' She looked worn.

I watched people heading to and from the Green, toward Acton Green Tube and some heading back up toward Acton. It was strange to see people going about their business, probably totally unaware they were being watched.

'I had just about given up,' she continued, grabbing a rancid-looking coffee and drinking deeply, 'and then I saw this.' Her voice was cool and she barely made eye contact.

She paused the image.

I leant in toward the screen, not really sure what I was looking at.

'There. Is that the woman you were talking about?'

I stared hard at the grainy image and as DI Ward zoomed in, I shot bolt upright, my legs starting to tremble. 'Yes, I think that's her.' It was hard to be sure, the image was so fuzzy, but her outline now looked so familiar.

'Unfortunately, I haven't found any footage of her face but it seemed to match the description you gave me.' She glanced down at her notes; my statement. 'A woman, five foot seven-ish inches, black coat.' She tapped the screen. 'I haven't seen Paul and Amy, though.' She glanced at me.

'Yes, but you haven't seen me either?' I challenged.

'No.'

'Well, you know I was there so that doesn't prove Paul is telling the truth.' My breathing had quickened. 'Can you zoom in a bit more?'

'It wouldn't make much difference. I mean this is sadly not much to go on but at least we have a positive sighting. And you're sure this is the woman you saw talking to Amy?'

'Yes.' I was sure because the same sickly dread washed over me.

'OK, well I'll keep looking. Get one of the PCs to scan the day before and after too.' She nodded, rubbed her eyes with her forefinger and thumb. 'Any more thoughts on the therapy? We need you to help us here.'

I shook my head. 'I told you I'm not going down that route. You just push Paul on why he's lying.'

She gave a nod. 'Fine.'

'Are you pushing him?'

'We're doing everything we can.' She stood up. 'Though, I'm not sure you're doing everything you can.'

I left the police station feeling like time was running away like sand in a timer, yet nothing had changed. As I emerged on the steps I looked up and down the road. I felt like someone was watching me. Perhaps exhaustion was taking its toll and, with it, I was becoming increasingly paranoid. But a sixth sense told me I wasn't. I looked up and down the street, my gaze searching the buildings, the passers-by. As I scanned the road, my eyes caught a movement in one of the windows above me and my eyes came to rest on the second floor of the police station.

DI Ward stood in the window watching me. My breath caught and, seconds later, the detective moved away. Her belief in me was ebbing away; sadly my own belief in what I thought to be true was ebbing too.

CHAPTER 9

Once outside, I phoned the one person who would understand. It took me a few seconds to find her number in the back of my Filofax; DI Ward had taken my phone off me so they could check out details on the call. I didn't think their forensics would stop at that. I had found the brick-like Pay-As-You-Go I kept in the kitchen drawer, for emergencies. As I waited for her to pick up, I realised that in not telling Faye, the person most like a mother to me, I had been pretending that none of this was happening. It was easier to believe that I would wake up from this nightmare if I didn't admit to being scared to anyone.

Now, it was time to face reality.

'Faye? Oh, thank god. You're at home.'

'Sophie. What is it? You sound awful.' Faye's soft Irish lilt threatened to crumble my resolve as I walked hurriedly down the police station steps. I didn't want the detective to see me break. She might read it as yet another sign of guilt. 'It's just gone 9 am. Of course I'm in. What on earth is the matter?'

I filled Faye in on the last twenty-four hours.

'Oh, Sophie…' Her voice trailed off. 'I wish you had rung me sooner.'

'You and me both,' I agreed as a wave of exhaustion swept through my body. 'Faye,' I nibbled at my lower lip,

'I need to find my little girl. It's my job to protect her and I… And I failed her.'

'Shhh, Sophie. It's all right,' she soothed gently down the phone. 'You have not failed her.'

'I thought life was about to change, you know?' I sniffled. 'I got cross with her. Just before she went missing. Now, I just wish I hadn't snapped.'

'Sophie, stop beating yourself up. You weren't to know.'

I started to walk. The cool air on my face felt good after the stuffiness of the interview room. I wasn't entirely sure where I was heading but I needed some space.

'Tell me what you think,' Faye said. 'Do you think Paul knows where she is?'

'How else would it explain the lies?' I said, turning into York House Gardens. A young girl of about Amy's age ran past squealing with delight as her mother pretended to chase her at full speed. She wore a Brownies uniform and her pigtails bounced up and down on her shoulders.

'Careful not to get your uniform mucky,' I heard the mother shout after the girl.

'It does appear Paul isn't to be trusted,' Faye continued. 'But would he do this? Really? Kidnap Amy?'

'At first, I thought it was impossible but the longer he spins these lies, I'm beginning to realise I might have never known what he was capable of.'

I told her about the phone call at the fair; the anniversary of Bethany's death.

'You know that night?' She had never been able to bring herself to say the words.

'Yes.'

Faye didn't speak.

'Faye?'

I knew she was finding this difficult. 'That Doctor Hurst said it was safe to say you weren't there, that you were suffering from anxiety-related blackouts. That finding out your best friend had, you know, years after your parents… Well, you thought you had been there.'

'But the thing is, Faye, this woman seemed so familiar. I swear she was there that night.'

'Sophie, darling, Bethany was never found. It was suicide, that's what they said.'

I could feel my frustration mounting. 'Yes, that's what everyone *said*, but maybe it's a cover-up.' I cried uncontrollably now. 'Maybe I'm not bloody mad, maybe I was there with Bethany and maybe this woman was there.'

I told her about the photos.

'Look, no matter what anyone thinks about Bethany's death, there are facts glaring us all in the face. Bethany died twenty years ago, on my birthday. Twenty years later Amy disappears. I receive a call, I receive photos. This is someone who wants to hurt me, or wants me dead.' My voice cracked. 'Or Amy dead.'

Faye gasped. 'Don't talk like that, Sophie. There will be some innocent explanation.'

I couldn't do this any more. The light-headedness had returned and I stumbled forward a couple of steps and, without warning, my legs collapsed beneath me and I fell onto my knees. The sound of the little girl still squealing grew achingly louder.

What I presumed was seconds later, I came around and found the mother of the girl gazing at me with concern. 'Are you OK?' she asked, her hand resting on mine. 'Shall I call an ambulance?'

I shook my head and focused on breathing deeply. 'Would you mind just helping me to a bench? I think I'm just feeling a bit faint.'

'Of course not,' the woman said and I gathered my phone off the pavement before being gently steered to the nearest seat. The girl hid behind her mother's leg.

'Are you sure I shouldn't call someone for you?'

I shook my head and smiled gratefully; the dizziness had started to pass. 'No, you've been very kind, thank you.'

'OK, if you're sure you're all right?'

I nodded. 'Just been very tired recently.'

Her eyebrows furrowed and then relaxed. She smiled. 'Come on, you,' she said to the girl. 'Let's do your laces up. We're going to be late.'

The girl sat down and looked up at me. She smiled goofily and offered me a gummy bear from her pocket. It was covered in grains of sand.

'I'm sure the lady doesn't want that, Melissa.' The mother smiled apologetically.

I took the sweet and smiled at the girl. 'Thank you, that's very kind. My favourite colour too.' It took everything in my power not to hug her and hold her tightly against me. She was a younger version of Amy and, as she busied herself with the badges covering her sash, my heart swelled with longing. I wanted my little girl back. Holding the sticky sweet in my palm, I was reminded of prising open Amy's small hand less than twenty-four hours ago and watching the lolly fall to the ground.

After a few minutes, the girl jumped off the bench and waved goodbye.

'Take care of yourself,' the woman said over her shoulder.

I thanked her again before I realised my phone was ringing.

'Hello?' I answered quietly.

'Sophie, are you all right?' Faye sniffed; I knew she was trying to hold herself together for my sake.

'I'm fine,' I lied. 'Just lost signal.'

Faye's pregnant pause told me she knew I was lying.

'Sophie, I'm worried about you.' She added, 'If you need me I'm always here for you.' She hesitated and

I could sense she was trying not to cry. 'Please let me know if there's anything I can do. Your parents would be so worried.' She paused. 'Are you feeling yourself lately or...' Her voiced trailed off. 'I mean, I know that sometimes you get a bit confused.'

I didn't like where this was going and I promised to phone with any further news before hanging up.

I sat on the bench for a while watching the world go by. The sun glinted off a large bronze figure of a man walking his dog; a piece of art commissioned by the council. The gleam hit my eyes as I shifted forward on the bench to try and read the plaque beneath it.

I was suddenly struck by an image.

My memory was hazy. A knife. I closed my eyes, let out an audible gasp as I could almost feel the prick of the knife's point in my back. I shook, my stomach swirled with anguish and the lapping waves of nausea trickled in and out of my brain. I urged my mind to think further, to remember anything. A fragmented image of a hand and I squeezed my eyes shut even tighter. But then all I saw was black. The same black that had erased my memory twenty years ago, and I had woken up in my own bed.

I opened my eyes, my knuckles white as I gripped my handbag.

It was time to meet the clinical psychologist.

CHAPTER 10

Darren Fletcher had agreed to meet me straight away because of the urgency of the case. He was stood outside Acton Green Tube station. He wore scruffy jeans and a navy blue wool jacket. He was busy making small talk with the florist as I exited. He approached me.

'Sophie? I'm Darren.'

We shook hands.

'How are you holding up?'

'I'm not.'

'You're doing well,' he said.

'How do you know?' I arched a brow.

'I mean, you're here. You're trying.' He gave another small smile. 'It's admirable.'

We walked toward the green.

'I know this is probably hard for you, but I thought whilst the fair is still here, it might jog another memory.'

The rides and tents were indeed all still in place, only this time, it being mid-week, they weren't lit up and instead the green had assumed a deathly solitude about it.

I looked to where the candyfloss seller had been set up. There was nothing there now. My eyes smarted.

Darren looked at me. 'Tell me what you're thinking.'

'That's where Amy was when she disappeared.'

'Right.' He caressed his unshaven chin. 'And where were you?'

I walked a few metres on. 'Here.'

'OK, close your eyes, Sophie.' He looked around us. 'There's no one about, so try to relax and remember the sights and smells of the day.'

I nodded.

'What could you smell?'

'Um,' I hesitated. 'Candyfloss, hot dogs, Paul's cologne.' I opened my eyes. 'Even though he wasn't there with me at that point.'

'OK, close your eyes again, Sophie. That's really good. How did it feel? Was it warm?'

'Yeah, it was pretty warm. The sun was on my face.'

'OK, and then you had a call. So you got your phone out of your bag?'

I nodded. 'I got my phone out and I was looking over there.' I pointed, not opening my eyes.

'Right, and this woman's voice, did you know right away that this was the same woman who spoke to Amy earlier? The same one you saw outside the hamburger joint?'

'Yes.'

'And how do you think you came to that conclusion, because I presume you had never heard her voice before?'

I hadn't thought about that. 'Gut instinct, I guess.'

I sensed Darren shuffle slightly. A couple walked past chatting, then stopped as they came up alongside us. I opened my eyes, suddenly self-conscious. Darren smiled.

'Don't worry, it's London. They won't have thought anything of it.'

I nodded, closed my eyes, willed my mind to focus. 'Yes, I knew it was her. I could just sense it, the woman's voice sounded so familiar, like a voice you would never forget.'

'OK, did you hear anything else? Maybe in the background?'

'No,' I started, and then my eyes snapped open. 'Yes, I do remember. I thought I heard someone calling my name.'

'Could it have been Amy?'

'No, it was really similar to the voice on the phone.'

'So this woman was speaking to you and you could hear another person calling your name? A woman or a child? Go on, try and go further with that, Sophie.'

'I didn't think anything of it, thought it was just some woman nearby, a strange coincidence, you know? But come to think of it it's like there were two of them on the phone.' I squinted into the sun.

Darren came up and held my arm. 'That was good. Really good.' He gestured in front of him. 'Let's talk about Bethany. Tell me about when you first met her.'

We walked and talked, and I felt comfortable.

'As soon as I saw her, I knew it was love. Bethany was beautiful.' I blushed. 'I mean not in that way, but she had a magic about her.'

He nodded and I went on.

'She wasn't beautiful in an obvious way, no. She had a slightly wonky front tooth and when she was sad,' I paused, 'which turned out to be quite often, it's hard to explain but it was as if her face didn't emanate the same glow, the same wonder.'

'What did you feel about Bethany when she was sad?' He gently kicked at some leaves as his foot hit the grass.

'I loved her in those moments as much as any. Because, on those few occasions, she needed me. I always wanted her to need me because she knew I needed her.'

'Why did you need her?'

I shrugged. 'I'm not sure, I think it was because she just got me. No one, not even my boyfriends,' I stopped, 'including Oliver, ever got me like she did.'

'So tell me about when you first met.'

We rounded the green now and started heading back on ourselves.

'We had introduced ourselves briefly on the first day. She had been dropped off by her mother and, I could tell, her mum was relieved that Bethany had met someone who might look out for her daughter. To be honest, Bethany hadn't struck me as the kind of girl who needed protection.' I chuckled. 'She had bags of confidence. Or, at least, I had thought she did. Within minutes of introductions, we were swept out the door by our other housemates and we all headed to the student union bar. I tried to talk further with her, but I was jostling for her attention. The guys couldn't keep their eyes off her!'

'Did you find her attractive?' Darren was gazing into the distance as we spoke.

'Yes, I mean she had long legs and tanned arms – she had clearly been in the sun over the summer.' I smiled. 'In contrast, I was pasty – I hadn't got out much, not since the accident – choosing to spend my time in my room.'

Darren slowed. 'The accident?'

I swallowed hard. 'Yeah, I remember it had been a warm evening when they came to the door. I tried to take in what the young WPC was saying.' I stopped now. 'She was telling me my parents were dead. A car accident.'

I gave Darren a sidelong look. He was frowning.

'It wasn't until the police woman had driven me to the hospital and I was asked to ID my parents that the tears came. After that, there was no consoling me.'

'So, you were eighteen?'

I nodded. 'Yes, Faye, the cleaner, had brought me meals and tried to chivvy me along but, for two months, I wouldn't speak to anyone. I realised now, it must've been hard for her too. My parents had been her family, and me, her daughter. I had no other family: we depended entirely on one another.'

I felt old wounds reopening and I willed myself not to cry now.

'Go on,' Darren encouraged.

'Well, walking along that night, heading to the union, I was amazed I was even at university. I had received my A-level grades in the midst of that bleak summer and I had barely registered the two As and a B. It had taken a lot of persuasion but, in the end, Faye had won: "It's what your father would have wanted for you," she had said.' I paused. 'She was right.'

'So you're walking to the union and do you ever talk to Bethany?'

'Yes, eventually. I desperately wanted to join in the conversation but I was shy around her.'

The October breeze blew across my face and reminded me of our conversation that night.

'I remember she asked me if I was cold and she gave me her jacket.' I gave a small laugh. 'I remember her smile made me go weak at the knees.'

'What exactly was so attractive about her?'

'Well, even more than her physical beauty it was this strange power she had. It kind of left me wanting to be her.'

'Later, did you feel jealous of her? Did she have something you wanted?'

I stopped walking again and Darren turned to me, his face open. I wondered if I really could trust this man. I felt like I was talking about subjects that I shouldn't admit to anyone, let alone a therapist working for the force. I wondered if this was somehow a leading question.

'Yes, I was jealous of Bethany.'

'Why?' he pushed.

When I didn't speak, he said, 'Sophie, I'm trying to make you remember and sometimes that hurts, I know.'

'I was jealous of her ability to have people eating out the palms of her hands,' I hesitated, 'mainly me.'

He nodded. 'OK, so what else do you remember from that night? Anything?'

'Yes, I asked her about her tan.' We had started to walk again. 'And apparently her father had paid for some expensive holiday for her and her mum, but he hadn't gone. It was clearly a really sore point as she didn't speak to me for the rest of the evening.'

'Were you upset by that?'

'Yes,' I admitted, 'ridiculously I was. I had only known her for all of five minutes and she already had me feeling guilty.'

'So did you guys make up that night?'

'Yes, I remember, on the way home, I hung back again. I was still wearing her denim jacket; it smelt floral, like the perfume she wore. She told me to keep the jacket and said she didn't like to speak about her dad. She never went into why.'

'What did you say?'

I shrugged. 'I think I apologised and I remember being relieved because that's something we had in common. She didn't like talking about her dad and I didn't want to talk about my parents and the accident.' I nodded, thinking. 'Yeah, I felt good after that. Like I had found my soul mate. In fact, she was like the sister I never had. I needed her.'

Darren nodded, gave a small smile. 'Sophie, you're doing really well.' He pursed his lips before continuing, 'So, you think your past is important in finding Amy?' I nodded. 'And I agree. What we need to do is find out why now. Why twenty years later?' He waited for my confirmation. Again, I nodded. 'OK, why twenty years later, you believe the person involved in your friend's murder is linked to Amy's disappearance.' He pinched the bridge of his nose, thinking. 'Do you know if Bethany had any troubles at university with a stalker? Or someone who maybe developed some sort of obsession with her?'

I stopped abruptly. 'What do you mean?'

'I mean you believe your friend was murdered. We need to figure out why.' He studied my face. 'I mean when you talk about her, Bethany sounds like an intriguing person. She clearly had some sort of hold over you.'

I took a sharp intake of breath. 'She never had a hold over me,' I corrected him, even though I was lying. 'She was just the family I didn't have any more.'

He smiled at me gently. 'I didn't mean it in a negative way. I meant exactly that: she was your friend, a kind of sister.' He started to walk again. I jogged a couple of steps to catch up. 'So, be honest with me, Sophie, it's the only way this is going to work if you're honest with me. Bethany meant the world to you?'

I nodded. 'Of course.'

'What did you feel when perhaps her attention was on somebody else?'

I pushed my tongue around the back of my teeth, holding out on an answer.

'Sophie?'

'Like there were three of us in a relationship.'

'OK,' he nodded, 'so we need to figure out who had that same feeling, but heightened, toward Bethany, and perhaps in finding your friend's killer, we find Amy too.'

We had arrived at the Tube again, come full circle.

Darren pulled his coat more tightly around him, the wind had started to pick up. 'So, how do you think that went, Sophie? How are you feeling?'

'Drained, but a bit more hopeful.'

'Sounds pretty normal, then.' He gave a small smile. 'All in a day's work.'

I gave a small laugh, felt my shoulders loosen. 'I feel like I'm on the brink of discovering something. Like the person I am today is going to meet the person I once was.' Bubbles of excitement had started to form in the pit of my stomach. 'I think that we could do it, you know, find Amy.' My eyes suddenly smarted with tears, despite the excited knotting in my stomach. 'I need to find my daughter.'

My phone started to buzz. It was DI Ward, she spoke fast: they had just confirmed a press conference. She said it was important to put our message out there as anyone could be listening: the abductor, Amy, a member of the public who knew something.

Darren offered to drive me, told me he had actually come by car. He moved through the London traffic with confidence.

I didn't speak, my palms starting to sweat at the thought of the press conference. It made the whole thing far too real.

'Don't worry, Sophie. It'll be fine. You're in safe hands with DI Ward.'

I nodded, unconvinced. 'It feels like I'm having to share my grief with the world.' I gave him a sidelong glance. 'Whereas this feels private. I mean, what if the public think I'm a fraud?'

'Why would they do that?'

I shrugged. 'I don't know. I guess I don't trust many people. When I've opened up before, I've been judged, told I'm delusional. Who's to say they'll think anything different now?'

He pulled up outside the station, killed the engine. 'Sophie, this isn't about you. It's about finding your daughter.' His kind eyes rested on mine. 'Just focus on that.' He tapped the steering wheel with his forefinger. I watched him do it eight times and willed him to tap a ninth. I told myself, if he tapped a ninth time, the press conference would go well. He brought his hand down to his lap, and my heart beat a little faster.

'I'd like you to keep a journal. Write down anything that comes to mind – any past experience. Doesn't matter what.'

I sighed. 'The problem I have is that I'm never sure if my memories are true or in my imagination. All those doctors telling me I'm delusional, makes you question yourself.'

'Listen, it doesn't matter, there's as much truth in the made-up as there is in reality.'

Before I got out, he asked, 'Do you remember the name of the perfume Bethany wore?'

'Yes, it was Chanel No. 5,' I said, barely skipping a beat and frowned. 'Why?'

'Have you got any?'

'Yes.' I didn't tell him that I had the very bottle Bethany had used before she died and the CD we had played on repeat in the weeks leading up to her murder. It was my secret; just a couple of things to remind me of her.

'Great. Can you bring it with you when I see you next? We'll use it to evoke memories. Smell is one of the most powerful tools.' I nodded and opened the car door. 'You'll be fine. I'm on your side.'

It was then I decided I liked him; that I thought maybe I had finally found someone I could trust, and with a lighter heart, I entered the station.

CHAPTER 11

As I opened the door to the station, I found Paul stood with a young man I didn't recognise. He introduced himself as Tom Dixon, a Family Liaison Officer, looking after Paul. Fiona joined us. The situation wasn't a million miles from the family courts. Paul had his team and I had mine.

Fiona smiled at me and suggested we make a move toward the conference room. She told FLO Dixon the conference was due to start in a couple of minutes.

'How you doing, Sophie? How did it go with Darren?'

I started to explain but DI Ward had arrived and stood beside me.

'OK, Sophie. I'm sure Fiona has already explained that it's best if you read out the statement we've prepared.'

'What does Paul read out?'

DI Ward explained, 'I think it's best coming from you. As the mother.'

Paul had now joined the group and FLO Dixon hovered over his right shoulder. His hand went up as if to pat Paul on the shoulder, maybe to placate him.

'I'm not sure it is necessarily better coming from Sophie, is it?' Paul queried.

'I really think it is, Paul. Look, if it doesn't work out, and we need to hold another press conference tomorrow, then I will consider you reading out a statement.'

Paul grumbled something inaudible but made no more fuss.

'OK, I'll speak first, then, Sophie, I'll ask you to say a few words.' The detective looked at us in turn. 'OK? Everyone happy?'

I shot a sidelong look at Paul and he met my gaze; a look of sorrow passed over his face. Less than twenty-four hours ago, Amy was in Paul's care, I was getting ready to meet Amy and Paul in Chiswick and it had been my birthday. Now, we were stood outside a room full of reporters. DI Ward had said the first twenty-four hours were crucial and that this press conference could produce valuable leads. I imagined Amy staring at a television set somewhere, watching our faces appear on the screen as we pleaded for her to get in contact. Or, if she was being held prisoner, that her kidnappers would see sense and let her go. These thoughts streamed through my mind, one after another.

As we entered, DI Ward directed me to sit in the middle, Paul on one side and she the other.

'OK?' DI Ward looked at both of us and we nodded.

An expanse of faces sat in row upon row of plastic chairs. I couldn't really focus on anyone in particular and it reminded me of the one time I had been cast as a main part in a school play. I remembered, then, feeling awash with nerves but once the lights were on me and I was running through the lines we had practised for months, I drew comfort from not being able to make out anyone's face or features.

DI Ward coughed and started, 'Ladies and gentlemen...' She talked for a few minutes, giving only the facts: Amy's appearance, location, time, and date. I watched her mouth move and I only tuned back in when she said, 'Obviously, as you know, the first twenty-four hours are the most important and we urge the public to help in any way they can.' Then she looked at me and nodded. 'Ms Fraiser.'

I cleared my throat and clutched the piece of paper in my hands. It was only then that I realised I was trembling and the words on the page kept bobbing up and down like fishermen's boats at sea. My cheeks started to warm and I looked to Paul for help. He went to take the piece of paper off me but I ignored the script, and the words just tumbled out of my mouth.

'Please, Amy, if you are listening, if you see this, please know that neither your father,' I said, looking at Paul, 'nor myself are in any way angry with you. We just want you home as soon as possible.' Tears filled my eyes and my voice wavered with emotion. 'If you have our daughter, please, please, let her go. She needs to be with her parents.' Paul grabbed my hand. 'Amy is so precious to us and we couldn't bear to think anything might have…' I breathed deeply. 'Please, give us our daughter back.'

I couldn't make out the reaction in the room but seconds later, a quiet, almost excited hum started up.

'Well done,' DI Ward whispered to me and then louder, 'OK, any questions?'

A tall, languid-looking man stood, his leather jacket swamping his frame.

'Is it true that your daughter doesn't live with you, Ms Fraiser?'

I straightened, my heart beating loudly in my ears. DI Ward was already on her feet.

'Please stick to the relevant information here,' she said quickly.

'And,' continued the same reporter, his voice rising over the rippling murmurs, 'is it true that you're an alcoholic?'

'I…' I started to speak, 'I haven't…' I was floundering, falling backward.

'OK, no more questions.' The DI already had me on my feet, her hand guiding me firmly out the door. We bustled out of the room one after another. My face was flushed and my cheeks prickled as the hubbub in the room rose to a deafening level. Outside, in the comparative quiet of the corridor, Fiona came up to me and handed me a tissue.

'You did well in there, Sophie,' she said and rubbed the top of my arm. 'Never easy.'

DI Ward headed over and smiled at me, but I noticed the corners of her mouth twitching. 'Sophie, that was great. Just what we needed.' She took the press statement off me; I was still clutching it in my right hand, stunned. 'Let Fiona drive you back home, OK? I'll be in touch.'

'How did he know?' I could barely speak, my throat cotton dry.

'Don't worry.' The detective tried to dismiss it but I could tell she was riled, which riled me in turn.

'This is going to look bad, isn't it?' My eyes scanned the detective's face; I knew she was waiting for the nation to turn on me. The headlines were already swimming before my eyes. *Alcoholic mother loses child at fairground. Child too afraid to live with mother; runs away.*

Stunned, I turned to follow Fiona, only to find Paul standing right behind me. He took a step forward and awkwardly rested his hand on my arm; I flinched.

'I'm sorry.'

'Sorry?' My eyes flashed. 'Did you let it out? Did you tell a reporter about our situation? Is this all because of the court case?' Spittle leapt from my mouth as I brought my face closer to his.

He shook his head, took a step backward. 'That this had to happen to us. I haven't told anyone anything.'

So many lies.

I tried to calm myself. 'Paul, talk to me.'

His gaze dropped to the floor and he started to move off. I grabbed his hand.

'Paul, please. I know you don't want me to have custody of Amy. Is this what it's all about?'

He remained very still, not looking at me. 'See you tomorrow, Sophie, at the next conference.'

'They might find her today,' I said, injecting false hope into my voice.

'See you tomorrow,' he repeated and I let go of his hand. He walked off to join FLO Dixon by the door.

Fiona came over. 'You OK?' Her eyes flicked toward Paul.

'I just want to know why he would do this.' I jammed my hands into my pockets. 'He loves her, Fiona, he loves Amy so much. That's why none of this makes any sense at all.'

When we turned the corner to home, I spotted dozens of vans outside and journalists getting themselves ready in front of cameras, photographers snapping pictures of the house and garden. Some of my neighbours had gathered on one corner of the street and I saw my neighbour opposite talking in earnest to a journalist.

'Oh my god.'

'Don't worry,' Fiona said. 'I need you to remember not to say anything. If you do, just state "no comment" and that's it.' She killed the engine and journalists and camera crew ran toward the car, their faces, notebooks and lenses up against the glass.

Fiona got out first. 'Move aside, guys.'

She opened my door and once I was out, kept her arm firmly around me as we made our way up the path to my house.

'Ms Fraiser, tell me about your time in the Priory.'

'Ms Fraiser,' someone else called over, 'do you know where your daughter is?'

'Ms Fraiser, your husband denies any knowledge of the fairground, is this true?'

My eyes stung with tears and I was shaking uncontrollably as Fiona guided me indoors. It took any last ounce of self-control I had to not shout at them, tell them they were looking at the whole thing from the wrong angle. What was more important? My issues with drink or finding my little girl?

Once inside, Fiona slammed the door shut and I collapsed against it, my breathing erratic. I rapped the back of the door three times with my fist and focused on steadying my breathing.

Fiona led me through to the kitchen. 'You did well. It's horrible, I know. I've seen it before. They're like a bunch of bloody hounds.'

'DI Ward did warn me but I had no idea how awful it would be.' I paused, my hands still unsteady. 'I think I'm going to go upstairs for a lie down.'

Once upstairs, in the privacy of my own room, I sat on the bedroom floor, holding the small passport photo of Amy and I scanned the news headlines online. I openly sobbed at the predictability of it all. Article after article outlining me as an unfit mother, and that Amy had been in my sole care, that a recovering alcoholic was not fit to look after her child. Then, the one that twisted my gut: *Father Denies Knowledge of Being at Fairground.* But, most sickening, most crushing were the endless comments in response to the articles from people, normal people, as they were swept along the tide of sensationalism.

Ruth07: Some women don't deserve children. I hope they find the child and lock the mother up for life.

AndyK: She's clearly deluded. Not fit mother.

Daisy: Let's hope the girl's not dead because then she'd be a murderer as well.

Dave: Bit odd the parents not agreeing on where they were. If you ask me, the woman's mental. Unfit mother.

My hands shook uncontrollably as I let the laptop slide from my lap, another sob escaping my throat.

I looked at the photo: I had failed my daughter. That's what everyone now thought. That's what I was beginning to think. Amy's auburn hair, similar to mine, wild with curls. Her cheeks were rosy and plump. If I closed my eyes, I could smell her shampoo and hear her laugh; the image was so vivid, I put my hands out to touch her.

'Sophie? Where are you?'

The front door shut and I heard Oliver pounding up the stairs. He entered the room, a large duffel bag over his shoulder which he let fall to the floor before sitting next to me on the carpet. He put his arm around my shoulders and I tilted my head into the crook of his neck.

'You staying?' I asked, pointing at his bag.

'If you want me.' He laced his hand through mine. 'What happened at the station?'

'DI Ward found the woman I was talking about, on the CCTV footage. Not sure it gets us any further, though.'

'No,' he answered simply, and a rift of silence opened up between us. 'I've bought us some lunch. Do you want me to go down and make something?' He wouldn't look me in the eye.

'You've seen the headlines?'

He nodded grimly. 'Yes, but people will forget. When Amy's found and Paul's revealed for what he is, they will forget.' He looked down at me. 'Eat something?'

'I can't eat.'

'Sophie, you have to eat. You need to keep your strength up.'

I nodded and Oliver lifted himself off the floor. I grabbed his arm. 'Oliver, will you help me?'

'Of course I will, I told you that last night. Sophie, the police will find her.' His certainty sent a pain through my heart.

'No, I mean will *you* help me? I don't think I can sit around waiting for the police to find Amy.' I spoke fast. 'I can't trust anybody because I don't think they trust me. Except Darren. Maybe Darren believes me.'

Oliver sat back down with a thud. 'You don't *trust* the police?' He looked at me, bewildered. 'So…'

'When I talk to the detective she appears less and less convinced by what I'm saying, how can I spend so much time trying to persuade the very people who are meant to be looking for Amy?' I laughed a brittle laugh. 'She'll be locking me up soon, giving me meds.'

'I don't understand.'

'So, I need to find Amy. Alone.' I paused. 'Or with you. If you'll help me.'

'But what are you going to do?'

I noted the singular and sighed. 'You've seen the papers. If people are not on my side, what can I do? I can't sit around, letting them all circle me like prey.'

He started to move off.

'Aren't you going to say something?'

'There's not much to say.' He didn't look around. 'If you leave, you'll make yourself look even more guilty.'

His words ran through my heart like a sharpened blade.

'Oliver, please.'

He turned, tears in his eyes. 'Just give me some time, OK?' He left and padded down the stairs.

I stared at the spot where Oliver had just been sitting. What had I expected? That Oliver would take me in his arms and tell me it was all going to be OK, that he would become a fugitive with me, the woman the nation hated? I curled up on the cream woollen carpet and gave in to the loneliness. In reality, I had been alone for years: my daughter lived with her father; I had few friends, no boyfriends.

The sound of my mobile cut through my thoughts: it was Fiona. She'd be back in an hour or so. How was I holding up? She was worried about me. I assured her I was fine and hung up.

It had suddenly occurred to me, lying there, that I hadn't checked the house thoroughly; what if it was bugged? What if someone was watching me in my own home? I stood, any tiredness quickly dissolving. Why hadn't I thought of that before? I needed to be sure that the house was safe from spies. My mind was spinning with possibilities: the police might not trust me, Paul might have planted something in the house. I knew it didn't sound a sane concept but then my daughter going missing and her own father denying it was, to me, equally irrational.

I started in the bedroom, and moved furniture aside, checked the corners of the room and under the bed. Once I had finished in there, I did the same throughout the whole of the upstairs. Minutes later, I was downstairs.

'Sophie? What on earth are you doing?' Oliver emerged from the kitchen.

'I need to check the rooms,' I answered breathlessly; there was no time to explain now. In my heart, I knew I had to get rid of Oliver if he wasn't going to help me. A sickening thought spun through my head: what if Oliver was helping someone else? He had come back into my life so suddenly and he seemed reluctant to assist me.

He pinned himself against the wall as I blustered past. 'Are you looking for something in particular?' He had followed me into the kitchen.

'Cameras. Listening devices. What if this place is bugged?'

'Seriously?' Oliver gave a small shake to his head. I shot him a look.

'Seriously. I've checked upstairs so far...' I scratched my head. 'Ah! The attic.'

I ran up the stairs two at a time and folded out the ladder in order to climb into the attic space. Once I was inside the fusty and dark room, I found the torch I kept up there and flicked it on, shining the light over the boxes of Amy's school reports, pictures, her old baby clothes, piles and piles of books. I felt around the edge of the small window, in case I was missing something with such limited light. Nothing.

Exhausted and dejected, I sat down on a box with a thud. From my position, I had a bird's-eye view of the road below. Kate wandered about her garden, picking out the odd weed. A delivery van pulled up a few houses away and a woman with a pushchair walked past. I looked longingly after that woman. In my head, I rewound the years, and I was there again, pushing Amy toward home, smiling at her over the top of the handlebar whilst she giggled happily at the funny face I pulled.

My gaze left the woman who had now rounded the corner and fell on the bins outside. I shot up, my eyes wide with disbelief. Seconds later, I was sprinting down the stairs, past Oliver prepping food in the kitchen and I flew out the front door. I ran over to the bins and plucked the lid off the first one, chucking it on the ground.

I gasped, frozen to the spot. My breathing had turned ragged, the ringing had started up in my head, piercing my thoughts. Oliver's hand was on my shoulder and no sooner had I fully comprehended what I was looking at, the world went black.

When I awoke, I found myself staring at Fiona, still lying on the grass. Her face was flooded with concern and she ordered Oliver to help me inside and settle me on the sofa.

'What about the…' I pointed at the bins.

Fiona frowned. 'DI Ward is on her way.'

I nodded numbly.

'Are they…?' She didn't finish her sentence.

'Yes,' I said, my voice unsteady, 'Amy's clothes.'

I looked back over my shoulder as Oliver led me inside. My heart surged with love at the sight of Amy's pink duffel coat. But then, just as quickly, it plummeted into the depths of my stomach: I wanted to know what it meant. Where was Amy? Was she alive? Why would someone put Amy's clothes in my bin?

Unless whoever had Amy wasn't just happy with that, they wanted to enjoy the ride too. What better way than to make me look guilty after the press had started to hunt me down than to put evidence of Amy's whereabouts on my doorstep? Make out I would kidnap my own daughter.

CHAPTER 12

Forensics had just finished bagging up the clothes. Fiona had made me a third cup of tea and, I'm not sure if it was just my imagination, they were also getting increasingly sweeter.

She sat opposite me now and had on a full set of leathers. There was something about the combination of her clothing and the fact that her feet couldn't quite reach the floor when sitting on one of the dining room chairs, that didn't match up.

'You into motorbikes?' I asked and realised I was making small talk again; it was a nervous habit, a way of taking the spotlight off me.

'Yes,' she laughed, pointing to the outfit, 'I wouldn't wear these out of choice.'

A small giggle erupted and I concentrated desperately on pushing the laughter bubbling up inside of me back down. It wasn't that I didn't want to laugh; no, quite the opposite, but laughter would easily bleed into hysteria.

'Sophie,' Fiona said, more seriously now, 'how are you holding up?'

'Great,' I lied, forcing a smile.

'Sophie.'

I frowned, my lower lip quaking. 'Not great. And a bit sick of all this.' I indicated the forensic team.

'Don't worry,' Fiona said gently, 'I understand. No one likes to feel like they're constantly being watched over.'

'No,' I agreed, thinking back to the clothes, 'no one does.'

'Are you OK, Sophie?'

'What do you think it means? The clothes in the bin?' I took a sip of tea; this cup was already cold but it gave me something to do.

'It's not my place to answer that but…' She started and stopped, her gaze moving to the figure entering the room.

'Sophie.' It was DI Ward. She grabbed another dining room chair and sat almost equidistant from Fiona and myself: the perfect triangle. 'We've been over what happened. You saw the pink coat from the attic window and went outside to check it out for yourself.' She scrutinised her notebook.

'Yes.'

'What were you doing in the attic?'

I pressed my lips tightly together before speaking. 'I wanted to find something of Amy's,' I lied. 'A picture she made me recently. She gave it to me last time I saw her.'

She raised an eyebrow. 'And you had already put it in the attic?' Her tone sounded unconvinced.

'Yes.' I shrugged, my nonchalance hopefully masking my sweaty palms and drumming heartbeat.

'Why do you think Amy's clothes were in your bin?'

'Someone's trying to set me up,' I answered simply.

'Set you up?' She sucked on the end of her pen. 'You mean the woman from the fair?'

I felt as if we were raking over familiar territory. 'Yes.'

'Right, well, as you know, forensics have taken the items and will examine them.' She clicked the pen a couple of times whilst she gathered her thoughts. 'Is Oliver Dyers here?'

I narrowed my eyes. 'In the kitchen, why?'

'Just got a couple of questions for him.' She smiled and left.

Fiona tried to stifle a yawn. 'Sorry,' she mumbled.

'Don't be.' I sat back in the sofa. 'I know how you feel.' Grabbing a cushion, I placed it on my lap and started to smooth over its cover. 'You know DI Ward...'

'Hmmm?'

'Is she good?'

Fiona grinned. 'Yes. The best.'

I cocked my head to one side. 'Really?'

'Really.' She whispered now, 'Yeah, she can be a bit, you know, abrasive but that woman's good. Really good.'

I needed to know more. 'OK, but she doesn't trust me, does she?'

Fiona looked surprised. 'What makes you say that?'

'I don't know. Stuff she says, her body language around me. Everything, really.' I nodded toward her. 'She's not as understanding as you.'

Fiona blushed. 'She's just different that's all. She's not good at not knowing the facts.'

I smiled despite myself. 'Must be hell in her job then.'

She grinned. 'Yeah but makes her work damned fast.' Her face grew sober. 'She'll find Amy.'

I nodded tiredly. 'I need to believe that.'

After a while, Oliver reappeared in the doorway to the living room and I heard the front door slam shut.

'All OK in here?' he asked.

Fiona, ever the sensitive one, felt the tension and excused herself. 'I'll be in the kitchen. More tea, anyone?'

I smiled gratefully. 'Not for me, but thanks.'

Oliver gazed tenderly at me. 'I'm sorry for questioning you earlier. It's just what you're saying about not trusting the police.' He paused and cleared his throat. 'Just a lot to take in, you know?'

'I know. I'm the one who should be apologising.' I looked at him steadily and whispered, so Fiona couldn't hear, 'I just needed you to understand why I'm finding it hard to trust the police. I really do believe I need to find Amy myself.'

'But don't you think you might be putting yourself in danger?'

'Oliver, my daughter is out there somewhere and I need to find her.' I looked around the room. 'I don't even know if this room is bugged. What if she's been listening in this whole time? What then?'

'Who is *she*?'

I reached out to him, he moved closer, and I took his hand. 'I'm trusting you to keep this secret. I understand if you feel you can't help but I needed you to know what's going on.'

He smiled, his eyes watering. 'You're as stubborn as the day I met you. God help me.'

I was about to answer, when the phone rang. It was Zander, my boss; he had seen me on the news.

'Zander, I told you I'm *fine*.'

'How can you be fine, Sophie? When I turn on the news and I see all this, well, I was…' I sensed he was trying to grab at a word that wouldn't send me reeling. 'Shocked.' He decided on *shocked*. It sounded very English, upper class and entirely ridiculous. A local mugging would be shocking, and this was bigger than that.

'Yes,' I replied honestly. 'It is shocking to me too.' I peeked out the curtain and a dozen or so flashbulbs went off in reply.

He talked hurriedly and I thought I picked up on a hint of nervous excitement in his voice.

'Zander, do you mind if I phone you back another time?'

The six o'clock news had used an old photo of Amy and Paul taken last year. DI Ward had given them the photo.

A separate and more recent one of me at a legal awards ceremony, downloaded off the Internet, stood alongside it.

'What can I do?' Zander continued, ignoring my obvious plea for him to leave me alone. 'I mean they're just hounding you, the press.'

'Yes, but you can't do anything, Zander, thank you. I won't be in to work for a while. Until I find Amy.' My voice caught. 'If I find Amy.'

'*When* you find Amy. Of course, of course.' I let the silence hang awkwardly between us, my patience wearing thin. Zander finally said, 'Right, well…' He cleared his throat. 'Let me know if I can do anything for you. You're like family to me, you know?'

'Sure.' I willed him to hang up. 'Thanks.'

I pushed the phone back in its cradle and slid down the wall until I was sitting on the floor. It had been a long day.

'You OK?' Oliver appeared in the doorway to the kitchen.

'My boss.'

'Sounded like he was pretty concerned.'

'For his company's reputation.' I wasn't stupid, I knew why Zander had been phoning; worried clients were going to fall by the wayside overnight.

Fiona coughed to let us know she was returning.

'Guys,' she smiled at both of us, 'I'm going to head off but I'll be back tomorrow to take you to the next press conference, OK?'

'Thank you for everything,' I said.

She nodded. 'I'm always on my mobile, OK?'

Once we heard the front door close, Oliver leant heavily on the doorframe. 'DI Ward didn't beat around the bush. She wanted to know if it was coincidence that I turn up on the scene and Amy goes missing.'

I remained quiet.

'You don't actually think the same do you?' He righted himself, searched my face for answers.

I tried to remain impassive, despite the niggling doubt at the back of my mind. I mean, hadn't Oliver always wanted to play happy families? Life was so black and white to him. He had come back, wanting the old me; the 'me' before Bethany had died. That me didn't exist any more. Or at least, it was suppressed.

'No, of course not,' I said, turning on a reassuring smile, 'I mean that's ridiculous, questioning you. Is that really all they've got? At this rate, Amy will just turn into a number on the missing persons register.'

Oliver nodded and visibly relaxed his shoulders. 'Just her job, I guess.'

Then I thought about Paul. A man who had never made out he wanted to play happy families, and yet now was lying to me, the police. Why was I focusing on Oliver when it was really Paul who was unable to tell the truth?

'What are you thinking?' Oliver looked at me, concerned.

'Why they're not pushing Paul. He's the one who claims not to have been at the fairground.' I feigned slapping my head. 'Oh no, that's right, I'm the fruit loop alcoholic who *makes stuff up*. Paul is *innocent*.'

'I guess they have to explore all options,' he said mildly, and once again I was torn: maybe Oliver had done something to Amy, maybe he wanted us to be together. Just us. His reaction to Amy's disappearance at times felt so bland, so non-committal. It was angering and unnerving all at once.

'What's that supposed to mean?'

'That nothing is as it seems.'

'What are you trying to say, Oliver?'

'I'm just saying, th-that,' he stammered, 'I can kind of see where the detective is coming from. You know, that nothing is very clear at the moment.'

I lifted myself up off the floor and tried to ignore the knots forming in my stomach. Suddenly defiant, I walked toward him. We stood inches apart.

'I think it's best you leave. For good this time.'

Oliver's face grew quietly livid.

'You know what, Sophie? What your problem is? You can't stand people questioning you. You don't want to admit that maybe your story does sound a bit strange. I come back, make contact again and you want me around when it's convenient. At university, you would break up with me and you would push me away. Then you would reel me back in. I fell for it over and over again. Now, you're doing the same.' I could hear the bitterness in Oliver's voice. Years of unresolved tension had begun to surface.

'I will go, Sophie. Because you're not yourself right now. I'll come back when you're calmer. But do me a favour and just think about what you're doing. What you've always done. You use people and dump them when you don't need them any more.' He stopped abruptly and I looked at him. 'Why do you keep pushing me away? One minute you want me here and the next you don't. You're like two people. So tell me, why? What have I ever done to deserve the way you treat me?'

His questioning was visceral and raw and I stood, unmoving. I couldn't tell him the truth: that he had been easy. When I needed him, he was there, willing to be my boyfriend and when I wanted Bethany's attention, he would disappear. Only, I realised with bubbling resentment, he never disappeared entirely. The thing is, I wanted to play happy families with him. I really did. In fact, I craved a happy family, the idea of one. But the reality was that I had never made that connection with anyone. Amy was my family and that was just fine.

He continued, 'You just don't get how selfish you are and you don't see that I love you. I always have done. I want to help you find your little girl.' His voice had softened but the words remained coated with a sticky unpleasantness. 'God only knows, I can't imagine what it would be like if I never saw Annabel again. If you think about it, we're kind of the same like that. I see my daughter every two months if I'm lucky. I want to make sure you find your daughter.'

I felt defeated, and moved toward the window. My heart thundered in my chest and I didn't trust myself to speak. He was right, I needed him and I was pushing him away – again. He had been there for me in the Priory, and he had come back into my life a month ago telling me he loved me and wanted me back – I hadn't asked questions, I was grateful for the companionship – and now he wanted to help me find Amy. My selfishness matched his selflessness.

The sun was setting fast. Another day gone and Amy was still missing.

'Sophie, you have to let me in. If you want me to help, let me in.' Oliver put his hand on my shoulder. 'Let me in, Sophie.'

I turned to him and cradled his face in my hands. 'I'm sorry. I truly am sorry. You deserve so much better. I sometimes wonder what our lives would be like if…'

'I know. I know…' he said and added, 'and I'm sorry. I was out of order.' He took me in his arms. 'Come here.' A few moments later, he said, 'You know you've never told me you love me, Sophie.'

I looked at him and I started to say it, but something stopped me. It was dangerous to need someone, to rely on someone: I knew that. I had loved my parents and lost them too young, I had loved Bethany and lost her. Love was too easily lost. I knew that my search for Amy was up to me, and me alone. I couldn't involve anyone else for fear of putting Amy's life at risk. But also because I wasn't sure if I could really trust Oliver. I'm not sure if I could really trust anyone.

Oliver led me to the sofa and we sat down, leaning back into the cushions. His strong hands gently caressed my hair. My eyelids grew increasingly heavy and I started to drift off. After a few minutes, Oliver slid his arms underneath me, and carried me upstairs. Gently, he placed me on top of the covers and bent down to take off my shoes. He tucked a blanket around my body and before he had even left the room, I closed my eyes. I felt him watching me and I held my breath, waiting for him to leave the room. It was like he could see straight through me, he knew and understood stuff about me that even I didn't want to acknowledge. I buried myself further in the duvet and wondered if he really would do anything – including kidnap my child – to have me all to himself.

In the morning, he was gone. He left a note telling me he would return tomorrow evening, to call him on his mobile if I needed anything. My heart and mind wrestled with his absence. Shivering, I went back into the bedroom and climbed under the duvet. The world was a cold and lonely place. The empty house a reminder of everything missing in my life and, yet, I preferred it like that. No one prying into my business, no one searching my face for answers I couldn't give.

I set my alarm, ready to meet Darren at lunchtime and fell into a fitful sleep.

Darren had come to the house. He had asked me to dig out all my photos of my time at university. I looked at them now, scattered across the table and gently fondled them one by one. The perfume bottle was there too.

'OK, Sophie, you're doing really well. I need you to concentrate on your senses.' He smiled gently. 'Like we've done before. Sounds weird but our memory is not confined to images, we can smell and touch, too, if we allow our minds to open up.'

I nodded, unsure.

'OK, let's take this one here.' He picked up a photo of Bethany and me, with people dancing in the background. Something about the image made my heart momentarily flutter with anxiety. 'Now, this looks interesting. When do you think this was one taken?'

'I was nineteen,' I said, not skipping a beat. It was as if my heart and mind had memorised it.

'OK, would you mind opening the perfume and smelling it?'

I took off the lid and spritzed some of the musky droplets onto my wrist, breathing it in deeply. I hadn't allowed myself to open the bottle before now. My breath caught as a fresh tide of grief washed over me, and I choked back a sob.

'OK, I know this is hard, but are you ready to start?' I nodded. 'Now I want you to close your eyes.'

He started to talk in his drawn-out, dulcet tones causing me to feel almost sleepy and I felt my body and mind giving way to the past.

'Tell me what you can smell.'

'Smoke,' I answered softly. 'Lots of cigarette smoke. Weed too.'

'Is it hot? The room?'

'Yes, too hot.'

'OK, what else can you see or feel?' I could sense him nodding encouragement. 'Just tell me everything you remember.'

'The party – organised by some third years – was heaving, the house overflowing with students and drink.' I stopped and let out a small gasp at how clear Bethany's face was in front of me.

'What is it, Sophie?'

'Bethany.' I put my hand out, gesturing to the thin air. 'It's the first time I've seen her that clearly in such a long time.'

'That's good. That's a good sign.' He paused. 'Go on.'

'I ignored everything but Bethany that night. I remember she moved her hips with ease to the bass.' I blushed. 'It was kind of sensual, you know?'

'Yes.'

I didn't want to open my eyes, I felt self-conscious now and my eyes started to well as the image faded.

'Sophie, just relax. I don't care what you say to me. This is about you now and what you can access.' He waited. 'Relax and tell me who else was there.'

I nodded, took a deep breath and the image came back, but now Oliver was there.

'Oliver was there and he said to me something like, "Are you listening?" He was shouting to me over the music.' I startled myself at remembering such detail, opening my eyes. Darren was nodding and I closed them again. 'Oliver asked me to repeat what he had just said.'

'And could you?' Darren asked. 'Had you been listening?'

'No, I hadn't.' I cleared my throat. 'I remember focusing on Oliver, his face was all expectant. I started to tell him that he had been talking about his match, but I stopped because I hadn't actually listened to more than a few sentences.'

'Why hadn't you been listening?'

'I had spotted Bethany.' Again, no hesitation.

'What was Bethany doing?'

'Dancing.'

'Tell me about her dancing,' Darren encouraged.

'She shifted effortlessly from side to side, her arms winding gracefully above her head, a spliff in her hand.' I paused, my heart suddenly pounding against my chest.

'Go on. What happened next?'

'A guy, tall and blond, edged his way closer to her.'

'Right, and what did you feel?'

'I felt jealous.'

'OK, this is good, Sophie. Why did you feel jealous?'

'Because he was snaking himself around her body and they started to,' I paused, reddening again, 'writhe against each other. I remember the blond guy leant down to her and whispered something.' I let out a small sob. I sensed Darren stop writing. 'Then Bethany tilted her head back and flashed him a smile and wink.'

'What did you do then?'

'I didn't move and I remember Oliver staring at me, then Bethany, in turn.'

'What did Oliver do?' Darren's pen started to scratch the surface again.

'He came over. Asked me something like, "Have you and Beth fallen out or something?" Then he pulled me into him.'

I shivered now at the memory of his touch, when all I had yearned for was Bethany.

'He joked about. Asked me if I wanted to show Bethany and this guy how to really dance.' I snorted now. 'It was funny in the sense that Oliver's got two left feet, but I remember hating him. I remember wishing he would go away.'

'Why's that?'

I opened my eyes now, looked at Darren. 'I wanted to know why I couldn't have one night where, like Bethany, I'd be confident enough to dance alone and have guys approach me? It was like watching your sister being more popular than you.'

He nodded, pensive. 'Close your eyes again, Sophie. Keep going if you can.' He waited until I had settled. 'What did you do next?'

'I remember pushing Oliver away. Told him I was too hot and that I needed to go outside, get some air. He asked if he could come.' A fresh wave of guilt washed over me. 'I had said no.'

'What did Oliver do?'

'He walked off and I turned, trying to make my way through the throng of students dancing in the front room in order to get out.'

'OK, go on. What were you feeling at this point?'

'Confused, a bit depressed.' I waited, tried to delve further. 'I started to make my way out but someone tapped me on the shoulder. I turned and saw Bethany.'

'What did she do?'

'Asked me where I was going. I told her I was getting some air.' I let out a small chuckle. 'The blond guy clearly didn't take to the interruption and tugged on Bethany's elbow but she shrugged him off, shouted something in his direction.'

I smiled now, remembering how satisfying it was watching him jerk his head back in surprise and saunter away.

'Keep talking aloud, Sophie. It'll be helpful to me later.'

I did. I told Darren how I remembered Bethany had pulled me toward her. We stood inches apart. I could smell her perfume, just like the night we first met: the scent of wild flowers on a sweet, spring breeze. Bethany's face glistened with sweat and I thought how alive she looked. How beautiful she looked.

'She asked me to dance with her and I panicked.'

'Why did you panic?'

'She was so natural at dancing, I didn't want her to be disappointed in my dancing.'

'So you said no?'

'No, she took my hands in hers and put my arms around her waist.'

'What did that feel like?' Darren asked.

'Safe. She had an amazing way of teaching me to do things I was afraid of,' I giggled, 'like dancing.'

I felt Darren smile back.

'So she guided you?'

'Yes, I remember looking into her eyes and thinking how dark they were, so rich.'

'That's good, Sophie. A good memory.'

'She gave me the spliff.' I furrowed my brow as that memory jolted me out of the happy place I had been. 'And I didn't really want it, but I took it. She said it would relax me.'

'What did you feel when you found yourself smoking it and yet, by the sounds of it, you didn't want to?'

'Confused that I felt a need to impress her all the time.'

'Can you remember what the atmosphere in the room was like?'

I squeezed my eyes more tightly shut. 'Yeah, the music was making the floorboards shake and it was boiling. Too hot. I remember Oliver watching me. Watching us.'

'What did he do?'

'Just stood there staring, a strange look on his face.'

'Can you define the look? Was he angry?'

'Possibly.' I nodded my head. 'Jealous too, I guess.'

'What happened then?'

'Bethany, I think she saw me look over at Oliver and she walked off. I went to see if Oliver was OK and, by the time I made it across the room, he had disappeared.'

'How did you feel at that point?'

'I felt my head start to pound, I remember feeling sick and dizzy. I don't remember much after that. Possibly I had had too much of the spliff.'

My eyes snapped open, disturbed by the clarity of the memory.

Darren said, 'Do you know why Oliver came back into your life recently? Has he given you a reason?'

The warmth of remembering Bethany's body close to mine was replaced by a feeling of cold, hard uncertainty.

'He said he loves me, that we were good together.'

'And were you?'

'Yes, I think so.' I shrugged, my lower lip quivering. 'I mean we were, it's just that Bethany held this power over me.'

'Are you homosexual?'

'No.' I was surprised at how quickly I responded. 'No, I'm not. But I realised with Bethany that she drew me in, in a way I've never been able to understand to this day.'

'You needed her?'

'Yes, I needed her.'

'Did you need her more than Oliver?'

I cleared my throat. 'Yes.'

'Do you think Oliver has anything to do with Amy's disappearance?'

'No,' I said quickly, then added, 'I don't think so.'

'And how do you feel now that Oliver is back?'

'Happy,' I said firmly and a moment later admitted, 'and a bit scared.'

'Why scared?'

'Because he reminds of a time I want to forget.'

Darren pursed his lips before asking, 'Do you think you can trust him?'

I remembered my doubt only hours before. 'I think so.' I shook my head. 'Actually, I don't know. If you're asking do I find it strange he comes back into my life weeks before Amy goes missing, maybe. But do you know what it's like to never know who you can trust?'

Darren blinked. 'You won't believe it, but to an extent, yes I do. It's why I started working these cases. I want to help people like you.'

I nodded. 'Then you'll know that I don't trust anyone but somewhere, deep down, I know I need to trust someone or I'm not going to find my little girl.'

'OK, I think it might be helpful if you ask Oliver what he remembers, specifically about Bethany. Does he believe she was murdered?'

'No, he's adamant that it was suicide. In fact, he gets angry when I mention it.'

'How does that make you feel?'

'Confused.'

'Do you think it would be useful to get Oliver to sit in on one of our sessions?'

I couldn't tell from the tone of his voice if DI Ward had put him up to that or if he genuinely thought Oliver's presence would help.

As if reading my mind, he said, 'Sometimes having someone from your past sitting with you as you explore a trauma can help.'

I nodded. 'If it helps find Amy, let's do it.'

CHAPTER 13

Later that day, I phoned Paul's mobile. He didn't answer right away but, on the third try, he picked up.

'Paul?' I needed some answers and I wasn't going to allow him to fob me off this time. Only, he didn't say anything and all I could hear was the sound of heavy breathing. 'Paul?' I tried again, less sure of myself this time.

The phone went dead.

'You have got to be kidding me,' I muttered. 'First the lies, and now he hangs up on me. I don't think so.'

I rang his number again, ready to give him a piece of mind.

This time he picked up right away. 'Sophie?' he answered.

'Oh,' I replied, not bothering to hide my sarcasm, 'you feel like talking now? What was that about? Hanging up on me?'

'I didn't hang up on you, Soph,' he said and I could hear the exhaustion in his voice.

Then, it dawned on me. 'Oh. Sarah.'

He sighed deeply.

The thought of Sarah comforting my ex-husband when he was lying about our daughter's disappearance was galling on so many levels. Surely, he should be focusing on searching for our missing daughter, instead of playing happy families with Sarah. I imagined Sarah crying fake tears whenever she looked at Amy's latest drawing on the fridge, or when she looked in Amy's room.

I clenched my jaw: I was Amy's mother, Sarah even living in our old family home was a violation. It's not like she could replace me as Amy's mother.

As if reading my mind, he said, 'I need companionship too, Sophie. You've got Oliver…'

'How did you know he was back?'

'Fiona let slip that he was staying at yours. If you ask me, a bit odd, don't you think? Turning up weeks before Amy goes missing.'

'A bit odd? What, a bit like you claiming you weren't at the fairground with me? That kind of odd?'

'Sophie, I'm not lying. I wasn't there with you. Nor was Amy.'

He had delivered the line so many times in the last forty-eight hours, I was starting to believe it.

'OK, Paul,' I tried another tack, 'what were you doing at lunchtime and during the early afternoon of Saturday?'

'I was out shopping.'

'That's all you're going to tell me?'

He sighed. 'There's not much to tell you, to be honest.'

The irritation bubbling beneath the surface quickly turned to anger. 'Not much to tell me? Are you kidding?' I pounded my fist on the kitchen counter. 'That's just it, Paul. There is a lot you need to tell me. Sure, if we hadn't been together on Saturday and Amy had gone missing, you might look like an innocent party in all this, but you were there. Don't try and convince me otherwise. Over the last couple of days there have been moments when I've almost believed what you're saying, but,' I gave a small, definite shake to my head, 'you will not make me out to be mad. Though, you're doing a good job. I can even feel the DI's trust waning. You know I would never hurt Amy, don't you, Paul?'

Silence before Paul cleared his throat nervously.

'I know you would never hurt Amy,' he said quietly, but I sensed he wasn't convinced.

'Would *you*? I didn't think you would but maybe I was wrong.' My body trembled now and I battled to regain my composure. 'Paul, tell me where Amy is. If you know where she is, just tell me.' I stopped shouting, changed tack, tried a softer approach. 'I know you wouldn't put Amy in danger. Do have any idea where she might be?'

Again, he was reticent before he spoke. Only this time, when he did, I heard the emotion in his voice. 'No.'

'Paul.'

'No,' he said more firmly.

Was it just me or did he sound scared?

'Is someone threatening you, Paul?' I said in a low voice. 'You can tell me.' I knew I shouldn't say too much. What if someone was listening in on our conversation? I had no idea any more when it was safe to speak: maybe it was never safe to speak. 'Paul, I'm worried that it's something to do with the night Bethany was murdered.'

'Bethany committed suicide,' he said, weariness tingeing his voice. 'We've been through this.'

It occurred to me that, if he were frightened, I would have to find another way to press him for information.

'OK, do you know who has our daughter? If you can't speak but you know, please do something to let me know.' I paused. 'Anything, Paul. Please.' I waited, my hand clasped firmly around my mobile. 'Please, Paul.'

Still nothing.

'OK, just answer me this, is she safe?' I wanted to scream and shout: just answer me, tell me what you know.

Paul's breathing had grown increasingly raspy; I could sense his inner turmoil, his anguish.

'Paul, you have got to tell the police what you know.'

But the line went dead. He had killed the call. I slumped down on the kitchen floor; my chest was so tight I couldn't breathe and I laid my head on the cool flagstone floor. Still gripping the mobile, I hugged it to my chest and curled up into a tiny ball on the floor.

CHAPTER 14

Fiona dropped her bike helmet when she saw me. It hit the parquet floor in the hall with a resounding thud.

'Sophie!' she yelped.

'Fiona?' I answered, barely enough energy to speak.

'Good god, Sophie,' she said, taking me in her arms. 'You gave me a fright.' She explained later that she could only see my feet and had immediately thought the worst. 'I thought…' The lines around her eyes creased with concern. 'You haven't taken anything have you?'

I shook my head. 'Nope.'

Relief passed over her face. 'What are you doing down here then?'

'I don't know,' I said, trying to right myself. 'I guess it all got too much.' I had been told not to phone Paul.

Fiona pursed her lips. 'Maybe you should see a doctor.'

I didn't answer and bit my lower lip, determined not to cry again. Too late. My eyes moistened and I wiped my already red-rimmed eyes. Fiona sat next to me, leaning up against a kitchen cupboard door and rearranged my head so that I was lying on her lap. She started to stroke my hair like I was a young child.

'I can't even imagine what you're going through, Sophie,' she said soothingly and I inhaled the scent of laundry conditioner on her jeans. 'You're coping so well.' We both knew that was a lie but I didn't argue, not as long as she allowed me to remain where I was. 'Amy would be so proud of you.' I flinched, guilty at the realisation that I was lying here being comforted when she was out there in need of my help. I sat up; my head rushed with the sudden onset of light-headedness and I waited for the feeling to pass. 'Sophie?'

'I'm fine. Honestly.'

'I'll make you something to eat.' Fiona lifted herself off the floor. 'I expect you haven't eaten today, have you?'

I shook my head miserably. 'No, but I'm not hungry.'

'Sophie, you need your energy. This is your body's way of telling you to look after yourself.' She started busying herself in the kitchen and she grabbed the loaf from the breadbin. 'Going a bit stale but nothing the toaster can't fix.' She looked at me. 'Would you mind putting the kettle on?'

'OK,' I agreed, although the last thing I wanted was another cup of tea.

Once I had filled the kettle with water and switched it on, Fiona asked me to chop a couple of tomatoes. I looked at her dully and nodded, before I set to slicing the tomatoes. Then it was spooning sugar into the teacups, pouring the milk, buttering the toast, until I realised she was sat, on a stool at the end of the counter, watching me. A small smile played at her lips.

'What?' I asked, defensively. Then I realised, she was getting me up and moving. This was her way of showing me I could do it; I could cope.

'I'd like a bit of mustard on mine whilst you're at it.' She grinned.

I smiled and took the jar, opened it and started to dab mustard on one side of the bread. 'I see what you're doing.'

'I'm not doing anything.' She laughed. 'OK, maybe I am. A bit.'

I handed the sandwich to her and one cup of sugary tea. 'Here you are.'

'Ta.' She bit into the bread. 'You're a dab hand at sarnie-making.'

I brought up a stool and joined her. It wasn't long before I had wolfed down the sandwich and gulped back the tea.

'I guess I needed that,' I said, wiping my mouth with the back of my hand.

'I'd say.' Fiona laughed, still with half a sandwich to go.

I chuckled. 'Thank you.'

'For what?'

I cupped my head in my hands, my elbows leaning on the counter. 'For being here.'

'Where's Oliver?' she asked with as much nonchalance as she could muster. 'I was surprised not to find him here. No way would he have allowed you to get in such a state.'

'Oliver's gone,' I stated flatly.

'Gone?' She raised an eyebrow.

I sighed deeply. 'I'm pretty hard to live with at the best of times, let alone when something like this happens.'

'Bet you're not that bad,' she said, rising from the stool and filling up the kettle again. 'Tea?'

'No, thanks. I'm drowning in the stuff. He said he'd be back. Tonight.' I shrugged. 'But, we'll see.'

'Yeah, well, he seems like the kind of guy who'd stick to his word.' She caught my eye. 'He loves you a lot.'

A lump rose in my throat. 'I know. Sometimes I think I've forgotten how to let someone love me, you know?'

She strode over and put a hand on mine. 'I know. But you deserve to be loved, Sophie, just as much as anyone.'

I nodded, swallowing hard. 'I can't think about it though. I just need to get Amy back home safe and sound. That's all that matters right now.'

'Speaking of which, once I've finished this, we'll head over to the station for the next press conference.'

I nodded, told her I'd go upstairs and change. As I headed out the kitchen door, Fiona's mobile rang. The caller didn't wait for any introductions or niceties before speaking and Fiona kept saying, 'Uh-huh.' I lingered in the doorway, watching her beseechingly: was there news?

Fiona finally spoke, 'I'll tell her. Yep, we'll be there in an hour for the conference. Bye.' My heart sank: it couldn't be good news if the press conference was going ahead. 'Yep, bye.'

'What is it?' I pleaded. 'Is it bad?'

'Nope, quite the opposite.'

My heart lifted. 'They've found her? They know where she is?'

Fiona frowned. 'Sorry. No, not that good.'

'Oh.' My shoulders fell.

'The CCTV footage. There's been some developments.'

'Developments?'

'That's all I know.'

I headed upstairs to change, to ready myself for whatever came next.

CHAPTER 15

DI Ward met us on the steps to the station. As we approached, I watched her suck the life out of a cigarette and drop it to the ground, stamping it out with her boot. She didn't look happy.

'The CCTV,' she said brusquely, 'you heard there's been developments?'

'Yes.'

'Let's walk and talk.' She addressed Fiona. 'Give us five?'

We walked away from the building.

'We think we found Paul on the CCTV footage.'

'Really?' I smiled, triumphant.

She sighed. 'From the day before.'

'Oh.' My face fell. 'What was he doing at Acton Green the day before?'

'He says he was picking up your birthday present, purely coincidental.' She pressed her lips together. 'It doesn't prove much but we're talking to the guy he bought your present from.'

I furrowed my brows. 'I never got a present.'

DI Ward stopped walking, nodded. 'OK, Paul says he gave you a necklace.'

I raised one eyebrow in response.

We joined Paul and Tom Dixon outside the pressroom. DI Ward nodded to Paul and opened the door. We were late: there wasn't time for small talk. Paul shot me a questioning look. He probably wanted to know why we had arrived together, what we had been discussing. I broke off eye contact and joined DI Ward on the platform. Paul sat to my left. I wanted to speak to him alone.

I stared at the ground, until DI Ward invited me to speak.

When I looked up, I spotted the man who had asked about my drinking and my mouth went bone dry.

'We so desperately need to find Amy,' I said. 'Our lives are falling apart. She's my little girl and none of this makes any sense.' I nodded, went to say something else but I didn't.

Paul picked up where I left off. He surprised me by grabbing my hand and squeezing it tightly. 'We need our daughter back. Please if anyone knows anything, get in touch.'

DI Ward nodded. 'Any questions?'

The same man stood up. My stomach turned.

'I've come to understand that there are some discrepancies between the mother and father about where they were on Saturday afternoon. Is that right, Detective?'

DI Ward looked at him. 'I am not able to comment on that.'

The journalist continued unabashed. 'Ms Fraiser, is this true?'

I glanced at DI Ward but she didn't miss a beat. 'Please, Sir, I told you already. We are unable to comment on such matters.' She scanned the room. 'Anyone else?'

A woman raised her hand and got to her feet. 'Ms Fraiser, I'm so sorry to hear about what happened.' She paused and I smiled gratefully. 'But do you think there's a possibility that your daughter has run away? We are reporting a kidnap but I understand that your relationship with your daughter was, um,' I watched any kindness dissipate, 'difficult.'

My stomach turned and DI Ward was about to interject, but I put my hand up to silence her. 'I love my daughter very much and just because I don't live with her doesn't mean I don't do everything in my power to protect her.'

'But mightn't she have run away?' The journalist now aimed her question at DI Ward.

'We are looking into all possibilities. Whatever the case, a young girl of eight is missing.' DI Ward nodded her head, and added, 'Please remember that.'

We were marched out of the room and once outside DI Ward turned to us, her jaw clenched. 'Right, I need to know now, have either of you talked to the press?'

'What?' I jerked my head back. 'No, I haven't.' I looked at Paul. 'Have *you*?'

His eyes widened. 'What? You think I've been talking to the press?' He shook his head. 'You really are mad.'

'Well, how the fuck did that man find out that we can't agree on being in the same place at the same time? And more importantly, how did he come to think I was lying?'

Paul just looked at me, blinking. 'Did he actually say that? That you were lying? Do you think you might be getting a bit paranoid?'

Anger flared inside me and I brought my face inches from his own. He looked at the ground. 'You cannot do this. You cannot make out to everyone that I'm delusional.'

After a few long seconds he met my gaze. 'Soph, you know better than anyone what's going on.'

'I haven't got a clue what you're talking about.'

'You were the last to see Amy.'

'Paul, you know nothing about me.' I swallowed hard. 'Not any more, anyway.'

'Sophie,' he whispered hotly, 'just get some help. Find our daughter.' He strode off.

Tom caught up with him and I heard the FLO say, 'The detective wants a word.'

'About what?' Paul said, his voice fading as the door closed slowly behind him.

Tom looked as if he were trying to pacify Paul and, as they re-entered the building, I heard Paul whisper angrily, 'It was a long time ago, so what? She can have my consent but there's nothing to see.'

I watched them mount the stairs, straining to catch their conversation but soon they had gone, the only sound their heavy footsteps on the linoleum staircase and corridors that made up the labyrinth of the police station.

CHAPTER 16

I listened to the sound of the kitchen clock. I had waited for hours for the detective to ring me, tell me that she had finally forced him to admit the truth. Surely that was why the detective had wanted to talk to him. She had some information that allowed her to back him into a corner. Fiona had driven me home and, after much persuasion, left me alone on one condition – I called her if I needed anything.

'Anything,' she had repeated, giving me a big hug. 'Remember, I'm here for you.'

I looked at my watch: it was 11 pm. Now that Fiona was gone, I didn't know what to do with myself. I thought briefly about food but decided I wasn't hungry; sleep, but my mind raced with facts and snippets of information. I needed to go out, to walk and think.

I strode into the front room and peeked out the curtains. Half or dozen or so news crews remained but there was no movement. They appeared to be asleep in their vans.

I craved air, I felt trapped in my own home, and I decided to face the mob outside. Pushing down any anxiety, I wrapped myself up warm in a duffel coat, a scarf and a beanie hat. I'm not sure why, but I felt safer in the knowledge that most of my face was covered either by the scarf or the hat.

I stepped out and waited for a reaction but, when there was none, I slipped past the vans, headed right at the end of my drive and, by the light of the orange street lamps, walked briskly away. I strode fast around the block and when I crossed back, decided it was better to make the return journey on the other side. I waited a few minutes, stuffed my hat and scarf in my pockets and headed back. The reporters still hadn't appeared to have noticed my escape as I dipped in and out of the unlit sections of pavement. I eventually sat on a wall, away from the street light, and looked at my own house. Strange to feel your own house was as much a lion's den as the outside world.

I scanned the other windows and my eyes came to rest on the top floor of another Victorian semi. The large windows were lit up and the occupant hadn't bothered drawing the curtains.

A woman stood silhouetted against the light and I watched as she talked and laughed. She appeared to be cooking: perhaps for a guest. Moments later, as if she could feel my eyes on her, she came to the window, peered out. I froze feeling like a Peeping Tom. She shook her head and drew a curtain across one window and looked out briefly again before doing the same with the second.

I stood up and prepared myself to head back. But something out the corner of my eye stopped me in my tracks. I backed up a couple of paces, glancing behind me as I went to ensure I didn't collide with my neighbour's recycling box or step into the street lamp's light, and turned my head fully to the right.

There was a person, in an old Ford car, watching my house.

A cold prickly sweat worked its way over my body and I moved half a step back in order to get a closer look. The person's dark clothing, and the reflection from the street lamps, made it impossible to make out their features or build. I needed to get closer and I edged toward a small wall dividing the two houses.

From here, I could see it was a man.

I moved one further inch to my right, my eyes never leaving the car.

My mind worked quickly; I knew I couldn't do anything sudden as he might drive off. A cat wandered up to me, mewing. The animal was moving in circles around my legs and it lazily made its way up to the house's porch.

The man looked in my direction now and I stood stock-still. He started the engine and moved off and, without thinking, I took a deep breath and started to run after the car. Blood rushed in my ears and I squinted, desperately memorising the number plate.

Panting hard, I ran to the end of the street and watched as the retreating car easily sped off toward the river.

I snuck back inside, my mind buzzing as I tried to figure out who the man could have been.

I phoned DI Ward. She answered right away. I could tell she had not been asleep yet.

'Sophie?'

'There was a man,' I spoke fast, 'outside my house. Watching my house.'

'Are you sure?' DI Ward was typing on a computer as she spoke, I could hear the clickety-clack of keys being struck. 'What were you doing outside? I thought we told you, for your safety, you need to stay inside the house.'

'I needed air.'

She sighed. 'Sophie, I'll look into it. Don't worry yourself. Get some sleep.' She cut the call.

I stared down at the phone in my hand. DI Ward clearly thought I was delusional, that there could have been no one watching me. Despair washed over me. If the police didn't take me seriously, then how were we going to find my daughter?

I spotted a USB stick on the side and remembered it was the video of Amy's first school play Paul had sent me. I hadn't been allowed to attend, even though I had asked if the rules could be bent just this once. Paul, out of pity I suspect, had sent me a video of it. I imagined Sarah and Paul sitting near the front, proud as punch at Amy's delivery of her lines. I clenched my stomach at the thought of Sarah watching Amy like she had given birth to her.

I sat at the kitchen island, my old laptop (this one had been released back to me, the others were still with forensics) whirring as I watched the video on loop. Paul zoomed in on Amy's face; she had that nervous habit I had, of nibbling her lower lips as she waited for her turn to speak. Then, irritatingly, I noticed how Paul turned the camera toward Sarah who, as I had suspected, looked on delightedly at *my* daughter. But I didn't want to see Sarah's face over and over again, that's not why I watched the video on loop. It was because at the very front, I thought I had imagined it but then I saw her again and again and again.

The woman walking down Oxford Street, the woman at the fair, was sat watching my daughter act for the very first time. The back of the woman had a ghostly familiarity about it and she was wearing that black coat again: it was undeniably her. Every time I saw the silhouette of her shoulders and head, my certainty grew. It was her, there was no denying the woman had been there that night. I tapped the play button three times before I allowed myself to watch it again, and again. I would show DI Ward in the morning, and prove to her that I wasn't mad. I felt sick that this woman had been in our lives all along. She must have been laughing at us, the way we ignored her clues.

The weather took a turn for the worse overnight but I stayed up, moving to the sofa instead. At some point, I registered it was half four in the morning and I woke up suddenly. The laptop had slid in between the cushions and I had developed a painful crick in my neck. I manoeuvred myself off the sofa, albeit slowly, and tried to shake off the grogginess.

It was only then that I realised there was a light on in the kitchen. Had I left it on? No, I clearly remembered turning it off. I rose quickly, the hairs on the back of my neck stood to attention. Noiselessly, I grabbed the empty vase from the centre of the coffee table and tiptoed toward the kitchen. My legs wobbled beneath me. The previous night's events flashed through my head and I gripped the vase even tighter.

The door was within arm's reach. I could just about make out the sound of someone's deep breathing over the ticking of the clock and I counted to three. Adrenaline pumping fast around my body, my heart beating crazily, I charged into the kitchen. Barely thinking, I swung the vase to and fro.

'What the hell?' a voice shouted.

I froze, grabbing the vase to my chest and gasped. 'Oli!'

He was stood up against the counter, his face pale. 'Bloody hell, woman.'

'How on earth? What are you…' I started before I burst into laughter, placing the vase on the side. 'I thought you were…' I broke down. 'You…' I couldn't form any words.

'You silly woman, you nearly killed me,' Oliver said, catching his breath, his face tight with panic.

'What the hell are you doing back? How did you get in?'

'You left the door unlocked.'

I tried to remember if I had. 'Why didn't you knock?'

'I did.' Oliver looked at me. 'You can't have heard me.'

'Why are you back?' I said again, trying desperately to soften my voice, push down the fluttering in my stomach.

'I was worried about you.'

'Why?' I was still on the defensive.

'Because you haven't been the same recently. It feels like we've gone back twenty years and your head is all over the place. I can't walk away from you, Sophie, I never have been able to. Especially now, when you clearly need someone. I want to be here for you. Let me be here for you.'

I nodded slowly. My phone buzzed. It was DI Ward.

'I need to ask you a few questions before the press conference,' she said. 'OK?'

'Yes, fine. I've got something to show you too.' I glanced at my laptop, at the USB stick.

CHAPTER 17

DI Ward sat me down. We were in her office this time.

She hovered, almost as if unsure how to start, and then said, 'Tea? Coffee?'

'Tea, please.'

She nodded. The kettle in the corner was already boiling, and I noted that she only made me one, not herself. We didn't talk as she made me the drink and then she sat down. Her eyes were red, tired.

'What do you think about the car, the man outside my house?'

She nodded, ignored me. 'Your ex-husband, Sophie.' She skimmed over some scribbles in her notebook. 'He owns a security company? What do you know about it?'

I shrugged my shoulders. 'Not much. I mean what do you want to know?' I studied her face. 'Why aren't you answering my question about the man?'

'Has he owned it long?' DI Ward pressed. Back to the subject of Paul.

'He owned it long before we met, if that's what you mean.' I narrowed my eyes. 'What's this got to do with the investigation, Detective?'

She pressed her lips together. 'Maybe nothing.'

'Why don't you ask him?' I wasn't trying to be smart; it just seemed strange to be asking me questions about

Paul's career when he was just downstairs waiting for the conference to start.

'I have,' she replied simply. 'I asked him what he did before he set up his own company. I've looked up the details. He started his company up in 1992.'

'Right…' I couldn't see where this was headed.

'He was twenty-five. Told me he hadn't gone to college, left school at sixteen and travelled the world a bit. This all ringing a bell?'

I nodded, rubbing my hands together to try and warm them up. 'Yeah, of course, why would he lie about something like that?' I sighed. 'What does this have to do with Amy?'

The DI skirted the issue. 'I've had one of my officers do a bit of a background check on Paul. You know, phone up the various companies he quoted at us. See if they've got him on record. Most of them had but here's the thing…'

'Yes?'

She tapped her pen on the table. 'Between 1988 and 1991, we can't find any record of Paul's employment, he's not registered on any electoral role and yet…'

'Go on.' I moved forward in my seat, waiting with bated breath.

'His bank account was looking more than a little healthy.'

I shook my head. 'I don't understand. What does that mean? What does "more than a little healthy" mean?'

'He appeared to have gone from working as a night guard at the local supermarket, earning just above minimum wage, to the big bucks.'

'So, what has he said? Surely, there's some explanation.'

'He says,' she watched me carefully, 'that there has to be some mistake.'

I stuck out my lower lip. 'So, there you go.'

'You're suddenly on his side, Sophie?' The DI cocked her head to one side. 'Last Saturday, you wanted him charged with the abduction of your daughter and, now, you don't find that sort of information incriminating or strange?'

'I just don't see what it's got to do with Amy's disappearance.' I stuck my jaw out. 'I want to know why you're not answering my question about the man outside my house. I'd say you're ignoring my safety at the moment, Detective.'

She nodded slowly, avoided eye contact. 'Just thought you might be able to offer us some insight into Paul, that's all.'

'Well,' I said, more defensively than I intended, 'I can't.'

'Clearly.' She looked at her watch. 'When you met Paul, remind me when that was?'

'My final year at university.'

'Ah, yes, of course. Amy was born the same year?'

'Uh-huh.' I nodded, swallowing hard. My throat was dry and I slurped greedily at my tea. 'That's right.'

'Paul was doing well when you met him?' She blinked slowly. 'His house is certainly very nice.'

A tickle in my throat made me cough. 'Yes, we've always lived comfortably.'

She sucked air through her teeth. 'Well, yes, he had a good amount of money to invest in his company. Especially for a start-up company. Very good indeed.'

'What do you want me to say? You have to ask Paul these questions. I never asked him how he got the money to create his business.' I shook my head. 'I never thought to question it but, then, why would I? It's who he was, you know? The company was who he was. I didn't need to ask questions.'

DI Ward nodded briefly. 'Fair enough. So he owned this company when you met him, in a club? So he's the older man, were you attracted to the older man?'

'I was told I met him in a club, but that was the night Bethany was murdered.'

'Told you met him in a club?'

I clenched my jaw. 'I've been over this. Yes. I woke up in my bed and Paul had brought me back. We hit it off but I don't remember a club, I remember going out with Bethany.'

'OK, so he's the older man with a successful business that you don't ask any questions about?'

'If you're going to go down some Freudian route of him being like a father figure I've never had,' I said hotly, 'you'll find he's about as far removed from my father as you can get.'

'Sophie, you're getting very edgy.' She sat back.

'What does Paul say about all this?' I was almost afraid to ask but I needed to know. 'He gave you consent to look at his accounts?'

'Yes, he did.' She shut her notebook. 'He says he was doing odd jobs. Cash in hand type of thing and, as for the money in his account, we must have made a mistake.'

'I guess that's all there is to it.'

She smiled. 'Maybe. Except it's unlikely my officer would make a mistake. But, moreover, a bank couldn't make up the kind of figures I'm talking about.'

She stood and I did the same.

'You ready for the press conference?'

I nodded. 'What about the man I told you about? Don't you think it's important? I mean you could put one of your guys outside the house and they could...'

I saw it then: the slightest flicker of something in her face. And then it dawned on me.

'That was one of your guys, wasn't it?'

'It's for your own safety.'

I looked at her. 'Then why the secrecy? Surely, you'd want me to feel safe?'

She didn't say anything. Clicked her pen twice. I willed her to do it again.

I got it. 'You don't trust me.'

'I didn't say that. We should get to the press conference.'

'Why are we having another press conference so soon?' I asked.

'I want to press the public, put pressure on whoever has Amy.' She looked at me. 'Do you know what I mean? Let's really hit close to home. Talk about the things that you, as her mother, understand about Amy better than anyone else.'

'Like?'

'Like talk about her favourite toy. Let's try and highlight the maternal loss here. Not sure that message is getting out there.'

'What is that meant to mean?'

'You and Paul feel detached from the proceedings, if I'm being honest. I need more from you in particular.' She looked at the door. 'You only have to read what the press are saying, Sophie. It's time we get the press focusing on Amy again.'

'As opposed to?'

'You,' she said bluntly.

I was feeling slightly unnerved by her insinuating looks. I couldn't let this go. 'How are we ever going to find my daughter, if you're not on my side?'

'I am on your side.' She paused, opened the door. 'You have to understand my predicament. Paul and you can't agree. I have more than one mystery to solve if you think about it. There are two sides to every story but only one of you is telling the truth.'

I held up the USB stick. 'I have something to show you.'

She took it from me, frowned, and we sat again. She stuck it in the side of the laptop and I waited for the video to appear. I pressed play and paused it within moments of it starting.

'That's the woman, there.'

'What?' DI Ward squinted at the screen.

'That's the woman at the fair, who's got my daughter.'

'She looks different to the one on the CCTV footage, Sophie.' DI Ward studied my face, I felt myself flush.

'No, I'm sure it's her.' I looked again. 'See the black coat, the shape of her shoulders.'

'She looks different to me but I'll keep it, show the officer who's scanning the CCTV footage.' She stood. 'Thanks.'

'Is that it?' I stood too, wondering why the DI wasn't taking this evidence more seriously.

'Not much to go on really, Sophie. We don't have an image of this woman's front. As far as I'm concerned that's just a woman, probably a parent, wearing a black coat.'

She walked out the door and I followed her out the room and back down the long corridor. Paul and Tom were waiting outside the pressroom. DI Ward opened the door, nodded at the both of us and we started to follow her in. I hung back: Paul could sit next to DI Ward. The room fell silent and the journalists readied their cameras, notebooks and Dictaphones.

The DI began. 'Right, ladies and gentlemen, let's get started then. OK, Ms Fraiser will speak first.'

I cleared my throat, gripping the note tightly. 'I once told Amy a story.' I found a camera lens and started again. 'Darling, do you remember that story, the one about the princess whose family loved her so much? She was loved so much, just like you are.' My voice cracked. 'Please come home, darling.' I let my head hang. 'Please, let her go whoever you are.'

DI Ward nodded her silent approval.

'We just want our daughter back. Back where she belongs,' Paul said.

DI Ward warily asked if there were any questions.

A woman stood. 'Is it true that your friend was murdered at university? That you think the person behind that might have kidnapped your daughter?'

I looked at her, blood roaring in my ears.

The same woman continued, unrelenting. 'I spoke to an,' she consulted her notepad, 'Oliver Dyers. He says you've had a lot on your plate recently. That you're trying to get custody of your daughter again? He says that you've been reacquainted recently.' She was just reading her notes now, matter-of-fact, no emotion. She looked up from her pad, her eyebrows raised. 'He says he's always wanted to be with you, that you would make a great couple. Sounds like a happy scenario, Ms Fraiser, don't you think? Just you and him, no children.'

I sat stock-still. Oliver. Oliver would speak to the press about me? About us? Make out we're in some loved-up, honeymoon phase?

'Please,' DI Ward came in, I could feel her bristling, 'this is not a time for personal attacks. Let's be professional.'

'I do not believe Oliver would talk to you,' I said, my voice threatening to crack.

'Well, I have ways of getting information out of people,' she said, causing a small ripple of laughter.

They really were predators, I thought, my hands shaking.

Another lady at the front rose from her chair and smoothed her skirt. 'I understand that you are due in front of the family courts in a few weeks? I imagine you would do anything to ensure you gain custody of your daughter.'

Her words were less a question and more a statement. As if she had already decided, along with the rest of the pack of journalists in front of me, that I had done something to Amy. I didn't move except for clasping my trembling hands together. Tears pooled in my eyes.

'OK,' DI Ward said quickly, 'I'm afraid we are unable to comment. These questions are unhelpful, to say the least.'

The DI had risen from her seat, and she firmly placed her hand on my arm, guiding me forcefully from the room.

I felt my legs weakening and I stood in the hallway, numb with shock, questions racing through my head. Fiona told me she would just be a couple of minutes then she would drive me home. I just nodded and manufactured a smile but remained silent. Everybody's faces loomed in and out of shot, their mouths appeared to move more slowly, their words came out like an actor's on slow-speed.

'Are you sure you're OK?' Fiona shrugged on her biker jacket. 'Come on. You look unwell. I'll take you home and you can rest up.'

I followed: mute.

Fiona stopped to exchange a few words with a colleague. Stepping away from Fiona and the small group of people gathered outside the pressroom, I got out my mobile and rang Darren.

I was seething with anger just thinking about Oliver talking to the press. I wanted to believe that he had been conned, that he wouldn't have let me down like that. Surely, she must have tricked him. I thought of the female journalist: she said she had ways of gaining information. What did that mean? I was torn between desperately wanting to trust Oliver and yet, on the other hand, wondering why he had come back into my life, out of the blue.

I recognised then that Oliver might remember something about me, about Bethany, from all those years ago and that it might help me remember something: he might hold the key to accessing my erased memories.

When Darren answered, I said, 'Can you meet me at the house right away? I want you to talk to Oliver too. I think you're right that he might help me remember something.'

He agreed to set off right away.

Fiona allowed me to sit in silence on the journey home.

'Come on then, love,' she said, hopping out her side and opening the car door. She held out her arm as if I was an invalid but I took it. We fought our way through the throng of journalists who had suddenly come to life like moths to a light. Guiding me to the house, Fiona hurriedly stuck the key in the lock but Oliver beat her to it and opened the door for us. His hair was dishevelled; he looked as if he had been napping.

'All OK?' he asked, as Fiona led me to the sitting room.

'I think Sophie's exhausted. She suddenly looked very unwell back at the station.' She didn't go into the details of the press conference; I expect she thought that conversation was my prerogative. Once she had settled me on the sofa with cushions behind me, she nodded for Oliver to follow her through to the kitchen. Minutes later, I heard the front door close quietly and Oliver reappeared.

'Fiona says you're not well. That something happened at the conference. She didn't say what.'

I shook my head, bit down hard on my lip. 'I'm fine.'

'Well, you're clearly not.' He kneeled on the floor next to me. 'What can I get you?'

Anger coursed through my veins, my mind buzzing with questions about why he would do that to me: why he would speak to the press, make me look like an uncaring mother. Make it look like I just wanted Oliver in my life and that we were better off without Amy.

I felt a ball of cold dread sitting in the pit of my stomach and suddenly, I realised, that he wanted me to need him.

It was like we were back at university. That look he was giving me now was the same look he gave me when I had been with Bethany: jealousy. He was jealous. Was he back, all these years later, to seek revenge? Would he take my daughter?

Oliver was looking at me intently. I realised I wasn't speaking. I daren't speak, because I needed him to talk to Darren. If I shouted at him now, Oliver would run.

'Darren wants to meet with both of us,' I finally said, my voice monotone, covering up the tide of nausea and anger I was feeling.

Oliver stood, I saw him clenching and unclenching his jaw.

'It's not a set up,' I continued, trying to placate him. 'Darren genuinely thinks it would be helpful.' I looked at him. 'Please.'

He nodded slowly. 'OK.'

Minutes later, the doorbell rang and I jumped up, rushing to the door.

I let Darren in.

'Sophie, are you OK? You look shaken up. Has something happened?'

I searched his kind eyes. 'I'm fine. Oliver's through here.'

Oliver shook hands with Darren, his jaw twitching with irritation.

We sat at the kitchen table.

'OK,' Darren said, smiling at me. He was trying to encourage me to relax. I clearly looked as wound up as I felt. 'What I thought might be helpful is if we talked about that party you were telling me about the other day, Sophie. I believe Oliver was there, wasn't he?'

'He was.' I nodded. 'You know the party at Steph's house? It was a huge house party. You had just told me you were thinking about travelling to India over the summer.'

'So you had been listening,' Oliver said, the bitterness apparent.

I pulled a face.

'So, I think what would be helpful, Oliver, if you don't mind just telling me what you remember from that night. What was the atmosphere like?'

'What do you mean?' Oliver was being sullen.

'I mean was it hot in there or...'

'Yeah, it was boiling. It was like the middle of the summer and there were loads of people dancing, what would you expect?'

'It to be hot,' Darren agreed, showing no emotion, 'and do you remember much?'

'No.'

'OK, Oliver.' Darren smiled at him now. 'We're doing this to help Sophie find Amy.'

Oliver nodded slowly. 'Fine, yeah, I remember quite a lot actually.'

'OK.' Darren smiled.

'I remember that Sophie wouldn't stop drooling over Bethany.' He looked at me, and I stared hard at the table top, my fingers silently tapping out three, six, nine. 'I remember that I was trying to talk to Sophie and she wouldn't stop staring at Bethany. Sometimes I swear Sophie was so obsessed with Bethany, I wondered if she might suffocate Bethany with her adoration.'

I let out a small gasp. His words were so abrasive.

'What did you think about their relationship?'

'They were like two peas in a pod.' He looked straight at Darren. 'Like sisters. One minute they loved each other and the next they hated each other. I don't think it was very healthy to be honest.' He smoothed the table with his hand. 'I mean they started doing stuff by themselves. Never told the rest of us where they went. Then the drugs.'

'I didn't…'

'Sophie, please,' Darren said, put his hand up. 'Give Oliver a second.'

'What do you mean, you didn't?' Oliver furrowed his brow, shook his head in disbelief. 'You and Bethany spent most of your life smoking weed or, on occasion, taking some sort of pill. You guys were always off your heads.'

'How is this helping?' I asked Darren, my heart beating faster, my left hand now gripping the table leg.

Darren brought out the photo of me and Bethany, the one at the party. The one that had started this whole memory off.

'What does this make you think of?' Darren held it up for Oliver.

Oliver grabbed it, pushed his hand through his hair. 'I took this photo.'

'Did Sophie ask you to?'

'Yeah, her and Bethany were arguing.'

I whipped my head up and stared hard at Oliver. 'Arguing? We weren't, we were dancing together.'

'No,' Oliver said, 'you had both taken some pill. That's what you told me anyway, and it certainly looked like it. I remember because I was trying to keep an eye out for you, make sure you didn't do anything stupid.'

'Right, Oliver. This is good. Please go on,' Darren said.

'I came up to them in the middle of this argument, tried to break it up.'

'What were they arguing about? Do you remember?' Darren scribbled something in his notebook.

'Yeah, Sophie had flipped. She had like turned into someone else and she was going on about Bethany being ungrateful. Her words were more choice than that but, essentially, she was screaming at Bethany, telling her she should appreciate her family more. That she was lucky to have one.'

I exhaled loudly, shook my head. I hated Oliver in that moment, and I hated him even more now. We had been dancing together, not arguing. I remember thinking that Bethany should be more appreciative of her family, but I certainly didn't shout at her, like Oliver was making out.

I saw that Oliver's hands were shaking now. 'I'm sorry, Sophie, but it's the truth. You asked me to take this photo of you two together. You put your arm around Bethany and shoved the camera in my hand. I remember thinking it was an odd thing to do, but took it anyway.'

'I didn't.'

'You did. That's why Bethany's not smiling.'

I looked down at the photo. She was smiling, kind-of. I knew her better than anyone else, she was smiling.

'What happened after the photo?' Darren asked Oliver.

'Bethany walked off and Sophie blacked out.'

'You were jealous,' I said, my voice low, threatening. 'That's why you're saying this now. We didn't argue that night.'

After a few more minutes, it was clear Oliver and I weren't going to agree and Darren called it a day. Suddenly we were left alone. I asked Oliver to go to the shops for me, get me some aspirin. He tried to apologise about the session with Darren, said he didn't know what came over him. Before he left, I decided I couldn't ignore the horror I had been through in the pressroom, and told him about the journalist.

'What?' He looked shocked. 'I would never, Sophie, you must know that. Come on, it's me we're talking about.' Then I saw the flicker of recognition pass over his face. 'Oh god, there was one woman at the grocery store. She said she was a good friend of yours.' He looked at me. 'Shit, I'm such a fucking idiot.'

I knew then I couldn't trust Oliver. He was not the caring family man I had once thought he was. There was something in his recollection of the woman at the grocery store that struck me as untrue. Oliver was a savvy, intelligent man; I was pretty sure that if he was looking out for me, he wouldn't even have entertained this woman for one minute.

There was no one I could trust. I couldn't trust DI Ward. She had sat someone outside my own house, to watch my every move. I couldn't trust Paul. He lied and continued to lie. There was no one.

My eyes wandered the length of the kitchen; something didn't feel right. It was as if someone had been in my house, but nothing looked like it had been moved until I caught sight of a piece of paper peeping out of what I called my 'secret' drawer. My breath caught, I rose slowly from the chair and moved toward it, treading softly. The drawer was where I kept my medicine, my personal bits and bobs including all the house keys. I didn't remember putting a piece of paper there. Plucking the paper from the drawer I skimmed the text and gasped. The words were made up of cut-out newspaper letters and stuck down. I imagined the woman at work: latex gloves, tweezers, glue, all by the light of her task lamp. It read:

You have forty-eight hours to find Amy.

Do not tell the police or she dies.

P.

'P'. There it was, that one initial, and I realised she was back: 'Polly'. The same woman who had clearly been so jealous of Bethany and me at university had returned. I thought then of Bethany's doll, those glassy pale blue eyes staring out of a pallid face, her small rosebud lips pinched. I remember joking that her eyes seemed to follow you around the room. The all-seeing doll.

It was then I realised I had to find Amy. Alone. Whoever this woman was, she was bitter and twisted. 'Polly' had harboured some sort of hate for me for all these years and she was therefore, I believed, capable of anything.

I ran upstairs and grabbed a change of clothes, cash (I couldn't use my card), my phone and a small box of memorabilia I kept under the bed: my only memories of Bethany. I don't know why but something told me it might hold some answers. I left using the French doors and the back gate. I had checked the front: it was too risky. DI Ward's informant, three journalists outside wanting to know where I was going and the chance of Fiona reappearing, and Oliver about to return, put the front of the house off-limits.

CHAPTER 18

I slunk further down into my coat, and headed toward the Tube. My heart was hammering in my chest. What if someone saw me leaving? What if I was arrested? Then the police would *never* trust me. I felt as if I was falling: out of control, no plan, but I needed to find Amy. I could see that things were taking too long with the police. The officer outside my house unnerved me: it wasn't for my safety, I saw that now. The way the detective looked at me: did she suspect I had Amy? As I slipped between the closing doors of the Tube train, I remained facing away from the other passengers. As the train sped up and we left the bright light of the station and descended into the underground's depths, I caught my own tired reflection in the glass. I didn't look the same. The last few weeks had taken their toll. Ever since I saw that woman outside the burger joint.

I headed east, the number of passengers soon dwindled the further out we travelled, and I was relieved when the carriage only contained one other person. I glanced over, not wanting to draw attention to myself, and gasped inwardly. She looked like the back of the woman at the fair, the one at the burger joint, the one watching Amy in her play. My heart was racing, and I gripped the yellow pole, steadying my suddenly weakening legs. I could feel the familiar humming in my ears, the carriage had started to spin. Slowly at first, then faster.

I clawed my way to the nearest seat and gulped air. My eyes remained on the woman's back and I was just about to yell out to her, when I noticed a young girl by her side.

I held my breath. Was it Amy?

The doors were opening again. I needed to get to the woman.

'Stop,' I called. 'Please stop!'

She had stepped off, refusing to turn around, the girl at her side.

I flung myself at the window, my palms on the cool glass, as the train pulled away. The woman turned just as we sped away and I realised it wasn't her, nor was the girl Amy. My breathing had started to slow but the tears came fast.

I got off at Whetstone, my legs shaking uncontrollably after the attack. Walking as purposefully as I could, I made it past the transport police unnoticed and headed out. Within minutes I had found a B&B. I just needed a base for the time being, whilst I planned out my next move. I felt out of control, my nerves jagged. Just around the corner from the B&B, I spotted a corner shop and picked up a few supplies. I paid with cash and avoided eye contact with the man on the till: I did not want to draw attention to myself. Stuffing the items in my bag, I headed off quickly, head down.

Having checked into the B&B, I looked around the hotel room, grimacing at the mildew climbing the walls, the musty bed sheets and the bathroom reeking of stale cigarettes. I had chosen a rundown joint on the edge of London's North Circular. It seemed unlikely that anyone could spy on me here.

I took the small box of mementoes from inside my bag and emptied its contents onto the bed. It was mainly photos. A picture of Bethany stared out at me from the middle of the pile and I picked it up. When Bethany died,

I threw almost everything we had bought together away, plus letters, photos. I had kept the perfume, and the music – everything that reminded me of her death, out of respect. Even deleting most of our email conversations: each one a painful reminder of what I had lost. But this photo was different. I couldn't bear to get rid of it. She looked happy and carefree. Or was she? Oliver told me she hadn't been smiling in that other photo. No, she was happy in this one. I had taken this photo from her room when she died. It was a snapshot of Bethany on holiday with her mother, before I even knew her. A happy family photograph. I know Bethany would have wanted me to have it.

I heard shuffling outside. I dared not move, make a sound. Maybe it was the landlord, if he had recognised me, he hadn't commented. I had noted he was an overweight man wearing a white string vest, despite the chilly weather, and he hadn't bothered with the garden as stubborn weeds covered the small square lawn, the beds empty except for crushed Coke cans, empty bottles of vodka and condoms.

My only fear was his phoning the police, telling them my whereabouts, but he had barely registered my face, too interested in his cigarette.

I retrieved the note from my bag and read it again. The words swam before my eyes. I thought 'Polly' had disappeared the night Bethany died. As though,she realised that there were no longer two of us, that there was no need to be jealous any more because my best friend had died. Now, it was just Sophie, and she was fine with that. Only, clearly she wasn't and she was back.

Trembling violently, I sat heavily on the bed. Tears streaked my face and I looked at my watch. I needed to get back, tell the detective, show her the note, get her to up the search: to not tell the police would be crazy. But then my running away was crazy. She wanted this: she wanted me to chase her. But I had to do it alone. I felt a rush of relief that there was still hope Amy was alive and if she was, it was up to me to find her. I couldn't however brush away the guilty feeling that it was my past that had put Amy in danger.

I opened my bag. I felt around inside, looking for my phone, when I felt the familiar smooth metal of a can. Shoving the receipts and endless boxes of unopened medication to one side, I brought out a can of gin and tonic I realised I had bought from the shop. I didn't even remember picking it up. Looking inside my bag, there were a few more cans, sitting there, taunting me. It was then I knew how much I wanted to feel the warm liquid hit my veins, make me buzz. I wanted to feel the alcohol take hold, softening and blurring reality. Maybe I could have just a sip? Just to calm my nerves. I threw it on the bed but it sat there, almost mocking me. What harm could come of one can? I pulled back the tab and drank deeply, the fizz swishing around my mouth, and it didn't take long for the alcohol to bring on the familiar feeling of numbness. Only, it wasn't enough. I realised my hands were shaking, that a thin film of sweat now covered my face. I caught sight of myself in the mirror; it was like watching the old Sophie take off her mask and reveal her other self. I looked tired, I was trembling and I knew that having just that one can had set me off on a downward path. I eyed the other cans and picked another up, glugging the bitter liquid back, barely registering the taste but fully aware of the glorious rush of adrenaline.

What was I doing? I stared at myself in the mirror again. My daughter was missing and I was fuelling my body with poison. I ran to the toilet, lifted the lid and stuffed my fingers down the back of my throat. I heaved, but nothing came. Tears cascaded down my cheeks and I fell to the floor, my knees hitting the tiles. I rested my head on the back of the shower screen and I was filled with self-loathing. I knew I had to get myself together, that I was wasting precious time.

Looking at my watch again, I gave its face three taps and tried to focus. There was no time to waste. Forty-six hours remained. I stood up, moved from the bathroom to the window; a thin film of dirt covered the panes. A constant flow of traffic whizzed past, fumes lingering over the tarmac.

Turning away, I glanced at the passport photo of Amy; I'd taken it out of my wallet and propped it up against the bedside lamp. Looking at her gappy teeth and freckly nose, my heart ached with longing. How could I have even had a drink at a time like this? It was because I was no longer a woman in control. I could feel myself slipping into the darkness again. I thought about Paul. Is this what he had wanted? For me to trip up and fall, because he knew that my drinking was that bad it wouldn't take much to drag me back down again? I balled a fist and hit the wall. How could I have given in like that? I would not let Paul ruin me.

'Come on, you stupid woman,' I muttered to myself, staring down at the bed sheets and ran my tongue over my teeth, feeling the fur the G&T had left behind. My mind wandered and then I realised the smell of gin was so familiar, a memory lurking not far below the surface. I picked up my phone and called Darren.

'Can I come and see you? I've done something stupid.'

He didn't hesitate: I could tell from his voice that no one had noticed my disappearance yet.

Darren opened the door before I had a chance to ring the doorbell.

'Sophie.' He ushered me inside. 'Are you OK? Are you and Oliver OK?'

'Fine, yes, fine,' I brushed him off. 'I need your help.'

Once I had sat down, he looked at me properly. 'Have you had a drink?'

I nodded, started to cry. 'Yes. It got too much for me.'

'Because of Oliver and what he said?'

'Partly.' It was a half-truth.

'Have you taken your meds?'

'Yes.' I paused. 'I hate that I was so weak. I hate that even after so long, I still wasn't strong enough to resist it. But in a small way, I'm almost glad. The smell made me remember something, Darren. It must have been that trigger-thing you talk about.'

He gave a small frown. 'Look, for now, we need to forget about the drinking. The important thing is you clearly regret it. Let's focus on what it made you remember.' He took a swig of water, offered me a glass and asked me to sit on the sofa. 'Let's begin.'

'I remember a night out.' I looked down at my lap, shuffled slightly in my seat. 'We were part of an escort agency.'

When Darren didn't say anything, I glanced up. His face remained impassive and he nodded for me to continue.

'I had wanted to quit but Bethany convinced me otherwise.'

'So was this a particular occasion you remembered?'

'Yes, where I had said I didn't want to go in and she said he'd be angry.'

'How did that make you feel?'

'I guess I wondered what her priorities were.'

'You mean she wasn't listening to you?'

'Yeah.' I pushed my hand through my hair. 'Surely she should have been looking out for me? Listening to what I was saying. That's what family do.'

'But you weren't actually family.'

I sat up straight, challenged him. 'We were as good as.'

'She ignored your wishes, and then what?'

'Told me she was going in because she wanted to show her dad who was boss.'

'Her dad?' Darren crinkled his nose.

I brushed some imaginary crumbs off my trousers, three times. 'Yeah, she always banged on about how claustrophobic she felt around him, and doing something like escorting, that he wouldn't have approved of, was her sort of release.'

'How did that make you feel?'

I clenched my jaw. 'I called her an ungrateful bitch.' I paused. 'So Oliver was right, I did argue with her sometimes. I don't think we argued the night he was talking about, but maybe we did.'

Darren's mouth twitched. 'Why did you call her that?'

'Because she had a family. Not only that, she had a dad who cared enough that she didn't get involved in stuff like escorting.' I pursed my lips. 'I thought she was being selfish.'

Darren was busy jotting stuff down.

'So on these occasions, did you drink much? Drugs?'

'Yes, both.' I paused. 'I never wanted to. Bethany made me. So, yes, Oliver was probably right again, but Bethany made me.'

'Made you?'

'Told me that they would make me feel better after losing my parents and everything.'

'Didn't you think that you could say no?'

I shrugged. 'I guess what I meant to say was Bethany put pressure on me when we first knew each other, but I guess, if I'm being honest, I enjoyed it after that.' I pulled at a loose thread on my sweater. 'It kind of gave me a release.'

'So the drink, the drugs made you feel better?'

'Yeah, always at the beginning of the night and then I would wake up the next morning with a crushing sense of self-hate.'

'So would you say you got into escorting, drugs and drink because of Bethany? She essentially played on your vulnerabilities?'

I nodded. 'Yeah, she definitely introduced me to all of it, but I suppose I didn't put up much of a fight. The problem was I did too much of the drinking, the drugs, and I always blacked out. It was like each time it wiped my memory of who I had been.'

'Anything else?'

'No,' I said firmly. 'That's it. It's just I drank today and it made me remember that maybe Bethany and I didn't always see eye to eye. That maybe I've remembered her differently to how she really was.'

'It can happen. Another survival technique, if you like.'

'Do you think if Bethany was talking to you now, she would remember me as that angry person, as the one who called her things like an "ungrateful bitch"?'

Darren didn't speak for a few seconds. 'We all remember things differently.'

'She often said I had two sides to my personality.'

'Well, you know you've been through a lot but you're controlling it now, and that's the main thing.'

'Yeah.' I didn't feel very in control.

Darren nodded. 'I need you to come back tomorrow.'

'I can't.'

He raised his brows. 'Why?'

'Please, I just want to remember who did it. Who killed Bethany. That woman I've been seeing has my little girl, I'm sure of it.'

'I can't help you unless I see you.'

'It's all taking too long.'

He didn't say anything but I could tell I had said too much. I left, walking quickly down the street, only turning at the end. Darren was stood on his porch watching me.

I got back to the hotel room, unable to forget my anger at the way Bethany had made me feel. It was a memory I hadn't expected to have, a negative one like that. I picked up an empty can and threw it against the wall in frustration, then picked up the meds and threw them too. I couldn't bear the person I had become.

My skin crawled with goose pimples and I got up to dig out the electric heater I had found earlier. Turning it on full blast, the room soon smelt of burning dust but, in the small space, the temperature heated up fast. Sitting back on the bed, the springs sitting at awkward angles beneath me, it occurred to me that I needed answers, answers I couldn't find without the help of another source; someone I had used in the past to gather legal documentation. One name in particular sprang to mind. I picked up my phone, noticed the battery was getting low, and rang Jia. She didn't answer but I left a voicemail, explaining that I had a new number and that I desperately needed her help.

Placing the phone on the bed, I started to search through the pile of photos.

Amy's first shoe, pictures of my parents at Christmas; my father's paper hat perched clumsily on the top of his head, his cheeks glowing. My mother stood gracefully behind him, her arms hung loosely around his neck. Amy learning to ride, Amy aged seven on a bouncy castle. Then, at the bottom of the box, sat my wedding ring. But there was something else. A bracelet, its clasp tangled in a small mitten: Amy's when she was five. I drew out the mitten and carefully unlatched the clasp from the yarn. Holding the soft material up to my face, I rubbed it over my cheek and looked closely at the bracelet. I had found it in my pocket the morning after Bethany died. I don't remember if it was hers but it felt precious to me, a part of me; its gold had faded over time, the heart-shaped lock scratched. Holding it up to the light, I inspected the underside.

In small italic writing it read: *To Love is to Protect.*

I lifted myself off the bed and looked out at the bleak city landscape. The first drops of rain broke free from the clouds overhead and landed loudly on the windowsill. I wondered if the news had broken yet and I turned on BBC 24. My face filled the screen and below the ticker read: ALCOHOLIC MOTHER ON RUN: HAS SHE KIDNAPPED HER OWN CHILD?

My mouth grew dry, the remnants of gin at the back of my throat, and I shakily turned the small TV off. It was time to leave, I couldn't afford to stay in one place for too long.

CHAPTER 19

I rammed my belongings in my bag, leaving only the empty cans on the bed. The landlord was watching TV, and I slid past reception unnoticed, my heart beating loudly in my ears. Once outside, I walked fast down the street in the driving rain until I spotted the welcoming orange light of a free taxi.

'Where to, love?' the driver asked, switching off the light as I clambered into the back.

'Soho,' I answered.

'Anywhere in particular?' He started off, his eyes on mine in the mirror.

'Just drop me outside the Century Bar.' It was time to meet with my contact. I had met Jia in my early days at Thompson and Partners. She had been a whistle-blower for a major city bank and having gone into hiding decided to make her money finding out information the likes of me would never be able to access.

'Okey-dokey.'

The taxi driver had a run of good luck with the lights and the traffic was relatively light because of the hour.

I was soon stood on Shaftesbury Avenue and I rang Jia. She answered after three rings. Finally, a lucky sign.

'Sophie?' She sounded wary.

'Yeah, it's me.'

'Bloody hell. I've been waiting for your call. I got your message.' She sounded fraught. 'I saw you on the news. How you doing?'

'Fine. Well, not really. Listen, my battery is running low and I can't charge my phone up for now.'

'Where are you?'

'Soho.'

'Soho. Is that it? That's all you're giving me?'

'To be honest,' I admitted, 'I've got nowhere to stay tonight. I was at a B&B but I don't want to stay in the same place for too long, in case the police catch up with me.'

'Shit, Sophie. I'd invite you here, only…'

I nodded, even though she couldn't see me. 'I know the rules.' Rule number one for Jia: she preferred to do business over the phone, where possible.

'I need you to do me a favour. I'll transfer the money, the normal way, but will you help me?'

'As I always say, Sophie, depends. Fire away.'

'OK. I need as much info as possible on a woman called Bethany Saunders.' I filled her in on as many details as possible: obviously, I could be pretty precise about the date of her death. 'At Aberystwyth University, started in '89, studied law.'

'Leave it with me.'

I went to thank her but she had already hung up. After wandering through the backstreets of Soho for well over an hour, stopping only once to have a sandwich bought from a Spar, I decided to bunk down in the entrance of a shop. I couldn't risk checking in anywhere, using my card or even using my phone beyond what was necessary. The police would be out looking for me now and I sure as hell looked guilty now.

I wrapped my coat as tight as it would go around me but it was bitterly cold, making it impossible to sleep. After an hour or so, however, I felt my eyelids getting heavier. Sleep took a hold of me, and I didn't try to stop it. I wanted to escape this world, and enter another.

Then: *chink*.

I brought my head up quickly. My muscles immediately tensed, ready to fight. But there was no one there. I lifted myself from the ground and scanned the road. No one. That's when I noticed a two-pound coin, on the pavement, by my feet. I smiled. Some kind soul had thought I was a tramp, homeless. Reality clobbered me around the head: *I was homeless. Or, I wouldn't return home, until I had my daughter.*

A grumbling sound came from behind me. I swivelled around. A bearded man moved past me and sat down in the shop entrance. He handed me a bottle. Vodka. I could have; I wanted to, but I shook my head and sat back down too. The man stared at me and brought a brown hessian sack up around his chin. He would be my company tonight. I grimaced at the stale smell that came from his 'blanket' every time he moved. He knocked back a huge gulp of the vodka and closed his eyes.

He must have felt me staring and his eyes flicked open. I smiled apologetically and, in turn, tried for sleep once more. Moments later, I felt something scratch my hand and opened my eyes quickly. The man held out another hessian sack. He silently indicated that I should put it underneath me. I did, more by way of making amends for my ill-mannered behaviour. He nodded, happy that I had done as I was told, and once again returned to his slumber. I had to admit, he had a point. The warmth that came from having the rough material under me allowed me to drift off.

After a couple of hours of restless sleep, I opened my eyes. A rubbish truck was making its way up the side road.

The lifting mechanism screeched with every new load of commercial waste.

It was only after a few minutes of contemplating my next move that I realised the man had gone. I lifted myself up and folded the hessian bag in a neat square. Not sure how I could return it to the owner I carefully placed it in the corner.

I glanced at my watch. My heart quickened: I had thirty hours to find Amy.

The coffee shop on the corner was already open and I ordered an espresso and a croissant. Downing the coffee in one, I ordered another. A quarter of an hour later, I was ready; my eyes stung and I could barely string a sentence together due to tiredness, but I had a plan.

As I hadn't heard back from Jia, I headed to a library. Once I had secured a seat away from prying eyes, I started my search but I felt like I was being watched. Fear pricked the hairs on the back of my neck. I swivelled in my chair and my eyes came to rest on the librarian busy checking out books. She looked up. I gave her a small smile and turned back around in my seat.

I had feigned needing access to newspaper records for PhD research in criminology; I felt it was only partly a lie. Although I thought I must have read every article about what happened that night, maybe, just maybe, I had missed something. At first nothing came up. The pages took increasingly longer to load as my fingers tapped the keyboard vigorously. I couldn't think of any other keywords or sets of words. Familiar articles, their font and typeface now dated, appeared on the screen. But I had seen it all before. Then, I remembered the bracelet: *To Love is to Protect*.

It sounded so familiar, like something I had been told as a child. Maybe it came from a children's story or rhyme.

My phone started buzzing on the desk. The librarian glanced over and shot me a disapproving look.

'Hello?' I whispered into the phone.

'Sophie?' Paul's voice boomed loudly down the receiver. 'Why are you whispering and where the hell are you?'

I left the room hurriedly, my head down.

'Paul, why are you ringing me? How did you know this number?'

'You gave it to me ages ago. I tried your other phone, there was no answer so I gave this number a go.'

'Why are you ringing?' I repeated.

'Because you're missing,' he said simply. 'Because we're just about to do another press conference and you're not here, because Fiona just asked me if I knew where you were.'

'And DI Ward?'

'She's got officers out looking for you.'

'Right.' I leant up against a wall. I didn't know if anyone was listening in; I didn't want to give too much away.

'That's all you're going to say?'

'I'm looking for Amy.'

'Alone?' he asked incredulously.

'Yes.'

'Where are you?' he repeated.

'I can't tell you.'

He lowered his voice. 'Sophie, be careful. You don't know what you're dealing with.'

'I can't just sit at home.' I risked being heard and said, 'She told me I have forty-eight hours to find Amy. And that was last night.' I turned and pressed my forehead to the wall. 'Paul, you need to go and get our little girl. We can do this,' I hit the wall gently with my clenched hand, 'together.'

'Sophie, I have to go.'

'Wait,' I said quickly, 'one thing, will they do it? Will this woman kill her if I don't find her in time?'

Paul hesitated. 'Sophie, just come home.' Desperation tinged his words.

I knew I had to stay calm if I wanted him to tell me more. 'Paul, please.'

Silence: the gulf of unanswered questions sat stagnant between us.

'Paul, just tell me where she is. I'll deal with it. I won't involve you. Just tell me where Amy is.'

I knew he had to know Amy's abductor or else why would he be lying? My best guess was the woman was threatening him somehow, she had some sort of a hold over him.

He killed the call and I kicked the wall with my foot in frustration. It felt as if I was going around in circles. I needed help but, as I couldn't ask the police directly, it was time to check in on Darren.

A woman answered. 'Darren Fletcher's office.'

I stopped breathing. I thought I'd get straight through.

'Would you like me to connect you?' asked the woman.

'Please.'

She hesitated; I could hear the rustle of paper. 'Bear with me. Let's see if he's free.' She clucked down the phone. 'No, I'm afraid he's got another patient. Could you ring back tomorrow?'

'Not really,' I answered frankly. 'When will he be free?'

'He's in sessions for the entire day.' She paused. 'Oh, wait a sec. Can I ask who's calling?'

I debated that one. 'Sophie. Sophie Fraiser.' I cleared my throat. 'I am a patient.'

'Ah, OK. Then that's a different matter.'

'Really?' Was that a good or a bad sign?

'Yes. Darren has left a note here stating that, if you were to ring, I must tell him. Apparently, a matter of urgency.' She dropped her business-like guard.

Without further delay, she put me through to his office.

'Sophie?'

'Yes, it's me…'

'Where are you?'

'I need to see you.' I swallowed hard.

'Everybody's looking for you.' He sighed deeply; it sounded as if he had the weight of the world on his shoulders. 'The DI's onto me. Wants me to tell her as soon as you get in contact.' He hesitated. 'She doesn't, however, know I'm still willing to help you. To a point, though, you understand? I know you're not going to tell me where you are and so it would only play on my conscience if I didn't guide you where I can.'

I nodded. 'Did you show her your notes so far?'

'No, patient confidentiality. Until I consider you to be a danger to the public, I can't give her access to them.'

I felt a brief glimmer of hope: maybe the DI would see that it was all coming together.

'Sophie,' he said, his tone grave, 'it would be easier if you came back.'

'I can't.'

He breathed heavily down the phone.

'Darren, DI Ward told me that you managed to crack a case using exposure therapy. I read about it. Why is it not working for me?'

'It is working, Sophie.' He hesitated. 'It is working but the thing is you have to be willing to open your mind up entirely. You see, if you hold back because, say, you're scared of what you might remember, we will always hit a wall.'

'How do I do it then? Not hold back?' I pushed him.

'The thing is, Sophie, it's a double-edged sword. Your mind is protecting you by not allowing you to entirely return to the time of trauma. In some cases, when a person's mind is fully accessed, they have never recovered.'

'Darren, I *need* to remember who killed Bethany. I need to unlock everything. Please,' I encouraged. 'I've got a bracelet that I found after she was murdered. It says "To Love is to Protect". Do you think this method might help even figure out if that quote is relevant?'

He sighed. 'This person DI Ward is referring to remembered not only the events they had supressed but a great level of detail.'

My breath caught. 'Could I do it? If I am really willing to try?'

'Potentially,' he said quietly. 'In fact, I had been thinking the same thing but I'm afraid of the repercussions in light of your state of mind.' He paused. 'What I'm saying is, it's a risk.'

'OK, but I'm willing to take it.' Then I had a thought. 'But how do I know I can trust you? How do I know you won't tell the detective we're meeting?'

'Because,' he cleared his throat, 'as I said I have to honour patient confidentiality. However, if I think at any point you are putting yourself or the public at risk, I need to go to the police.'

My heart leapt with joy. Finally, someone I could really trust. 'Thank you, thank you.' Tears spilt down my face.

We agreed to meet away from his house in two hours. I came off the phone and scanned the milling crowds of academics and visitors to the library. A quick peek at my watch told me it was mid-morning and clearly everyone had decided to go for coffee at once. As I struggled against the tide of people and made my way back toward the reading room, I felt someone's eyes on me. Looking back, over my left shoulder, I thought I saw a person in dark clothing move in and out of my peripheral vision. I collected my locker key from beside the computer and headed downstairs to fetch my belongings. Grabbing the duffel bag from the locker, I walked fast out of the library and checked for any unread messages from Jia or Oliver.

There were none and, as I stepped out onto Euston Road, I went to put the phone in my bag when I felt someone collide with my right arm, sending me flying as I crashed heavily against the building wall, falling to the ground.

'What the…' I shouted angrily, my mind trying to catch up with what had just happened.

I lifted myself off the pavement, ignoring the pain that tore through my right arm as I scanned the crowds for anyone running or familiar. There was no one.

'Are you OK?' A woman was beside me now: she wore a business suit and smelt of expensive perfume. 'Here's your bag.' She handed me the small duffel bag. 'And your phone.'

The phone was smashed into three or four pieces and I could tell it was broken, never to be fixed. I smiled gratefully, biting back the stinging tears. 'Thank you so much.'

'Did you hurt yourself?' She frowned, waiting for me to check.

'No,' I lied, not wanting to show my face should she recognise me.

'I just saw you suddenly fall to the ground,' the woman was saying. 'Like you had blacked out or something.'

'Someone ran into me.'

'Oh, do you want me to call someone for you?'

I shook my head, wishing she would go, and checked my bag. I stuffed everything back in: keys, Bethany's CD, and a dented can of drink.

'Are you sure you're all right?'

Suddenly aware that the woman was waiting for an answer, I forced a smile and took the risk of looking up at her. 'Fine, thank you.'

I zipped up the bag, my fingers not cooperating as pins and needles set my fingertips on fire. I flinched with the pain and the woman held my arm now.

'Perhaps I should take you to A&E?'

'I'm fine,' I mumbled and hurried off in the opposite direction to where I had been going. After I rounded the corner, I stuffed my broken phone into the outside pocket of my bag and made tentative steps toward the edge of the kerb to hail a cab. It was time to see Darren again. He had said we should meet at his friend's house. It was too risky for me to return to his. This is when I knew that Darren really was on my side.

CHAPTER 20

The taxi driver let out a low whistle as we drove up to the large Regency house.

'Nice pile,' he murmured. 'You live here?'

I shook my head. 'No. Just a friend.'

He grinned at me in his rear-view mirror. 'That's the kind of friend you want to keep on side.' He glanced at the meter. 'That'll be nineteen-fifty then, love.'

I nodded, took out my wallet and handed him a twenty. 'Keep the change.'

'Much appreciated,' he said in his East London accent. 'You'll be wanting a receipt?'

'No, you're all right.' I started to climb out of the car.

'You're the lady off the telly, aren't you?' He turned in his seat now to get a proper look. He flashed me an apologetic smile. 'Sorry, I recognised you a while back but didn't think it my place to say anything. Do they think they're going to find your daughter?'

I nodded fast. 'They're very positive.' I was lying: what did I know? It had been over twenty-four hours since I had spoken to DI Ward.

Once I was out of the car, he wished me luck and sped off down the quiet road. I turned and stared up at the doctor's friend's house, suddenly aware that the police might jump out and arrest me. Arrest me, I thought ironically, for looking for my daughter. I basically trusted

Darren but, at the end of the day, he was employed by the police.

I dragged my feet up the steps, the pain in my right arm had become unbearable and it was slowing me down. Ringing the doorbell, I looked around me. I thought I was doing well as a lawyer, but this was another echelon of society altogether.

The door opened and I fully expected to be faced with a butler.

'Sophie,' Darren said. 'Am I glad to see you.' He took me in a firm embrace; more intimate than we had ever been previously as doctor and patient. It was strange to see him in his jeans and T-shirt in the context of this house, he suited his arty terrace much more. 'How are you?' He held me at arm's length and I must have flinched in pain. 'Sophie, oh dear, are you hurt?'

'Yes, it's my arm.' I explained the incident outside the library.

'Well, come through.' He smiled gently. 'Come through. My friend's a Harley Street doctor, said we could use his pad. Didn't ask any questions.'

I nodded and followed Darren through to a large sitting room off to the left. The fire was lit and a large lamp in the corner was on. The warmth was inviting and I allowed Darren to take my coat. He carefully peeled it from my body so as not to cause me further pain. Minutes later, he came back with painkillers and an icepack.

'I know it's probably the last thing you want to be doing in this cold weather, but honestly, it'll help with any swelling. I've got his cleaner onto tea-making duties.'

Pushing my sleeve up, I placed the icepack on the top of my right arm. A gentle knock at the door and Darren stood up.

I leapt up from the sofa, my heart beating faster. I fully expected DI Ward to walk through the door.

A woman entered the room.

'Hello,' she introduced herself, 'I'm Patrick's cleaner.' She put a tray down on the ottoman. We waited for her to leave, closing the door behind her before either of us spoke. If she recognised me, she didn't show it.

'So, has the DI been in touch again?'

'Yes. She came to my house and, well,' he paused, 'she asked me if I had spoken to you today.'

'And?'

He cleared his throat. 'I told her about patient confidentiality, but you have to understand that will only work for a while. Your daughter is missing. Technically, there's a life at risk here and if I feel you or your daughter's in danger, or any other member of the public, I'll be forced to disclose everything you've told me so far.'

I nodded, took a sip of tea. 'Please, Darren, I don't have much time. Tell me what you think we can do.'

He exhaled loudly. 'OK, as I say, I think we should have one final go at exposure therapy.'

'OK.' I edged forward on the sofa. 'Do you think I'm capable?'

'Yes, but as I said, I'm wary of the repercussions.' He furrowed his brows. 'Most significantly you could suffer hallucinations, imagine things. Perhaps in light of your medical history, this might be a greater risk for you.'

'I will do anything to find Amy,' I said firmly.

'OK.' He picked up a file sat on the table next to him. 'I can show you the study if you like.'

'No offence, I don't have time to be reading the terms and conditions.'

He pursed his lips, bunched his fist. 'It's about taking you back to that night, true age regression, so that you will feel and hear what you felt. We make a connection between the recent trauma, Amy going missing, with the past trauma of Bethany dying.'

'Would it explain then why, when we were back at the site of the fairground, I remembered hearing another woman's voice calling my name at the fair?'

'Yes, exactly. Although, I would say that the level of recollection you will have reached that day, with me, might not have been enough to re-experience that night. The voices,' he hesitated, trying to explain, 'might not actually have been real. Your mind is substituting one thing for another. Your mind was as near as it could get to what you actually heard, but that's not to say that the fact that your mind chose bells as the substitute is not meaningful. You could have been reaching further back to a memory of something someone's told you.' He paused. 'Like Bethany.' He was tapping his foot now, I counted every third tap. 'OK,' he said, clearly now fizzling with energy, 'you mentioned the bracelet on the phone. You said you found it in your pocket after the night Bethany died. Maybe the bracelet is Bethany's and the quote on it might be resonating with you in some way we can explore further.'

'What do I do?'

'Lie over here. I'm going to talk to you but the most important thing, Sophie, for this to work is you have to be willing.'

'Of course I'm willing! I want my child back. I'll do anything.'

He nodded. 'It's just when we started these sessions you were reticent, I need you to open your mind up fully. Remember why you're doing it.'

'Darren,' I said as I lay on the sofa, 'I have to find my daughter in a few hours or she dies. I will do anything. I think I can remember more about that night where

I got angry with Bethany. You know that I told you about it last time?'

He nodded and with that, I settled back on the sofa, closed my eyes and listened to him talking. He started to paint a scene. It wasn't a scene I knew and yet it was strangely familiar.

'OK, Sophie, on the count of three I want you to tell me where you are.'

'I'm in a taxi and it drops us off at the end of a long drive.'

'Who are you with?'

'Bethany.'

'Can you tell me what you can smell, what you can hear?'

'The taxi smells dusty mingled with Bethany's perfume.'

'Does the taxi driver have any music on?'

'Yes, there's some classical music on low. I don't recognise it.'

I became aware that Darren had started up some very quiet music.

'OK, continue, Sophie.'

'We get out of the taxi and we start walking toward a huge house. I remember thinking that it's now eerily quiet, no one around. Just us.'

Darren stops the music.

'Is it cold?'

'Freezing. I'm shivering.'

'Are you in the countryside?'

'Yes, in the middle of nowhere, near Aberystwyth.'

'How do you feel?'

'I remember feeling sick inside, like something bad is going to happen.' I swallowed. 'We're arguing. I don't want to go any further but Bethany tells me it's the last time. I hate her in that moment for having this power over me.'

'OK, does someone greet you at the door?'

'Yes, a man.'

My heart started to pound faster as I remembered his face. Darren must have sensed me starting to panic.

'Keep as calm as you can, Sophie. It will help keep your mind open.'

I took a deep breath. 'He was the diplomat, the man hosting the party.' Involuntarily, I put my hand to my cheek. 'It's suddenly much warmer.'

'Why, Sophie?'

'We've passed a room with a fire.'

'Do you go into that room?'

'No, he leads us upstairs and then – then…'

'Sophie, you are safe here, keep your mind open.'

'There are businessmen. Five, I think. Sitting in a semi-circle around the bed.'

'Why are they there?'

'To watch us.'

'Watch you?'

'Yes.' My breathing quickens. 'I didn't know it would be like this. We were asked to bring handcuffs, but I didn't know. Then the door was locked.' I let out a sob. 'We were trapped.'

'Sophie, shhh, you're doing well.'

I sensed Darren was nearer me now. 'What happens next?'

'I can't remember.'

'Try. I know it's hard but do try.'

'We snort some coke, I think. And drink.'

'How does that make you feel?'

'Light-headed. Sick.'

'OK, and then…'

'I don't remember what we did. I really don't.'

'Sophie, you're doing so well, keep going as long as you can.'

'There's a woman in the room.'

'Not Bethany?'

'No, another woman.'

'Who is she? Who is the woman?'

'I don't know! She's really familiar, but I don't know.'

'OK.'

'She has a gun and a knife. She…'

'You're doing well, keep going.'

'I'm screaming. Telling her no. Don't do it. I knock her arms out of the way, try and get the gun, but she's determined.'

'She has shot your friend? Sophie, has this woman shot your friend?'

'Yes. Yes. Yes. Bethany's head bounced backward.'

'What do you do?'

'I'm falling. Falling.'

'Where?'

'To the ground.'

'Anything else, Sophie? What does "To love is to protect" mean, Sophie?'

'I don't know!'

'Try, dig deeper, let your mind go.'

'The woman, she kept saying it, the woman who killed Bethany.'

'So, the bracelet belongs to the killer?'

'Yes. No…I don't know! I thought it was Bethany's. Maybe the killer knew about the bracelet.'

I sat bolt upright, a shadowy, forgotten memory attempting to push its way to the forefront of my mind.

'Sophie,' Darren was by my side now, 'are you OK? Here's a tissue.'

I hadn't even realised I was crying. Hot, furious tears cascaded down my cheeks. 'I feel like the answer is so obvious. Just then… I almost remembered something,

something that I know is so important. But, just like that, the thought had disappeared.'

Darren nodded gravely. 'I can understand that. Your mind automatically shuts out pain, grief, anxiety and in order to remember, you need to open your mind even further.'

I blinked. 'How do I do that?'

'The only way,' he took my hand, 'is to face your fears.'

'You make it sound so easy.' I withdrew my hand and twisted the tissue round and round into a tight knot.

'It's not easy. But your greatest fear is also your greatest strength.'

I smiled weakly. 'That's deep.'

He patted me on the hand. 'Your greatest fear is losing your daughter?'

'Of course.'

'Anything else?'

'Yes, feeling like I know the woman who killed Bethany. How I can get so close to remembering.'

Darren considered this for a minute. 'Well, maybe until you allow your mind to face the fear of finding out exactly that, we won't be able to go any further.'

I was about to ask him how I go about getting over that fear when Darren's phone rang. He looked at me, his eyes not leaving mine as he answered.

'Yes, OK,' he said to the caller. 'Yes.'

The one-word answers and I knew who he was talking to: the police. I ran for the door and out onto the street. I didn't look back once.

CHAPTER 21

Without a mobile, I couldn't ring Jia. By now, she might have more information on Bethany; moreover, she might have something on her father. I knew she'd be unhappy if I just turned up on her doorstep but, without a phone, I couldn't think of another way of contacting her.

Two buses later, I was in Soho. It was rush hour: agency workers and media types spilt out onto the roads and into the nearest bars and restaurants. I crossed Shaftesbury Avenue, walked under the gateway to Chinatown, and headed for Jia's workplace. She lived in an amazing apartment with panoramic views of the city, but worked out of a bedsit in Chinatown. In her line of work, finding out information that most people could never legally get a hold of, she felt safer hidden away.

I walked down the steep steps leading to the basement and knocked twice in rapid succession, followed by a pause, and then twice again.

The door opened a crack. 'Sophie.'

I could just make out a sliver of her face. 'My phone is broken,' I explained.

'Come in.'

I shuffled through the small opening and Jia shut the door directly, pulled the chain across and double bolted it.

'Had some problems recently,' she said in her Chinese-London twang.

'I know you prefer to do business via the phone but, as I say, my phone was broken and…'

She looked at me and grinned. 'I've just got to be careful, you know how it is, but I'm glad you came.' She came over and hugged me tight. 'How you doing, Sophie?'

I struggled to find the words and she gestured for me to sit. 'I'm… I'm… I just want her back.' I wiped away tears with the back of my hand. 'There's so much going on, stuff I can't tell anyone. Things no one can understand. But the woman who's got her…'

'You know who's got Amy?' Jia sat beside me, rubbing my back with her hand.

'Not exactly but I think it's related to something that happened years ago. I just have to figure out who's behind it and why my ex-husband is involved.'

'Paul? Really?' She stood up, started busying herself with the kettle.

'Really.' There wasn't enough time to bring her up to speed on the session with Darren. 'Jia, did you find anything out about Bethany? I can't stay long but if you have something, anything, I need to know.'

'Coffee?'

I shook my head. 'I really need to get going.'

She abandoned the kettle and sat down.

When she didn't speak, I pressed her. 'Jia.'

'OK, but I believe you might think I'm a liar.'

'What do you mean? Please, Jia, tell me.' I caught her eye. 'I have twenty-four hours to find Amy or she will be killed.'

Jia nodded slowly, her gaze cast downward at the pile of papers on the coffee table. She picked up a pencil and studied my face.

'Bethany is an illegitimate child.'

I jerked my head backward. 'What? She never talked about her family but I didn't think it was because of something like this.'

'There's more.'

I looked at Jia, my eyes imploring. 'Tell me.'

'You've met your friend Bethany's mother?'

I nodded. 'Yes, a few times but only briefly and I never met her father. She didn't like talking about him. I think she was ashamed of the money he pushed her way but, also, she acted as if he suffocated her.' I thought back to the bracelet: *To Love is to Protect.* Suddenly the engraving made sense. Were they the words of a man who, perhaps, hadn't known that love – too much love – could push someone away, not bring them closer? That Bethany wouldn't have entered that house if it hadn't been for her desperate need to prove something to herself; some sort of independence.

'As I say, she was born out of wedlock.' Jia sat upright, the lamp behind her creating a kind of halo effect: like she was about to deliver some great truth to me.

'Jia, please.' I reached inside my bag to retrieve my wallet. Taking out two fifty-pound notes, I placed them on the desk.

'Bethany's father is Zander Thompson.'

'Zander?' I gasped and gave a small shake to my head. 'But he's my boss. How can he be my best friend's father?' My hand went up to my mouth as I tried to take it in. 'My dead best friend's father.' I looked at her, uncomprehending. 'Are you sure?'

'I know. When I got hold of her birth certificate, I couldn't believe it either. At first, I thought it was no one of importance but I looked into his background and made the connection. That's when I found out, he owns the firm you work for.'

My head was spinning: I wanted the world to right itself but, instead, I was discovering that those people I knew, those people I could trust, were involved in a web of lies. A web so sticky, so tangled, I was in mortal danger of being dragged into its very centre and left flailing.

'I'm sorry,' she said.

It was time to leave. We stood and she hugged me at the door before releasing the lock. I walked up the stairs, my eyes squinting against the bright daylight and heard the door slam behind me.

I needed answers: it was time to find a phone and a computer. Once on Shaftesbury Avenue, it was easy to signal a cab.

'Hampstead Heath, please.' I climbed into the back, grateful for the dark quiet space to think. I needed somewhere safe and Faye's house was as close to that as was possible at this time.

It wasn't until I went to pay the driver, I realised Jia had tucked the fifty-pound notes back into my bag.

Within minutes, Faye had taken my coat, sat me down and put the kettle on. She had a tea towel in her hands which she kept folding this way and that.

'Sophie, why didn't you contact me sooner? I've been worried sick.' As soon as the kettle had boiled, she put the towel down. 'Tea?'

I nodded. 'Please.'

'I noticed you weren't at the press conference yesterday. I saw it on the news. Paul was there but you weren't. That's when I knew something was wrong.' She paused. 'Then that female detective turned up on my doorstep an hour later.'

'What did she say?'

She cocked her head and poured the boiling water into mugs, her hand visibly trembling. 'She said your Family Liaison Officer couldn't find you. Did I know where you were?' She cleared her throat. 'I said no. Which was the truth but it got me thinking.'

She had her back to me now and I could see her shoulders quivering gently. I rose from the chair and came up behind her, putting my hand on her shoulder. She turned, her face wet with tears.

'Aw, Faye. I'm truly sorry.'

She sniffed. 'I was just worried, you know? You're like a daughter to me and I thought, at first, I thought…' She fished out a hankie from inside her cardigan sleeve. 'I thought you might have done something stupid.'

'Stupid?' I nodded: the realisation of what she was saying dawned on me. 'Kill myself?'

She grimaced at my blunt wording. 'Yes.'

My heart twisted with guilt. How could I put the one person who understood me so well through this?

'Faye, it's fine. I'm fine.'

'Sophie, it's just you know and I know that there are two sides to you. That things haven't always been easy.'

'I'm trying to find Amy myself.' I nodded with a false confidence. 'I think the woman who has Amy killed Bethany. She's come back to find me.' I knew, for Faye's sake, I needed to keep the details brief.

Faye cupped my chin in her hand, her skin crepe-like and clammy. 'Are you in danger?' I didn't speak. 'You must be careful. Please.' She turned now, her movements awkward. 'You think this person has Amy?'

'I'm pretty sure.' I took the mug from her. 'Faye, do you mind if I use your computer and phone.'

Relief passed over her face. 'Of course, what else can I do?' She needed to feel useful.

'I'd love to stay the night too. If that's OK.'

'My goodness,' she smiled now, 'of course it is. You are always welcome here, you know that. I'll make you a good supper too. Get your strength up. I don't think you know how thin you've got.'

I gave a small smile. 'It's certainly one way to diet, but I wouldn't recommend it.'

'Just like your mother... You don't know your own beauty, darling Sophie. Inside and out.'

She told me to use the spare room: she had put fresh bedding on in case I turned up.

'And you know where the computer and phone are. Help yourself.'

I nodded gratefully. 'Did the detective mention anything about that night?'

'She asked if I knew anything about it or the time you spent in the Priory. She was on her way to see someone called Darren. A doctor of some sort.'

'That's it?' I pressed.

'She said she was going to look into that night.' Faye frowned. 'But couldn't be sure it would amount to much.' Faye reached into her pocket and took out a card. 'I've been told to ring her if you turn up.'

'Please don't.'

Faye paused, deliberating. 'But don't you think it would be for the best?'

'No, I can't trust them.'

She nodded slowly, unquestioning. 'I'll put supper on then.'

I headed upstairs, turned on Faye's ancient computer and dug around in my duffel bag for the photo of Amy. I struggled to find it and quickly emptied the bag of its contents. It was then that I brought out what I thought was Bethany's CD but a wave of panic moved over me as I quickly realised it wasn't. Bethany's was there too but this new one, I didn't recognise. My mind flashed back to the library and falling to the ground. My breathing grew shallow as I realised someone had planted it in my bag.

Sitting quickly in the office chair, I loaded the CD and double clicked on the disk icon. The hard drive whirred into action and I sat back, waiting.

A pair of eyes filled the screen and I watched in horror as a large image of Amy's face slowly panned out to reveal that she was tied to a chair, her mouth covered in duct tape. I struggled to breathe, my chest tight. Amy thrashed about in the chair, lashing her head from one side to the other. She was so much thinner too.

I screamed before ramming my fist into my mouth, fearful Faye would hear me. Tears streamed down my face and I put one hand up to the screen, caressing her image with my forefinger.

On the CD, I could hear the scraping of wood against wood. Seconds later, Amy's face came up inches from the lens. She was so close: I could make out the individual freckles on her nose and the small scar above her eyebrow where she had fallen off the swing aged five. She had been so brave about the stitches. I touched her image with my hand again.

'Amy, sweetheart.'

A voice at the door and a gentle knocking: 'You OK in there, Sophie?' Faye asked. 'You sound upset. Can I come in?'

'I'm fine,' I called back, my voice wavering and paused the CD. 'Honestly.'

Silence ensued and I thought Faye might have left but seconds later, she said, 'Sophie, supper will be ready in half an hour. OK?'

'Sounds great.' I forced a bright and breezy tone.

After a minute or so, I heard Faye's footsteps on the stairs.

I pressed play again and realised Amy was speaking. I leant in, my face right up to the screen. The room she was in looked strangely familiar. I could see past Amy, out the window, and I felt like I had been there before. I could just make out a metal sign on the wall behind Amy, it read: Shamrock Place.

She whispered, 'Mummy, please can you stop this. Please help me.'

I was shaking uncontrollably. I needed answers and used Faye's landline to phone Zander, my boss's, mobile. I knew the number off by heart because, I realised guiltily, of the number of times I had to phone to say I'd be late or request an extension. He had not once argued with me, or made me feel bad.

There was no answer. I tried again. Instead I phoned Thompson and Partners' main line. It was time to find out why Bethany's father had employed me all those years ago. It was out of hours, but only just, and worth a shot. I knew Bex, the receptionist, hardly ever left the office before seven. She went straight from the office to some gym class pretty much every day.

Clearing my throat, I dialled.

'Thompson and Partners Limited. How may I help you?'

Relief shot through me. 'Bex, it's me. Sophie.' Silence. 'Sophie Fraiser.'

'Hi, Soph.' She sounded panicky. 'How you doing?'

Why did everyone keep asking me that question: it felt so pointless but I answered anyway. 'You know, not great.'

'Hmm. I can imagine.'

'Actually, Bex, I was wondering if you could put me through to Zander?'

'Right.' I could almost hear the clickety-clack of her bright red manicured nails moving over the keyboard, drumming the edge of the desk. 'He's actually on a call right now. Can you call back? Or I can get him to give you a ring?'

'Don't worry, I'll call back later.'

I hung up the phone but I had already decided I needed to see him in person. To see the whites of his eyes when

I told him I knew who his daughter was. Gathering my coat and wallet, I made my way downstairs and explained I was just popping out for a bit.

'Oh no, Sophie. I've cooked your favourite. Lasagne.' Faye looked dismayed.

'I'll be back before you know it. But you go ahead and eat.'

'Sophie, do you have a mobile?'

I remembered mine had been broken into smithereens and I shook my head.

She handed me her phone: even more brick-like than the damaged one upstairs. 'You never know when you might need it.' She scribbled her landline number on a post-it note and passed it to me. 'I'll eat now but I'll warm some up for you later.'

I smiled appreciatively and hugged her close. 'Thank you.'

'Be safe.'

The night sky was clear. I wrapped my coat closely around me and tightened the belt. It would take me a good hour or so to get to the office in Temple but I needed to speak to him.

It was time to get some answers from Zander Thompson: my boss and Bethany's father. I wanted to know why he had never told me who he was, how I had come to be working for the very man my dead best friend hated. I certainly didn't believe the link was coincidence.

CHAPTER 22

I made the familiar journey down Surrey Street toward Thompson and Partners. As I neared, I could just make out a figure leaving the building: Bex. She didn't bother locking up because, just as I had thought, she wasn't the last to leave. In fact, the building was pitch-black except for one window.

Opening my wallet, I retrieved my card to access the building. As I swiped, I held my breath: it wouldn't have surprised me if Bex had cancelled the card. But she hadn't thought of that and I entered the building quickly and quietly, making sure the large swing-door didn't slam back on itself. The reception area was dark; the only light came from the tropical fish tank in the corner. An angelfish darted through the water, kicking up the sand on the bottom. I waited for my eyes to adjust before moving up the stairs. The office had, in some ways, become a home from home. But now, I was a stranger in a foreign land.

I knew I had to take Zander unawares. My ears were pricked: listening out for any movement but the only sound to cut through the murky gloom was the high-pitched hum of the pump in the fish tank. I felt for the first step and began the steady climb up to the fifth floor. Remembering Faye's phone, I took it out and pressed a key to power up the display. It gave me just enough light to make it to the first floor, after which, I used the eerie green light from the fire exit signs. As I neared the top, I stopped momentarily to catch my breath. I put the phone back in my pocket, dragged my hand through my scraggly hair and strode up the final few steps.

I could see Zander through the glass, sat at his desk, whisky in hand. The gentle sound of Mozart drifted over the still office space and, for a brief second, I just watched him. This man who I thought I knew. He looked different to me now. I wasn't sure if he had physically changed but there was something about his overall appearance that didn't feel right. Normally, Zander was a man in control: clean, pressed suits at all times, hair slicked back, shaven. I shifted my weight from my right foot to the left and a pen I had been carrying in my pocket fell to the ground.

Zander shot up, out of his chair. 'Who's there?' He strode to his office door and leant out. 'Who's there?'

I stepped out of the shadows. 'It's me, Zander.'

An expression of sadness, or remorse, flitted across his face. 'Ah, Sophie.' He took a tentative step out of the office into the darkness and I heard him fumbling about with switches before he flicked them on and the entire office space was bathed in a harsh fluorescent light.

'What on earth are you doing here, Sophie? It's so late. Has something happened?'

I stood rooted to the spot. My mind couldn't comprehend the situation or the man in front of me.

'I know who you are,' I replied simply, a small rumble underpinning my words; the organic beginnings of hysteria before it became fully fledged.

If he was surprised, he didn't show it. He turned from me and headed back into his office. 'Soda water?' He concentrated on plucking ice cubes from a bucket and dropped them into a glass. Slowly, he unscrewed the bottle cap and poured me a drink. 'Do you mind?' He indicated the whisky on his desk and I shook my head. Taking his own tumbler, he topped up the already neat whisky with another finger. 'I'm not sure I understand, Sophie.'

I sat myself down on the edge of his leather Chesterfield and he returned to sitting behind his desk. A nervous fluttering in my stomach and the sudden onset of clammy hands, took me back to our first meeting. Our interview had been more of a chat, less a grilling. I had walked into the job or, at least, that was what it had felt like. Now, I was beginning to wonder if Zander had dubious reasons for taking me on.

'You're Bethany's father.'

He raised his eyebrows. 'Bethany?'

I cleared my throat. 'Yes. Bethany Saunders. Your illegitimate child.'

He gave a small shake to his head. 'I don't know what you're talking about.'

'You don't know what I'm talking about?' I took a huge gulp of soda water. 'I have proof. You can't lie. I've seen the birth certificate.'

He leant back in his chair. Mozart had reached a crescendo and Zander appeared to be absorbing every last note. I waited, wondering how long he could keep up this façade.

'Why did you employ me? Did you know I was Bethany's friend?'

Zander eventually opened his eyes, put down his tumbler and swivelled the chair so as to face me head on. Up close, I saw that he really was a shadow of his former self. His shirt appeared to hang off his frame, his eyes looked sunken and he had a couple of days' worth of stubble.

'Sophie, any more news on your daughter? I've seen from the news that they're looking for you too now.'

I didn't know what to say any more. Previously, I would have told anybody, anything. I had believed that everyone was on side, apart from the custody battle; I honestly thought everything else was pretty straightforward. Now, I found myself thinking twice before I divulged any information.

'No more news,' I replied simply.

'I was so sorry to hear. I hope you know that.'

I stood up, the soda water sloshing from my glass onto the deep blue carpet. 'Why are you changing the subject? You're not answering my question.'

The Mozart CD stopped, whirring to a halt. An impenetrable silence descended on the room. I thought of the CD with Amy and her tear-stricken face and looked at my watch. I had less than twenty-four hours remaining. Time was running away from me like sand through my hands.

'Bethany never talked about you. Or, at least, she talked about how you just gave her money all the time and about how you wanted to protect her from everything.' I glared at him. 'You pushed her away, Zander. Did you know that? Your love for your little girl was too much.' I reached into my coat pocket and took out the bracelet, strode over to the desk and thrust it under his nose. 'Do you know what this is? Do you remember giving this to her?'

Zander took the bracelet off me and caressed the heart-shaped locket between his forefinger and thumb. 'I loved her,' he said, his voice rumbling with emotion. 'Yes, maybe I loved her too much but I couldn't fight it. She was my reason for living.' He looked at the bracelet. 'I don't recognise this, though.'

I grabbed the bracelet back off him. Lies. Everyone was always lying.

'But why didn't you tell me you were her father when you took me on? How did you know to take me on?'

He swallowed hard and I watched the rise and fall of his Adam's apple. 'Bethany talked about you whenever I saw her. She told me you were studying to do law too. So, it seemed natural to ask you for an interview.' His eyes glazed over with tears. 'Especially after she, you know. Took her own life. It felt like she would have wanted it.'

'But for all these years…' My voice trailed off.

'I never talked about Bethany to anyone. She was born, as you describe it, illegitimately and I've seen what that tag can do to you. It was the end of everything for me. My cosy existence just vanished overnight.'

'What do you mean?' I sat back down on the Chesterfield.

'My wife found out and we divorced. It was bitter.' He let out an empty laugh. 'In that sense, Sophie, we make good lawyers. We've both seen that side of life.'

I nodded, a lump forming in my throat. 'So your wife found out about Bethany when she died?'

He frowned. 'Yes. That night forced the truth into the open. My wife couldn't take the news. What would she tell her friends? Her husband has a child by another woman and now she's dead, killed herself?'

I remained unmoving. Did Zander, too, think Bethany had committed suicide? My belief in what I thought I had seen that night, what had happened that night, ebbed further away.

He continued, 'In the circles we moved in, that wasn't the done thing.' He paused, took a swig. 'The funny thing, the other woman, Bethany's mother, we weren't meant to be. It was a brief…' he reddened slightly, 'fling. But when I found out she was having our child, I couldn't bear the idea of never meeting her, getting to know her: my own flesh and blood. So, I kept in contact with Bethany. To be honest, Bethany often threatened to stop talking to me altogether.' He rubbed his eyes with the heels of his hands. 'All that stuff she said to you? About me being over-protective, thinking money can solve everything, she told me that stuff too.'

I nodded in silence. 'Didn't your wife ever suspect you of being dishonest? Whilst Bethany was alive?'

He pursed his lips. 'Yes, I think she did. But she never said anything. She was a stoic woman, wanted to hold it together for the sake of her reputation. Once I saw what that kind of thing could do to a marriage, I knew I couldn't afford to let it wreck my career too. So, I've never talked about Bethany or the night she committed suicide to anyone.'

'So, you never talked about Bethany when she was alive because someone might have found out you had a child with another woman and then, after she died, you continued in the same vein? Because it might have ruined your career.' I looked at him. 'Would it have, though? Ruined your career?'

'This firm is my pride and joy. It's not good press to air your dirty laundry in public.'

That comment felt pointed. I fiddled with the edge of my coat, rubbing the wool between my fingers. 'That night…' I didn't know how to continue.

'When she died?'

'Yes.' I chewed the side of my mouth nervously.

'I still never fully understood what happened that night,' he said, his gaze dropping to the desk. 'It was…' He tried to speak but I could tell he was fighting back the tears. 'Let's put it like this, I lost so much that night. More than most people will ever know.'

'It was awful for me too. My parents…'

'Yes,' he said. 'I know. They died a couple of years before?'

I nodded miserably. 'I suddenly had no one. Or, at least, it felt that way.'

'Yes, it must have been really tough on you too.' He took a deep gulp of the whisky and closed his eyes. I could almost taste and feel the warmth of the amber liquid. 'When she died, it was as if my whole world collapsed. My wife was divorcing me, Bethany's mother blamed her daughter's death on me, Bethany was gone and the only thing that made any sense was keeping the firm together.' He lifted his gaze and looked at me. 'Maybe she wouldn't have started escorting if I hadn't needed so much from her.' His recognition of his own failure as a father struck a sombre note with me. I, too, felt I was failing Amy and I didn't want to end up like the man in front of me: living a life of regrets after the death of a child.

'You knew about the escorting?' I was amazed.

'Yes, I feel guilty to this day that I didn't do more to stop her. She once wrote to me, told me what she was involved with and that she was doing it because she wanted to hurt me.' He went on unabashed. 'I took you on because I could see you were good but,' he smiled tenderly, 'you also reminded me of Bethany. I'd be lying if I said you didn't.' He stood up now. 'I'm sorry for not being honest with you, Sophie, but it was and is complicated.'

A wave of emotion washed over me: I was relieved to know the truth about Zander's connection to Bethany but I felt Amy was slipping out of sight: maybe Zander wasn't the answer after all. The clock on the wall behind Zander's head read nine o'clock. I had less than twenty hours to find my daughter or else I feared history would repeat itself.

Zander walked me down the stairs to the entrance to the building.

'Sophie.' he stopped me as I went to open the door, his hand on my arm. 'I need you to know I will do everything I can to help you get Amy back.'

I nodded slowly. 'I'm sure there's nothing you can do.'

'I know what it's like to lose a daughter.' He let go of my arm. 'Just remember I'm here for you. We're like family.'

I pondered this for a moment before stepping outside into the chilly night air. 'Hasn't the detective been to see you?' It suddenly dawned on me that he hadn't mentioned her but, I was sure, she would have made Zander a priority.

He glanced at me. 'Yes, I forgot about that.'

'What did she ask you?'

'If I had seen you… That kind of thing.'

'That's it?'

'Oh, and how I thought it unhealthy you spending time with Paul like you did last Saturday. She thought it strange a boss should take that much interest in your personal life.' He gave a small laugh.

I nodded. The detective had queried Zander's interest in my failed marriage. 'I already explained you're only trying to protect me.'

He smiled. 'Exactly. Keep loved ones close but enemies even closer.' He held the door open for me. 'Or, however, that saying goes.'

I smiled, stepped into the street and brought my collar up against the cold wind whipping through Surrey Street. A black cab scuttled up the otherwise deserted street and I could feel a panic attack coming on. I was no closer to Amy and everywhere I turned it seemed to be a dead end. I was surrounded by people who lied. My breathing was becoming erratic and I could feel my legs turning to jelly, the familiar humming in my head was getting louder and louder.

My mind couldn't register the fact that I had been working with Bethany's father for all this time. It just didn't make sense. On one hand, his lies felt like an enormous betrayal and, yet, I quite liked the idea that he thought I was like Bethany. It was what I had always wanted: to be like Bethany.

I felt the answer was so close and, yet, I wasn't quite able to access it. Why would this woman come back for me, why did she want to see me suffer? Had I wronged her in some way? I felt like I was being punished for something I didn't know I had done.

CHAPTER 23

I walked to a bus stop and took a bus to just beyond Hampstead Heath, deciding to walk the remaining distance to Faye's house. It was nearing eleven o'clock; a few late revellers spewed out of The Freemason's Arms.

'Hey, missy,' a large man, reeking of beer, slurred, 'you don't look too happy. Can't be all that bad.' This provoked a chuckle from his drunken buddies.

I ignored them, kept my head down and moved to the other side of the road.

'Bet she's frigid,' I heard him call out. Ordinarily, I wouldn't have cared: I mean, I could see they were drunk and trying to impress. Tonight, it stung: rubbing salt in wounds too big to ever heal. This wasn't the time to lose it; I knew that.

I watched a man in black tie trip up on the kerb and stumble toward the bus stop where he collapsed on a red bench, his head slumped forward in his hands. There was something about his black tie and the man's breath smelling of stale beer that grabbed at a memory in the recess of my mind. I stopped and stared as he started to undo his bowtie, and then I remembered. It was as if the latest session with Darren had unlocked a vault and the images were starting to flood back, their detail coming into focus.

I got out the mobile and Darren's business card and punched in the number. He answered on the third ring.

'Have you remembered something else?'

We didn't need introductions.

'Yes, I think so.'

'Talk to me, Sophie. From the night you think Bethany was murdered?'

'Yes.'

'Are you safe to talk? Where are you?'

'Hampstead Heath, I'll walk and talk.' I looked at my watch. 'But I haven't got long. I need to remember something now, Darren.' I decided now was the time to tell him about the note. 'The woman. She sent me a note. Said I had forty-eight hours to find Amy or she dies.'

'What?' He sounded alarmed. I wasn't sure if I imagined it, but I heard a clicking sound on the line.

'Is someone listening in?' My breath caught.

'No,' he said quickly, 'no.' He exhaled deeply. 'If this note is true, I might have to tell someone everything, Sophie. You understand? Like I said, a life is now at risk.'

I thought back to the note. It clearly stated that I wasn't to tell the police.

'Darren, I trust you and I'm telling you now, you can't. If she finds out you've gone to the police, she will kill Amy.'

After a few moments, he said, 'Tell me everything you remember.' His voice was terse.

'We hadn't spoken since the house party.'

'Because?'

'Because it had been quite intimate, I guess.' I paused. 'So I made sure I was up and out of the house before Bethany got up and, at night, Bethany stayed out late. Most nights she didn't return until four or five in the morning.'

'Go on.'

'I knew she didn't get back till then because I couldn't sleep a wink until I was sure she was back and I could hear her shuffling about her bedroom upstairs. I always wondered what she did, where she went but, in some ways, I think it was better I never knew.'

'OK.'

'We got a call from the agency a week later, asking if we would attend a black tie event. I was going to say no, unsure as to why I had ever joined, when I realised that it was an excuse to talk to Bethany; sort things out?' My question hung in the air for a moment.

'OK.'

'I told Bethany about the call. I remember I knocked on her door and she didn't answer right away.' I paused. 'When she did, she looked awful.' I put my hand to my mouth, choked back a sob. 'I should've known then that we needed to stop the escorting.'

I walked a bit, not speaking; Darren didn't pressure me. 'I found out later that she had been seeing men alone. Taken it further than we had agreed. She should never have died thinking she was only good for sex.'

'What did you say to her?'

My voice cracked. 'I pushed her to go with me.'

'Why did you push her?'

I bowed my head now, even though Darren couldn't see me. 'Because I wanted to spend time with her, because I desperately needed her to be a part of my life again. She had been distant with me since that house party.'

'Did she agree to go?'

'Yes.' I stopped now, taking a deep breath. 'But only because I pushed her. I can see that now.'

'Did she tell you where she had been going at night?'

'She just said clubbing.'

'Did you believe her?'

'No.'

I started to walk again, losing myself in the tree shadows.

'Are you sure you're still safe to talk on the phone, Sophie?'

'I don't know.' I let out the sob that had been building in my throat. 'I have less than eighteen hours to find Amy. Nothing feels safe!' I was hysterical. 'But I need you to tell me something. The doctors at the Priory, after Bethany was killed, told me that it was my mind's way of coping with losing my friend. A sort of displaced guilt. That it was easier to believe she had been murdered and that I probably felt like I could have protected her from suicide, but by believing it was murder, my mind was freeing me of guilt.'

'OK.' He was hesitant. 'And do you think that you did feel guilty about her dying?'

I noted he didn't say how Bethany died: choosing to remain on the fence.

'Yes.' I cried freely now, my breathing ragged. 'I'm the one who pushed her in the end to do the escorting, those final nights out were down to me. It had been her idea originally but, by the end, I realised that I could be closer to her during those times. She was all mine.' I looked out at the twinkling lights of the city. 'It's my fault.'

I sat on a bench now.

'Bethany had gone on about how she didn't think I would've liked the clubs she went to but, I realise now, she was protecting me from the truth that she was doing the extra escorting. We had always agreed no sex, but she had clearly gone down that route.' I wiped my nose with the back of my sleeve. 'I think she agreed to come that night because she felt guilty.' A bitter taste developed in my mouth. 'How ironic. Anyway,' I continued, 'we got ready as usual then met in the kitchen. It was our ritual. We had been to twenty or so events together over the past eight months with the agency and we always started with a couple of sneaky drinks in the kitchen, maybe a joint.' Darren made a sound that he was listening. 'It helped lessen any nerves,' I explained.

'Nothing else?'

'No,' I said, offended. 'Nothing else.'

'It's just Oliver thought you did other drugs.'

'Oliver is a jealous man.'

'OK, I've asked you before, but do you have any recollection of the houses you were taken to? It could really help you now.'

'Well, I remember bits of them but I have no idea where they were. I can see now that it was what the clients wanted, in case anything went wrong.' I let out a hollow laugh.

'Tell me about the evening you can remember, if you're ready.'

'At about seven, I turned off my music and gave myself a last look in the mirror. I remember I smiled at my reflection: I wore a long, black velvet dress that skimmed my slim figure and I had twisted my hair up into a chignon. I thought I looked good but, as I stepped into the kitchen, I wished I had tried harder.'

Darren's silence was strangely comforting and I found myself remembering details I hadn't even thought about at the time.

'I need you to focus, Sophie. Remember something about the house or your surroundings.'

I closed my eyes and pushed my mind to think. I gasped. An image spun into my mind. 'A cliff. I remember the house was near a cliff.'

'How do you know?'

'Because I can see Bethany lying by the cliff.'

'Why was she lying by the cliff?' He sounded on edge. The clicking sound was back.

'Because…' I held my breath, waited for my mind to open up but it shut down as quickly as I had stumbled across the memory. 'I don't know. It's gone.'

'That's good, Sophie.' He breathed deeply down the line. 'I'm going to have to tell the police, tell DI Ward.'

His words felt like a betrayal and I cut the call.

I thought back to the CD. I had recognised the room but I didn't know why. Then I remembered there had been a sign in view, behind Amy's head. It bore a four-leaf clover. I wish it had had three leaves. I pounded the pavement faster now. I needed to get back to Faye's, get on the Internet.

As I opened the front door, I expected the house to be plunged in darkness. Instead, I could hear the quiet murmuring of voices coming from the sitting room. My heart quickened and I shut the door gently behind me. I tiptoed toward the sitting room, the door ajar a few inches, and listened. But the voices had stopped: they knew I was there.

'Sophie, is that you?' Faye. Her voice sounded strained. 'Come on in.'

I pulled the door to, my mind racing with the possibilities of who might be waiting on the other side. As I started to close the door, it squeaked on its hinges, and I stopped, my breathing sharp and shallow. I decided to leave again and slipped back through the front door. I moved quietly across the front paved area and hid in the shadows between Faye's side alley and her neighbour's house. It was the police, I was sure of it. Though, there was no sign of a car.

I could feel a thin film of sweat covering my face despite the cold. I moved further back into the shadows as I watched a figure emerge from the house. I couldn't make out their features in the strip of light. I held my breath, willing them to leave. The person raised their collar around their ears, said something else to Faye and moved off. I waited with bated breath and then, as the person neared the end of Faye's drive, they looked back toward the house, their figure silhouetted against the street light, their features indistinguishable. I held my breath and watched as the figure disappeared down the road.

As soon as I thought the coast was clear, I went back inside.

Faye sat on the edge of the sofa; her gaze didn't shift from the television. She was trembling and blinking rapidly.

I finally spoke from the doorway. 'Faye.'

'Sophie, where have you been?' She jumped up.

Guilt swept through me; perhaps it had been wrong to turn up on Faye's doorstep. I walked toward her and sat on the floor by her knees. Reaching up, she allowed me her hand but the motion was stiff, awkward.

'Is that why you rang the police? Did you ring DI Ward? Tell her I was here?'

Her hand twitched in mine. 'I didn't phone anyone.'

I nodded. 'Who was here then?'

Faye moved her head now, looked down at me. 'It's just me.'

Unease flooded through me. 'Are you sure? I just saw a woman leave. Thought it was the police.'

'No,' she said and studied my face. 'Have you been drinking?'

'What did she look like?' I tried to keep my voice calm, despite the fluttering in my stomach.

'Sophie, have you been drinking?'

'No,' I lied.

She gazed at me, concern filling her eyes. 'You need some sleep. There was no one here.'

My stomach lurched and I moved toward the wall, steadying myself with my hand on the cool wallpaper. I couldn't tell Faye that the woman who had just been in her house had absolutely no right to be there. She would never sleep again. My gut instinct was right: that wasn't the police. That's why it had been such a low-key visit, that's why the lack of car: Amy's abductor had been in Faye's house. She was enjoying it; I could see that now. This was all part of her thrill. She had just let herself in through the front door and left again. That's why I had felt her eyes on me. She was playing games with me.

'Where did you go, Sophie?'

I shifted slightly. 'My boss.'

'Mr Thompson?'

Squirming under her gaze, I nodded. 'Yes.'

She didn't ask any further questions and I sensed her now inner disquiet. 'You should get some rest, Faye.' I squeezed her hand. 'You need sleep. We both do.'

'Your lasagne is on the side. I could heat it up in the microwave for you.'

I smiled apologetically. 'What kind of houseguest am I? Let me do it, you go to bed.'

She conceded and rose from the sofa slowly. 'See you in the morning, Sophie.'

'Goodnight, Faye.'

Once I heard Faye's footsteps on the stairs, I eyed her drinks cabinet in the corner and I lifted myself off the floor to take a closer look. Faye had never drunk much but was partial to the odd gin and tonic. I opened the walnut veneer cupboard door and peeked inside. The cupboard light came on automatically causing the familiar green bottle to glint: taunting me. I sighed deeply.

'Don't do it, Sophie,' I muttered to myself. 'Don't do it.'

But, surely, another couldn't hurt. Could it? It would just take away the pain, maybe it could rid me of the dull ache in my chest; fill the empty space where Amy used to be. I opened the cupboard door further and reached in for the bottle. It felt smooth and cool to the touch. I could almost taste it. Scrunching up my eyes, I willed myself to put it back.

A voice somewhere, Amy's voice, filled my head and I thought back to the CD. She needed me to be strong. But, on the other hand, I needed relief, to forget, just for a couple of hours…

With a shaking hand, I unscrewed the cap, my whole body strung out with tension. Every fibre of my being was in danger of shattering. I sniffed the clear liquid and it burnt the back of my throat. I wanted the release. I turned from the cupboard and threw the bottle onto the sofa, before collapsing onto the floor, my knees crashing onto the cream carpet. Silent tears tormented my body and I clawed at the rug. I thought I was losing my mind. Was this what it was like to go mad? Wiping the back of my hand over my cheeks, I tried to dry my tears. There was no point in abstaining from alcohol when my reason for living – Amy – was nowhere to be found.

It occurred to me that for every moment I spent crying, any hope of finding my daughter was quickly fading. I needed to do something.

I walked through to the kitchen, popped Faye's lasagne in the microwave and sat down heavily at the kitchen table.

A few minutes later, I grabbed the lasagne from the microwave, turned off all the lights downstairs and headed up to my room. I stopped briefly outside Faye's door and I was pleased to hear her steady breathing as she slept. Shutting the door to my room, I turned on the desk lamp and the computer. I was famished and ate the lasagne fast.

With a renewed sense of purpose, I remembered the sign behind Amy had read 'Shamrock Place' and I typed it into Google. An address came up for a small B&B on the outskirts of Dublin claiming to be 'your home from home'. But further down there was a picture of a large Victorian house with a wooden sign out the front: its emblem a clover. My heart skipped a beat. Clicking through the site, it quickly became apparent that Shamrock Place was an independent mental health unit in Holland Park.

I tapped my fingers on the desk and stared at the image of the Victorian house, thinking. Plucking a pen from the drawer, I scribbled a note to Faye on the back of an old envelope. Carefully, I opened the bedroom door and slinked back down the stairs. Within a few minutes, I had grabbed Faye's car keys off the hook, perched the note to Faye on the fruit bowl in the centre of the kitchen table, gathered my coat, checking it still held my wallet and Faye's phone before heading out the door. The clock above the hall mirror read twelve to five. My stomach did a somersault: the realisation that the deadline was today.

Not a moment to spare, I opened and closed the door as quickly and as quietly as possible and jumped in the car. Faye was bound to hear the engine but I hoped the note would go some way to comfort her. I started up the Honda. At the first twist of the key, the car sputtered and conked out.

'Oh, god. Come on,' I mumbled. I looked up at the house and Faye's light came on. I needed to leave before she asked questions. I tried again. 'Please, sweet Jesus, come on.' The engine coughed and died. I could have cried and hit the steering wheel in frustration. I tried for the third time, and it purred into action.

CHAPTER 24

I drove to Holland Park. The sat nav directed me down Holland Road, turning right into Oakwood Lane. I spotted Shamrock Place right away; the Victorian style house incongruous next to the Regency whitewashed building to its right, but most apparent was that it was boarded up. Plywood covered the windows and the entire building appeared to be derelict. I looked up and down the street and felt the shadows of memories shifting beneath the surface.

I got out of the car and walked up to the gate. It had a heavy, rusting lock hanging off it. I tried to prise it open, but no luck. Deciding that I might have more luck at the back of the house, I crept along the side passage, hoping not to be seen. A quick glance upward at the side of the building confirmed that this place was not habitable. More wood covered the gaping holes where windows once stood.

A gate at the end of the side passage prevented me from getting any further. I tried the latch, just in case, but as I had thought, it was locked. It wasn't high, no more than five feet, and I judged my chances of scaling it without breaking something were pretty good. I took a couple of steps backward and launched my right foot at the gate, using the momentum to grab onto the top with my right hand. My foot started to slide, and with my feet scrabbling against the wood like a hamster on a wheel, I used my left hand to drag myself up and over. I landed awkwardly in a heap.

But I had made it. A security light came on and I stopped, unmoving.

When no one appeared, I crawled along the ground to the large set of doors at the back of the house. The old Victorian stained glass was intact here. Standing up now, my back against the wall, I turned my head very slowly and managed a sidelong view of the outside. Disappointed, I realised there was nothing to see except an old sofa rotting in the long grass and a wrought-iron bench covered in moss.

I took a deep breath and turned my body 180, now facing the glass. My heart leapt into my mouth and I gasped, frozen, before relaxing: I was staring at my own reflection.

'You silly fool,' I whispered aloud, pushing down the feeling of *déjà vu*.

I came up close to the glass and tried the handle and it turned. I tentatively opened the door. It creaked on its hinges creating a cloud of dust. I coughed and, unable to see anything in the pitch black, closed the door again. I didn't know what I was looking for and, suddenly, the whole exercise seemed pointless. Backing away from the window, I looked down the long stretch of garden: at the end stood a shed.

I thought I might as well take a look: no harm done. Though it, too, was likely to be locked. The frost-covered grass crunched quietly underneath my feet. There was something about the smell of the earth and the stillness that transported me back to that night. I remembered the dampness of the drive; it had been raining all day and, unlike the clear sky tonight, a wispy layer of fog had drifted above the fields and the house's gardens.

Shaking off the memory, I pulled the latch on the shed door, not expecting it to give. But it did. Slowly, I tugged the door open. Its springy hinges squeaked noisily, and

I stepped inside, the door slamming shut behind me. The whistling, bitter winter winds couldn't reach me here and I was struck by the eerie quietness of the small, protected space. It was dark too. No street lamp, no moonlight, nothing. The infinite blackness threatened to swallow me whole and I took out Faye's phone. I pressed a random button and the screen lit up. It was hopeless; the glow lost to the cavernous darkness, like a single firefly making its way through the turbid black night.

I took a step forward, both hands out in front of me: my right hand held the phone and I used my left to feel my way in the dark. Without warning, something wrapped itself around my ankle and I tripped, grabbing a solid shape ahead of me in order to steady myself. I shone the light at the floor. Several lengths of rope lay at my feet like sleeping snakes. There was a chair and duct tape: this is where Amy had been sat. I looked up and on the wall was a sign for Shamrock Place. Quickly, I realised I had steadied myself on a box, a kind of packing box. I felt around for the flaps, pushed them back and shone the phone's light inside. The box, similar to the kind used in my office, was brown and would typically have been used to store records or files.

But this was holding recorded information of a different nature. My heart thudded loudly in my chest as I realised what I was looking at: the box was full of newspaper records and clippings. The first, on the top, a clipping of my face, next to it the headline read: *Missing child's mother doesn't show up for second press conference.* I put that cutting to one side and took out the next. *Child missing for over forty-eight hours: presumed dead.* I was afraid to delve any further.

The phone buzzed at me, indicating it had twenty per cent battery remaining.

Quicker now, I plucked out each article, skim reading the titles. *West London mother despairs as child goes missing at fairground; Fairgrounds no longer safe.* I reached the end of those articles and read other irrelevant articles taken from what looked like health magazines: *Mental health: more important than physical health; Dealing with depression; Jealousy: is it tearing you apart?*

The phone beeped this time: the battery sign flashing. The light caught the edge of another box and I ripped this one open. Time wasn't on my side and I had to work fast. Shining the fading light into the next box, my breathing uneven, I spotted a bible and magazines cut to shreds. Opening the bible, alarm ripped through my body. The page, clearly well thumbed, was coming away from the binding. Inside, somebody had scrawled over the actual text: *To Love is to Protect.* They had crossed this out and alongside it written: *Kill.*

Seconds later, the phone died.

CHAPTER 25

I decided it was time to confront Paul. He needed to come clean. The drive from Holland Park to Hammersmith took less than twenty minutes. Soon, I was outside the large red-brick Victorian house: this place held so many memories – good and bad – for me. We had chosen the house together; shortly after we found out I was pregnant with Amy. Money had never been an issue. Paul had his security company, I was being paid extraordinarily well for a lawyer in her early thirties. I realised now, with open eyes, that my more than generous salary was probably all part of Zander's therapy and his grieving process.

The house overlooked the river and, as I climbed out of the car, I remembered the parties we would hold in the garden, particularly the boat party. Every year, during the Oxford versus Cambridge Boat Race, we would entertain in style. A pang of regret at the way everything had turned out momentarily wrenched my heart. That was then, this was now. I knew that. But remorse sat heavily on my shoulders as I looked out at the river. Perhaps I was being nostalgic. After all, it was clear from the very fact that I was here to question my ex-husband, that the past held many dark secrets and that these happier times I remembered weren't the whole picture.

I walked up the path to Paul's front door and rang the doorbell. Less than a week ago, I had stood on the very same doorstep, with the detective, waiting with trepidation for what was to come. I could hear Paul's steps on the floor and he opened the door a crack, the chain still across.

'Sophie!' He almost looked relieved. 'I thought you had done something stupid to yourself.'

'Paul.' A gust of warmth escaped the house and rushed around my ankles. 'Can I come in?'

'Um, I'm not sure…'

'Paul. Is it because of Sarah? I'm not here to cause grief, I just need answers.'

He sighed deeply. 'OK. She's not here anyway. She's away on business.'

He pulled open the door and I stepped into the hall. Under the spotlights, I almost didn't recognise him. His eyes were totally shrunken, he couldn't have shaved for a few days now – perhaps Monday, when I last saw him – but, more alarmingly, he stank of alcohol.

'Have you been drinking?'

He wobbled slightly on the spot. 'Don't think you can talk to me about drinking.'

I pulled a face. 'No, probably not. You told me weak people drink in a crisis.'

'Did I?' he slurred and tipped ever so slightly my way.

'Yes.'

'Oh. Well.' He walked off now, in the direction of the sitting room. 'What are you doing here anyway?' He sat in an armchair. I noted the tumbler of vodka next to him. What I would have done to have a drink too. 'Didn't know if you'd ever come back.'

'Come back?' I sat on the ottoman by the window. 'I'm looking for our daughter, once I find her, I'm coming back.' I stopped, aware of what I had just said. 'I mean normal life will resume.'

'That's right,' he slurred. A small trickle of saliva dribbled down his chin and I tensed. 'Because you are loved-up with that man now, aren't you?'

'What would you care if I was, anyway?' Realising he meant Oliver.

He shrugged. 'I wouldn't.'

'Nice.'

'Anyway, would you?'

'Would I what?'

'Come back?'

'Here?' I laughed. 'Are you serious? After…' He gazed at me steadily. 'No. No, I wouldn't.'

'Just as I thought.' He picked up the tumbler and downed the remaining liquid.

'I know this is a bit rich coming from me, but it's not going to help you know.' I nodded at the glass.

'S'pose not.' He closed his eyes and, seeing that I might lose him to a drunken slumber, I rose from the ottoman. 'What do you want, anyway?' His eyes shot open.

'Our daughter.' I stood a couple of paces from the armchair, directly in front of him. 'I have until 4 pm this afternoon to find our daughter. You know where she is. I need you to tell me.'

'I don't know, Sophie.'

'I know about the house in Holland Park. I've just come from there. Who is she? This woman? I need to know where this woman's taken her.'

He bit his bottom lip and shifted in the chair.

'Will she kill Amy? Why does she hate me so much?' I felt like shaking him: ridding him of his drunken stupor and his lies. 'Tell me.'

'I don't know anything.'

'Paul,' I said, 'you know if our daughter dies, you will go to prison.'

'For what? You have our daughter.'

'But do you want our daughter's blood on your hands? Just tell me where to find her.'

He leant forward in the chair, his elbows resting on his knees, and rubbed his eyes with the heels of his hands. 'Shit.'

'Come on, Paul,' I coaxed. 'Is she listening now? Is this place bugged?' I turned a full circle, before my gaze came to rest on Paul again. 'I don't even care any more! What is she going to do? Kill me? I'd prefer she killed me and not our daughter.' I laughed hysterically now. 'I mean, it doesn't matter any more… Before, I was scared, but now I don't care. She clearly wants me dead. Like she wanted Bethany dead.' My voice trailed off, my last words hung over the room like a sticky sap falling from a tree on a muggy, thundery day. 'She's jealous, bitter and twisted.'

Paul's face was wet with tears. 'I don't know who you're talking about.' He paused. 'You showed up last Saturday with that detective and tell me our daughter's missing. Now you're going on about some woman who killed Bethany and now has Amy. And this woman wants you dead because she's jealous of you? Or something?' He was ranting aloud now; his thoughts making little sense.

I didn't know what to say, fearing my response might make him clam up even more. It was a tough one to call. 'Paul, you might not…' My tongue combed the roof of my mouth. 'You know, the court might understand that this was not your choice, this was under duress.'

He nodded. 'The court. Who cares about the court right now? Our daughter is missing.'

I nearly laughed. 'Who cares? You do! That's why you're lying, you want to make me look bad, get custody of Amy. You're working with this woman.'

'You've gone mad.' He was quietly seething now, his fists clenching and unclenching.

I pitied him in that moment. He spoke as though he was innocent, like I was the one who had caused all this. 'Paul, you're making out I'm mad. I've done nothing wrong.' I walked toward him now. 'Will you come with me? Help me find Amy? Tell me where she is. Who has her?'

With so many questions, he looked like a rabbit in headlights, unable to decide which way to move. 'You…'

'Paul. Please.' I bent down, took him in my arms now and felt his body relax next to mine. His shoulders bounced up and down as he sobbed. 'Is it just her? Is she working alone?'

He shrugged. 'I don't know who you're talking about.'

I swallowed hard, determined to get some information out of him. 'OK, if it's just one woman, surely she can't have this much hold over you.'

He buried his head in my shoulder, the stale smell of alcohol played on my already jagged nerves. 'Sophie, please stop.'

'Paul,' I whispered soothingly. 'Where is she going? Where is she taking Amy?'

'You need help.' He whimpered in my ear. 'Please get help.'

'Paul, I don't. You do.' I spoke even more softly. 'Do you think your house is bugged?'

'This could all be over so quickly if you were honest with yourself, Sophie.'

I was growing panicky with frustration. 'Do you believe that?' I stepped away from him now, holding him at arm's length. 'Paul. Our daughter is in danger. Forget us. Forget what's happened with us. That's in the past.' Tiredness took a hold of me as I realised he would never give me the truth. I didn't know why he was lying, maybe I never would. For the moment, it looked as if Paul was set on keeping it a secret and I had to keep running, chasing my own tail.

I sat down weightily on the sofa. 'OK, fine, you win. I can't keep asking. I'll just have to…' I stopped talking.

Paul whispered something, barely audible. I leant forward to catch it again but he didn't repeat it.

'Sorry, Paul, what did you say?'

'Only you know where she is.'

'What exactly does that mean?'

'Isn't that why you've been having those sessions with Darren? You've got some crazy idea that Bethany's killer has Amy? Well, what have those sessions told you? Anything?' He stared hard at the floor. 'Just bring our daughter back.'

He was right: it was time to go to Aberystwyth. My watch read seven o'clock in the morning. Daylight crawled in around the edges of the curtains and, now that I thought about it, I could hear the traffic out on the main road. It would take me at least five hours to get there and then I had to find out where the house had been.

CHAPTER 26

After a sluggish start through the knotty build-up of London traffic, I joined the M4 motorway. I put my foot down where I could but, approaching the second Severn Bridge, I was forced to slow. Memories spun through my mind as the traffic crawled across the bridge and I entered Wales. Then it was as if the closer I drove to where it all began, the memories became painfully clear.

I phoned Darren, put him on speakerphone.

'Sophie.' He sounded wary.

'Are they there?'

'Yes, they're listening.'

My stomach dropped, and I took a deep breath.

'OK, you have to believe me. The woman who has taken my daughter killed my friend, I'm sure of it.'

I heard a chair scrape in the background; imagined DI Ward getting up, them trying to trace my call.

'I think she's taken Amy to Aberystwyth, to a large house nearby.'

'OK,' Darren said slowly. 'Sophie, are you OK? You sound agitated.'

'Of course I'm agitated. I'm looking for my child. Do you want to help me or not?'

'Yes,' he said quickly and I imagined DI Ward nodding her head vigorously in the background. She didn't want to lose this call: her only contact with me.

'You know the evening I told you about before. Well, I remember the diplomat inviting us in. Bethany was angry with me. She hadn't wanted to go.'

'But you made her?'

'Yes, I made her. I wanted to have fun. She was always out, without me. I wanted to have what I deserved.'

'Which is?'

I looked out at the expanse of Welsh hills and suddenly felt so vulnerable. 'I deserved to spend time with people I loved and I loved her, like family.' I swallowed. 'It was *our* thing, you know?'

'OK, go on. Do you remember anything about the house?'

'It's near a cliff face, I told you that already. There were loads of rooms, like it was an old hotel. Not used any more.'

'What happened then?' Darren sounded exhausted.

'The diplomat told us to behave. There were five men sat in a semi-circle on a bed. They weren't that interested in us when we first went in the room.'

I stopped, waited for Darren to signal I should continue.

'Go on, Sophie.'

'They were drinking whisky, playing cards. Then this one guy did a couple of lines of coke. Bethany took some and then I did.'

'I thought you didn't do those sorts of drugs.'

'I did on this occasion. I needed to.'

'How did you know what to do?' Darren asked.

I cleared my throat, indicated and changed lane. 'OK, I might have done it a couple of other times.'

'Then what?'

'Then I drank whisky and I remember they handcuffed Bethany to the bed.'

'Was this agreed before you girls did this?'

'No.'

'Then you must have been scared?'

'I was.' I paused. 'Until I realised Bethany was in her element. She loved it.'

'How did that make you feel about Bethany?'

'Resentful.'

'Why?'

'She looked in control, I felt like I was floundering.'

'Then what happened?'

'A woman was in the room. This is where my memory is so muddled.'

I heard a chair scrape again. I didn't care if they were listening any more. I was closer to finding Amy than I had been over the last few days. I could feel it.

'A woman let herself into the room?'

'Yeah, I guess. I don't know because all I remember is a gun going off and Bethany's head bouncing backward.'

Darren's breathing had grown shallower. I imagined him listening, perched on the edge of his seat. DI Ward looking at him, nodding.

'Anything else, Sophie?'

'I remember Bethany looking at her killer and she seemed to know her.'

The ringing had started up in my ears again and I could feel my muscles weakening. I knew I needed to end the call and pull over before I had another attack. I indicated I was moving over to the side. I slammed on my hazards and held my head in my hands, willing my breathing to slow, and slowly, ever so slowly, the ringing sound disappeared.

DI Ward came on the line. 'Sophie,' she started, 'we need you to tell us exactly where you are. Your safety is our priority.'

I looked at my phone and cut the call.

Reaching down into the side pocket, I felt around for a pair of sunglasses, plucking out the contents and dumping them in my lap. A quick glance downward confirmed that Faye, like me, didn't keep spare sunglasses in her car or, for that matter, anything of use: a screwed-up chewing gum packet, pen and a small torch. The petrol gauge displayed almost empty and, spotting a sign for Magor services, I moved over to the left hand lane and came off.

The weather did a complete about turn and dark clouds shifted across the sky as I filled up with petrol. I figured there was enough time to sprint inside and buy a coffee, fearing I might fall asleep at the wheel. Having been to the toilet, I stood in a queue of two to order a double espresso from Costa. Across the way, in WH Smiths, a Chinese lady was using broad gestures and talking fast in a high-pitched voice. Her boss looked perplexed, shaking his head. The woman jabbed a newspaper in her senior's face.

'Yes?'

I focused on the spotty teenager in front of me.

'Double espresso, please. To take out.'

He followed my gaze as he struck the keys on the till. 'Two twenty-five.'

I handed over the correct change and he turned to the giant Gaggia machine. A couple of minutes later, he passed me a paper cup, shoving a plastic lid on top.

'What's going on?' I indicated the argument going on behind him.

'Woman says a child came up to her claiming to have been kidnapped.'

My heart dived into my stomach. 'Kidnapped?'

'Yeah, yesterday early morning, you know. I just started my shift, so I wasn't here.' He smiled. 'But then her mum came over and told her daughter to apologise.' He grinned now, the pockmarks around the corners of his mouth widening. 'You see it all in service stations.' When I didn't respond, he said, 'Enjoy your drink.'

'Thanks,' I mumbled, distracted, and took a sip of my coffee.

I wanted to talk to the woman across the way, see if she could tell me anything, anything at all. But it was hopeless. I didn't want to draw attention to myself and, besides, I knew where the answers lay. It wasn't with that woman. It wasn't here.

In fact, I was just over an hour off from where it all began; my mouth turned dry at the prospect. I walked hastily to the car, knocking back the espresso as I went, and jumped in. If that woman's sighting was correct, then I could at least continue forward in the knowledge that Amy was alive: for now.

It wasn't long before I hit the A-roads and I was taking no prisoners: flying around the bends and up and down the familiar Welsh hills. With each passing mile, the grey sky intensified and thunder sounded, clouds trembling on the verge of breaking. The rubbly, gorse-covered sides of the Ceredigion Valley grew steeper, sucking me in. It was as if the seaside town knew: today was the day. A sense of foreboding appeared to linger in the air; a valley shrouded in dark secrets. As I sped over the final crest, Aberystwyth came into view and the first drops of rain crashed down onto the windscreen.

CHAPTER 27

The seaside town appeared desolate as I drove through the centre toward the seafront. The odd person hovered in a shop entrance, cowering from the rain as it pelted the crumbling houses and shops. The weather kept shoppers at bay and I easily parked along the seafront. The waves crashed against the wooden pier; its thin stalk-like legs quivering as it fought the elements. The flashing lights of the arcades twinkled brightly through the deep-set fog hovering above the promenade.

I cast my eye over the length of the seafront. The buildings looked so familiar and, yet, not. In many ways, I could envision the younger me running along the seafront and laughing with friends on the beach as we barbecued. Yet, in so many other ways, this place had been as much a ghost to me then as it was today. In the last week, I had become less certain of what I knew or what I thought I had known. As if the past and present had become almost elusive, intangible: almost as one.

I needed to find the house. The house where it all began.

I used all my force to open the car door as I fought the thrashing wind. The sea air hit me smack in the face; I could taste salt on my lips, smell the seaweed. Drawing the collar of my coat up further, I bent my head against the driving rain and headed into town.

The nearest place open was a fish and chip shop. I pushed the door and paddled in, water dripping all over the floor.

'You win bravest customer award.'

I looked up, pushing wet strands of hair from my face and mouth and smiled half-heartedly. I was sodden right through, my wool coat water-logged.

'We've had no one in here so far,' he continued, in his sing-songy Welsh accent. 'Not that I blame them, mind. Who'd want fish in this weather? When you could probably catch one in your own backyard?' He chuckled heartily at his own joke.

'I was wondering if you could help me, actually.' I wiped the drop of rain hanging off the end of my nose with my sleeve. 'I'm looking for a house, maybe a former hotel, near the cliffs. I know it's not much to go on.'

He was busying himself with something, his back to me.

I tried again. 'Um…'

'Here you go, free.' He handed me a polystyrene cup. 'Tea. I presumed you take sugar.'

'Thanks.' I smiled and held the warm cup appreciatively. 'Just what I needed.'

'House you say?' His thick, bushy eyebrows furrowed. 'I don't know of no house like that. Well, I mean, can't you tell me anything else? Why you need the house, is it a National Trust property?'

'I went there once for an enormous party. A kind of secret party for the wealthy.' I knew how far-fetched it appeared. 'Oh. Never mind. I'll just have to drive around.'

'Are you that woman?'

'Which one?' I asked, pulling my damp hair around my face.

'The one with the child missing?' He smiled. 'You were in the newspaper again yesterday. Says you used to go to this university.' Beaming, he patted the countertop.

'I'd show you but I wrapped one of our customer's chips with it.'

I nodded. 'Right.' I sighed deeply. 'I really need to find this house.'

The man looked perplexed. 'OK, tell me again. A house that was once a hotel nearby?'

I nodded.

'In Aberystwyth?'

'No, on the outskirts somewhere.'

He tapped his chin thoughtfully. 'Just a second.' He left the room through a metal chain curtain at the back and returned with a plethoric-looking woman, a potato in hand. 'My wife, Morwen.'

'Yes?'

I explained again.

She smiled and looked at the man. 'Pete, you do know what she means, the manor house, ten miles or so outside of Aberaeron. It was on that programme a few years ago. Does that sound right?' She glanced at me now.

I shrugged. 'Possibly.'

'There's nothing for you in that place. It's derelict now,' she said. 'In fact, rumour has it some girl was murdered there but no one ever could confirm that.' She prodded her finger at me. 'You don't want to be going to a place like that by yourself.'

'The lady just needs to know where it is,' her husband said. 'Come on, Morwen.'

'OK.' She put down the potato, wiped her hands with a tea towel and pointed to a map on the wall. 'Let me show you.'

A few minutes later, after I had made her repeat the directions to me a good few times, I left the warmth of the shop and headed back out into the wind and the rain. The clouds were darker now and hung lower in the sky; the castle on the hill silhouetted against the stormy backdrop.

I climbed in the car, grateful for the shelter and cranked up the heater. Seconds later, condensation ran off the windows and I was forced to let some outside air in. The wind whistled past and the distant sound of thunder out at sea reverberated through the town. Gripping the wheel with clammy hands, my knuckles white, I turned the key, waited for the light and pulled out. The rain hammered the roof of the car making it almost impossible to hear anything. Anything: except for the sound of my pounding heart echoing in my ears.

CHAPTER 28

A quick glance at the clock: three forty-five. Fifteen minutes.

I passed through Aberaeron, as the woman had directed. The multi-coloured houses sitting alongside the harbour ordinarily looked so bright in the sunshine but, now, even they appeared melancholic. Boats skipped up and down on the rough water. One sole fisherman bravely readied his nets for the trip out to sea and the local grocer's shop was open for business but, otherwise, there was little sign of life.

Once out the other side, I came to a fork in the road and headed right, as I had been told. The lane was narrow, almost impassable and my headlights bounced off the hedgerow and stonewalling. I had no memory of the route; even as I followed what I presumed was the same road as the taxi twenty years previously. In fact, the further I drove into the Welsh countryside, the more unsure I became.

I thought about the techniques Darren had taught me and I knew I had to force a memory to surface. I needed to know I was heading in the right direction and that's when I saw it: the lighthouse out at sea. That night, just as today, I recalled the light as it bounced off the inky sky, over the choppy water and across the cliff face. Hitting a ridge in the road, the car jolted me upward and I focused my attention, once again, on the lane in front of me.

A light flashed on the petrol gauge: I was almost running on empty.

'Shit.' I hit the steering wheel, my mouth like sandpaper. 'Not now.'

I shifted gear. Three forty-eight. I had twelve minutes. Twelve minutes. My throat closed up and I pressed down hard on the accelerator: pushing the Honda to its max.

I hit a bend and overcompensated with my steering, sending the car violently veering across the road. The rain was coming down harder still and I could barely see a few feet in front of me. The light on the gauge flashed twice.

I was climbing higher, the car struggling to cope with the Welsh hills, and the lighthouse caught the car in its lamp's compass. The car started to slow and I could hear a strange thudding sound coming from the rear of the car. Moments later, the Honda spluttered to a standstill.

'No, goddamn it.' I punched the wheel repeatedly with my fists and cried out in frustration.

With no time to lose, I leapt out and started running instead, moving along the road at a pitiful speed, rain in my eyes. Tearing my coat off, I chucked it on the ground. The rain soaked right through my T-shirt and thin cashmere sweater in seconds, my jeans were sodden. A streak of lightning flashed across the purple-grey sky.

My legs couldn't go any faster; with no sleep and food I was working on pure adrenaline. After a few yards, my shoe caught on a rock and I stumbled forward, landing heavily on my hands and knees; gravel embedded in my palms. I lifted myself off the ground and I had nearly given up all hope as I reached the top of the hill.

That was when I saw it. The house where it all began.

CHAPTER 29

In that moment, as I stood at the end of the long drive, the last twenty years dripped away with the rain. Bethany was here. Or, at least, it felt as if she were. I closed my eyes and, for a second, I could almost sense her hand clasping mine, the electricity I felt just being near her. Even now, the memory of her was enough to create arousal in the pit of my stomach, a gentle but passionate longing for the woman by my side. Here I was, twenty years later, and I yearned for her touch, for the way she had brought me alive.

My eyes snapped open. She was not stood beside me and I gave a small shake to my head in an attempt to rid myself of her ghostly presence. I was here to face the past; I couldn't allow myself to be dragged back down into the quagmire of memories and secrets. I needed to focus.

Taking a deep breath, I started the walk toward the house. It was hidden from view, behind a small wood. The rain came at me in horizontal sheets but I was beyond caring, already soaked to the bone and numb with cold. Rivulets of water flowed down the dirt track and the pine needles glistened with water. Halfway up the drive, I stopped, drank in the memories before stepping forward again and, minutes later, the house was in front of me.

With every stride, the uncertainty of what lay ahead grew more intense, more suffocating. A small part of me wanted to run back onto the road, find the nearest house and get help. But there was no one around for miles and, even if I was lucky enough to find someone, it could be too late. Amy needed me now.

Walking quickly, my trainers squelched and stuck in the mud. I caught the first glimpse of the side of the house and swallowed; a small trickle of saliva worked its way down my throat.

I rounded the bend and the house sat in full view. Memories came crashing back. Years of sadness reflected in the derelict building. The windows were, as I thought, boarded up. However, the wooden planks had been removed from two of the windows.

Light flooded the front room, bulbs hung from the ceiling where the chandeliers had once been. A fire roared in the hearth as it had done twenty years ago. One floor up, another room was illuminated and I realised, fear creeping into my heart, that Amy must be upstairs. The bulb in the upstairs room flickered on and off and I thought back to that night. Bethany had died in that room.

Shakily, I walked up the front steps and stood just as I had done twenty years ago. I glanced to my right as if Bethany might appear. I didn't know who or what was on the other side. Swallowing hard, I pushed the door and, as expected, it opened.

She was waiting for me.

I walked into the hall, relying entirely on the light from the front room to make my way. The door slammed shut behind me and I jumped. My heart was beating wildly and, with pricked ears, I waited. The wind shrieked as it whipped through the cracks and crevices of the old house, the logs on the fire crackled in the hearth but, otherwise, the house was silent.

The house smelt fusty and dust hung in the air making it difficult to breathe. I crept slowly toward the staircase.

Out the corner of my eye, I caught something glinting in the darkness but pressed ahead, placing one foot tentatively on the bottom step.

A floorboard creaked and, as I turned, an arm grabbed me around the neck.

'Please,' I breathed heavily, the attacker's arm heavy on my throat, 'I can't breathe.'

She spoke, a voice muffled by cloth. 'You're late.'

I could tell she was slight but fit. I struggled to turn around, get a better look but with each throw of my body, her steady grip only tightened and I gasped for air.

'Please. I just want to see my daughter. Take me to my daughter.'

'How do you know your daughter's alive?'

I struggled to make sense of her words. 'What do you mean? She has to be alive.' I started to kick out frantically but she fought hard. 'Please,' I sobbed, 'tell me she's alive.'

'I can't do that.'

I swung my arm forward and elbowed her hard in the ribs. She recoiled and momentarily loosened her hold. Enough time for me to stamp on her foot, sending her staggering backward. I turned and peered at the figure as she emerged slowly from the shadows. Sheer terror seized me as I realised she was holding a gun. She smiled and moved into the light.

I gasped. 'You?'

CHAPTER 30

'Who do you think I am?' The woman smiled.

I gasped. 'Polly? Are you Polly?' The woman who had been more jealous of Bethany at university than even I had. My head was reeling and, with one eye on the gun, I moved backward. 'What the hell are you doing?'

She smiled, a demonic smile. 'We finally meet again, Sophie. I killed your friend and now I want you dead.' She flung the gun from side to side as she talked, my eyes never leaving it. 'And now I have your precious daughter who frankly deserves a better mother.'

I screamed, my hand flying to my mouth. It was hard to believe this woman was capable of murder, but I saw it now, that look in her eyes. She was more than capable. She was crazy, obsessed with me. Obsessed with Bethany. And now she had Amy.

'Where's Amy? Polly, where's Amy?'

She didn't speak, just looked at me: all-knowing. We stared at each other: the past rushing at us from all directions.

'It was you! All along, it was you... I told you to leave me and Bethany alone. And after Bethany died, you just disappeared. I thought it was over.'

'It's time you realised that you can't always get rid of your demons.'

'What do you mean by that?' I couldn't believe, after twenty years, I was staring into the face of the woman who had stalked me and Bethany, who had decided she wanted a relationship like we had. Like sisters. I had found a box of photos on my bed, once, of me and Bethany. Every single photo she had taken was of us together. The woman was nuts.

'Oh come on, Sophie. You know what I'm talking about. Your demons. The drink, the drugs, the counting to three. Like that's going to keep the demons at bay. Then there's me.' She smiled. 'Your other demon. Your stalker.' She laughed, it was a hollow, bitter laugh.

'You are no longer a part of my life. You have not been a part of my life for twenty years,' I shouted, despite my legs buckling with terror.

Polly sneered at me. 'The girl who can do no wrong at the firm despite turning up to work drunk, despite having endless time off for *therapy*.'

'Where's Amy?' I moved forward, I needed to get to my daughter. 'Tell me she's safe.'

'She's not safe. But she wasn't safe with you either, was she?'

She was enjoying this: it was the thrill.

'I think we should go upstairs to where it all began,' she said, her voice strung out, her eyes bulging with excitement. 'A trip down memory lane, you know?'

'You're sick.' I felt another rush of nausea.

She strode toward me, laughing, almost deliriously, and I stepped backward, falling hard against the stairs. Dragging me up, as if I weighed no more than a feather, she turned me around and pressed the gun to my temple. 'Let's go see where it all began.'

I gulped and shuffled forward.

'Come on, go,' she said, shoving me up the stairs, the gun knocking the side of my head as we moved.

'Where are you taking me? To see Amy?'

She laughed. 'I told you. She's as good as dead.'

I thrashed against her. 'No! She can't be. You never said that.'

She turned coy. 'Didn't I? Oh, because that's what I meant.'

We reached the landing. I knew she wanted me to head toward the light but I couldn't. Images of Bethany rushed at me. She pushed me hard toward the door, open just a crack, the light stuttering.

I flinched as she jabbed me once more with the gun. Polly told me to get moving and she propelled me into the room with such force I fell to the floor.

The last twenty years disappeared in that moment.

'Sophie, get up,' she snarled.

Scrambling to get to my feet, my head reeled, my eyes fixated on the spot where Bethany had died.

'Where's Amy?' I shouted. I wanted to get away from there, from the memories of the men looking at us with lascivious smiles. 'I need to see Amy.' I took my phone out. 'I'm going to ring the police.'

Polly shoved the gun in my face. 'Put that thing away.'

'No, this needs to stop.'

She scowled and held the gun up again, her once pretty face demonic. 'I know how to use this thing, you know?'

'Listen.' Fear pulsated through my body as I realised then exactly where Amy was. An image of Bethany by a cliff spun to the forefront of my mind. 'I'm going to the cliff. That's where she is, isn't it?' I needed Polly to take me to the exact location so I went on, played into her psychology. 'I want proof that Amy is…' I paused, unable to say the next word. 'Dead.'

She laughed again, almost overexcitedly. I realised this was all a big game to her. She was enjoying every moment.

'Polly,' I said, 'it doesn't matter if I don't ring the police anyway because they will be here any second now. DI Ward isn't stupid, she will be onto you.'

She stared at me. 'No, she won't. I've managed so far.'

'You're mad, I tell you!' The familiar ringing had started up in my ears again, I felt faint but I had to remain strong. I had to get to Amy.

'What did you say? Did you call *me* mad?' Anger replaced Polly's excitement.

'Polly.' I came toward her, adrenaline pumping through my veins. 'Just show me exactly where my daughter is.'

'Yes, OK,' she said and wiped the sweat from the top of her lip. 'You're right, we need to go to the cliff, let the fun really begin.'

Bile rose in my throat as I thought about the many stories I had heard about the cliffs; folktales and horror stories passed down from one university generation to another, from one local to the next.

Without warning, I felt the gun in the small of my back and looked over my shoulder at Polly.

'Go.'

I was guided out of the room, Polly hanging back threatening to shoot if I ran; adopting her acting role once more.

'For god's sake,' I screamed at her. 'We need to go faster!'

We stepped out of the house. The line of pine trees bent against the force of the wind, the rain slashing across our faces.

'Come on!' I shouted to her over the driving rain. 'Take me to see Amy.'

'Where's your car?'

'Up on the hill, but I've run out of fuel,' I said, my voice shrill. 'Please, Polly, come on!'

Polly shrugged, a picture of calm. 'There's a canister of petrol over there.' She pointed, her face lighting up with an excited smile. 'I was going to torch this place. You know, erase history.'

I ran to where she pointed and picked up the metal can. It was heavy and I stumbled forward under its weight. I looked back at Polly who stood unmoving. 'Are you coming?'

Begrudgingly she followed me up the hill as I jogged then walked back to the car, my breathing ragged. The rain came at us and the cold, coastal wind whipped around our already soaking bodies.

I snatched at the petrol cap, its smooth, wet surface impossible to grip. After another try, I managed to unscrew it and, lifting the petrol canister, poured the fuel in. Polly laughed delightedly as the canister kept slipping from my grasp. Once it was empty, I threw it to the side and I clambered into the car, indicating Polly to get behind the wheel.

She did as she was told but then turned, and looked at me. 'Actually, you know what, you drive.'

Exasperated I got out and we exchanged places. Polly climbed in the back seat.

'Polly, we don't have time to be messing about, just tell me exactly where my daughter is,' I shouted, my nerves jagged. 'We'll drive there now. This whole thing needs to stop.'

She laughed as she shut the door. 'She's by the cliff, like you guessed. But you would know that, wouldn't you?' She smiled, ran her tongue over her teeth. 'She's tied up, right on the edge.' Polly snorted. 'A bit like you.'

Horror shot through me. 'No! But Amy can't even swim.'

I started the car and after it sputtered to life, I sped off.

'Which way?'

'Go left at the end.'

I gave Polly a sidelong look, she was laughing hysterically and I realised she was totally out of control.

CHAPTER 31

We were fast approaching the cliff. I drove helter-skelter through the country lanes before cutting a right off the main road and down a dirt track. My mind spun with what lay ahead. Until I had my daughter back in my arms…

'You are taking me to see Amy, aren't you, Polly?' I yelled over the roar of the motor.

She didn't say anything and we hurtled forward, the headlights casting ghostly shadows over the trees. The thumping sound I had heard earlier from the rear of the car started up again only this time it was louder. I rounded a bend and as the sound grew more urgent, I realised the car might conk out and I came down harder on the accelerator.

'Where is my daughter?' I shouted as we sped toward the cliffs. The headlights swung left and right, randomly illuminating the craggy countryside. The cliff edge came into view and I braked but it took me a moment to realise that they weren't working properly. I wasn't going to stop in time and I started screaming.

'Sophie! What are you doing? You're going to kill us!' shouted Polly, her voice momentarily filled with terror.

I was doing eighty and we were only a hundred metres from the edge, but I couldn't stop.

'Sophie,' Polly continued shouting and simultaneously howling with laughter, 'brake!'

'I can't! The brakes aren't working!'

I looked at Polly's face in the mirror: she looked crazed. She sat forward, her seatbelt stretched to the max as she wriggled between the gap in the seats, jerking the wheel hard to the right.

'What are you doing? You're sending us even closer to the cliff edge.' I glanced her way as I felt the car finally respond to my foot on the brake.

We spun, once, twice and a final time, our bodies moved around the car like clothes in a washing machine. Sliding off the dirt track and into a ditch, the car rolled upside down and back around again before it hit a tree full force. My head pummelled the window repeatedly. The air bags whooshed open and then...

Silence.

Polly groaned before I heard a strangled cry from the boot of the car.

Amy. My heart plummeted as I realised that Amy wasn't on the cliff at all. She was in the boot of my car. I felt for the door handle and pulled it. The door wouldn't open. It was jammed. My heart quickened, realising I could smell petrol. Ignoring the pain in my head, I scrambled as fast I could to the other side of the car, pushing Polly's legs out the way. I tried it and, thankfully, it opened. The smell of petrol was overpowering now.

I ran to the back of the car and pulled open the boot. Amy was inside, her tiny body surrounded by bags of duvets and clothes, her mouth covered by duct tape and handcuffs secured around her feet and hands. She looked at me wide-eyed and I let out an overwhelming sob of helplessness.

'Amy!' I put my hands underneath her and using all my remaining energy I picked her up and turned, running in the direction of the slope. Glancing over my shoulder, I saw Polly crawling away from the car, her eyes never leaving mine.

No sooner had I levered us up the first rock, we were flung sideways as the car exploded: glass smashed and the tang of burning rubber filled the air. The heat from the flames rushed at us and I squeezed my eyes shut against the mirage of fumes. The smoke billowed upward and I brought my arm up across my eyes, the heady smell of petrol making my eyes water.

I turned and dragged Amy up the slope, my trainers struggling to find footing as I dug my nails into the gritty ground. Reaching the top, I looked at Amy.

She was alarmingly still, her face pale.

'Amy, darling,' I stroked her hair, 'who did this to you?'

I carefully peeled the tape from her lips and she whispered hoarsely, 'Mummy, please help me.'

Tears streamed down my cheeks landing on Amy's delicate skin and I tugged at the cuffs.

'Where are the keys?'

'I don't know, Mummy.' Her small body shook with sobs and her fingers held mine.

'I need to find Polly.' I gently lay Amy on the ground. 'Phone the police, an ambulance.' I took out my phone and realised I had no signal. I was plunged into a fresh wave of despair, of hopelessness.

I wiped the rain from my eyes and scanned the cliff top for Polly who had disappeared. Edging slowly toward the edge, I realised I couldn't see the water below but I could hear its roar as it thrust against the rocks and echoed back through the narrow space.

'Oh god.'

I looked back at Amy, tears silently streamed down her face. 'Mummy, please. I want to go home.'

'I know,' I soothed, 'but you're safe now. You're safe with me.'

She gave a small agitated shake to the head. 'Mummy, I don't want to die.'

I forced a smile. 'You're going to be fine. Everything's going to be fine.' I swallowed. 'Do you remember that story I told you once?' As I spoke, I carefully backed away from the edge. 'The one about the girl who was a princess.'

'Yeah…' Amy looked uncertain.

'Do you remember how brave she had to be?'

Amy nodded. 'Yeah.'

'I need you to be like that girl, OK?' I needed to think: I needed to get Amy somewhere safe and warm, but I didn't think I had the strength to carry her back to the house.

'OK.'

'I need you to be the bravest you've ever been.' I drove the lump in my throat back down. 'It's all going to be OK.' I paused to think, panic muddying any clarity I needed in this situation. 'How did Polly get you into the car?'

'Polly?' The tremble in Amy's voice was too much for me and I fought to stay in control.

'That's her name, that's the woman who took you.' My heart wrung out with guilt and panic. 'I'm sorry I let it happen. She's mad.'

Amy furrowed her brow and nodded. 'OK, Mummy.'

'OK.' I forced a smile. 'I'm going to find her.'

'Mummy, I don't want to die, I can hear the water… I'm scared.' She let out a small whimper and closed her eyes.

I knew she was getting increasingly cold, her body had taken on a blue tinge, and her eyelids fluttered as she tried to keep them open.

'OK, I'm going to get you out of here.' I indicated toward the dirt track; the black pluming smoke of the burning car a little way beyond that. 'You are so much braver than the princess I told you about.'

I glanced over the side looking for Polly and, as I stepped backward again, rubble and stones fell into the water below. The moon shone brightly, glinting off the seawater and I could just make out a black silhouette sat on a ledge further down. The narrow rock shelf jutted out precariously above the dark eddying water.

'She's down there,' I whispered to Amy, my breathing heavy, as I watched the stone face shift beneath me again.

'Where?' Her eyelids opened slowly and she strained to look.

'On the rocks.'

Amy, thankfully, couldn't see what I could: Polly had made her way silently down the rock face and now stood looking up at us.

I closed my eyes, despair washing over me. In the distance, I thought I could hear the sound of a car approaching. Carefully, I peeled myself away from the cliff edge and stood up, so happy the police had found us of their own accord.

A black Mercedes sped toward us and I repositioned myself in front of Amy. The car came to a standstill and I waited, my skin crawling with fear. A leg emerged from the car. It was a man.

'Paul,' I gasped, 'what the hell are you doing here?'

'I got your voicemail.' He shook his head, his face flooded with concern. 'I couldn't live with myself if something happened.'

I didn't remember leaving a voicemail with Paul. 'I didn't.'

'You did, Sophie. It sounded like you had been drinking. You told me you came back to where Bethany died. The cliff.' His voice cracked. 'How did you know she killed herself here?' He looked out at the sea: black waves sucking everything away with them. He wiped his eyes with the back of his hand. 'God, what an awful way to die.' He studied my face. 'Sophie, we need to go home now.'

'I didn't call you!' I gave a small shake to my head. 'I've found Amy though, but you need to help me.'

Paul gasped and alarm and confusion simultaneously crossed his face as he spotted his daughter lying a few metres from me.

'Oh my god.' His breathing was quick and shallow. 'What have you done?'

'What? What do you mean? Polly did this.' My hand rested on my forehead.

'Amy, darling. I'm here.' He ran over to her and scooped her up.

'Daddy!' She smiled at him despite everything and it tore at my heart. She was so brave. 'Help me.' Amy looked at me now. 'Please help me, Daddy.'

Paul stepped toward me with Amy in his arms. 'Who the fuck is Polly?'

'There's a woman down there. Polly. She stalked me and Bethany at university, she's the one who killed Bethany. And she's about to do something stupid again.'

He watched me for a few seconds. 'Bethany?' He shook his head. 'Oh for god's sake, it doesn't matter now. Where, Sophie? Where is this woman?'

'Down there.' I pointed. 'She's not very well. She hears voices. Or, at least, that's what we were told. She's suffered with schizophrenia for most of her life and this,' I gestured to Amy, 'is because she has stopped taking her medication. She's never been good about taking it. Or, at least, that's what I was told at university.' I looked at him, hoping he was beginning to understand the urgency of the situation.

'Sophie, let's just get Amy out of here, OK?' He indicated his car.

'She's got a gun, Paul,' I said, 'You can't do anything sudden. We can't provoke her in case she harms us. She'll do it Paul, honestly. She hallucinates.'

It was all coming back to me: one night in our third year of university. The kind doctor in the hospital had explained it to me; that Polly had attempted to take her own life because of Bethany and me.

'Fine. Well, let's call the police. They need to know we've found Amy. That the woman who had her is here.' He paused. 'When did this woman last take any medication?' Paul's voice was high, the panic clear. 'Did she say?'

'I don't know. My guess is a while ago. Maybe weeks,' I said. 'It's all my fault.'

'Why is it your fault?' he said, his frustration mounting.

'I should have remembered, I should have guessed that she had been so obsessed with Bethany, so why wouldn't she be obsessed with me, too?'

'Oh, for fuck's sake, I'm getting you both out of here.'

'Paul,' I breathed heavily, then realised he was right: this was my fight, my problem. 'You're right, forget Polly, get Amy out of here. Now!'

'No, you're both coming with me. *Both* of you.'

I watched as Paul shifted Amy's limp body into one arm and came toward me, grabbing my wrist with his free hand.

CHAPTER 32

I gasped, took a step forward, tried to wriggle free from his steadfast grip. 'What are you doing? Just get Amy out of here.' My eyes flicked toward our daughter. 'I'll deal with this.'

'What happened there?' He nodded his head toward the smoke.

'My car spun out of control.'

'Oh god.' He looked at me, his face filled with determination. 'Sophie, this ends now. You're coming with me.'

I ignored him, tried to get him to understand he needed to leave with Amy. Get our daughter to a place of safety. 'Polly was in there too. We hit a tree…' I searched Paul's face, adrenaline rushing around my body at high speed: like a band ready to snap. 'But she's down there now, she made it away from the car, down the rock face. Can you see her?'

'Sophie,' Paul looked at me, his face as desperate as I felt, 'we need to forget about Polly and go.'

Amy whimpered and Paul walked over to his car and very gently lay Amy on the back seat, covering her in a blanket.

'Come on, Sophie.' He strode back over, his steps full of purpose.

'No, you two have to go now.' I looked at Amy. 'She needs to be taken to a hospital, get her checked over.

'Not without you. Come on, let's go.' Paul peered into the murky crevasse. 'I can't see her, Sophie, where is she?'

'Down there. You see where the rock juts out?'

Paul shook his head. 'No.' Then he shouted down, 'What do you want from us, Polly?'

Silence.

I realised then it was up to me, she didn't want to talk to Paul. She wanted to talk to me. 'Let me go. She won't talk to you, she doesn't know you.'

Paul glanced back at Amy and then at me. 'Sophie, I'm not going to let you go down there alone.'

'Just leave with Amy whilst I distract her. She's got a gun.' I looked at him, my eyes searching his desperately. 'Please.'

Turning away from him, I started to slowly clamber down the rock face, my feet scrabbling against the slippery, rough surface. The rain was no longer distinguishable from the sea spray that stung my face like thousands of tiny needles. My hands had gone numb with cold and my skin was raw from clutching the rocky outcrops. When I reached Polly, she was backing precariously over the edge.

'Get him away from here! This is not about Paul. Get rid of him,' Polly screamed at me.

I could feel sweat forming around my hairline despite the rain and icy temperature.

'Maybe you'd like to talk?' I suggested.

'No, Sophie, there's nothing to talk about. This is where it all ends. You die here, the same way Bethany died here.'

I gulped, moved a couple of steps closer. 'What do you want from me?'

A hysterical laugh echoed around the rocks. 'Do you want to save your precious little girl? Like you weren't able to save Bethany all those years ago.'

'Please, Polly,' I pleaded. 'I need to understand what I've done wrong.' Polly didn't say anything and I risked a glance at Paul, up at the top of the cliff. He was on his phone, he'd clearly managed to get some signal. I hoped Polly hadn't seen. I didn't know what she might do.

'OK, we can talk,' Polly said, 'but you have to come closer.'

My heart beat wildly as I stepped toward the edge. My breath caught as my foot slipped and I threw my arms up, desperately scrabbling in the air for balance. A fresh wave of adrenaline surged through my veins.

The rocks were treacherous, covered in seaweed and algae. Eventually I found a smooth face of rock and made the final slide toward her.

'Ah, Sophie,' Polly whispered, 'so nice of you to join me.'

Her voice took me back twenty years, to that very same gleeful whisper in my ear as she watched my best friend die.

'Polly.'

I looked down. The waves would show no mercy to anyone as they smashed against the rocks. If you were lucky, you'd fall straight into the water, die on impact. If you weren't, you'd hit the rocks as you went down before finally plummeting into the dark water. Either way, there was no coming back from the hellish pit below. The further I walked toward the narrowest section of the ledge, the faster the wind lashed past, throwing me off balance. Polly was now stood at the very end.

'Now can we talk?' I hollered, the salt from the sea gritty in my mouth.

'What's there really to talk about?' She threw her arms up and manically pointed to the air around her. 'Do you see them? The others? They're telling me to kill you too, Sophie. They *hate* you.'

My fingers fumbled against the rock face, struggling to steady myself. 'When did you stop taking your medication, Polly?'

She laughed wildly. 'Sophie, you are the person who needs to take their medication. I'm fine without it, so don't start preaching. When did you stop taking yours?'

'I stopped a month ago and I've been fine without it.'

'Your demons will come back to get you. Just you wait.'

'I know I've got my demons,' I said, honestly. 'But I also know you're the one who needs help here. Bethany's dead. There's nothing here for you, any more.'

'You still don't get it!' She staggered to one side and fell down onto her knees. Against the backdrop of the moon and the cobalt sky, her hair flying off to the side, she actually looked quite beautiful. In fact, I saw Bethany in her. They both had that reckless force that was both scary and alluring.

'I do because in some ways, I'm just like you!' I paused. 'I got jealous of Bethany too sometimes! She was always so beautiful, so in control. Everything I wasn't. She had her family and I didn't.' I thought of Paul, up at the top, looking after Amy, my family. 'Do your family know you are here, Polly?'

She looked at me suspiciously. 'Why are you being like this, Sophie? Why are you being so understanding? Why now?' She looked around her. 'I always wanted what you and Bethany had. You were like sisters. I wanted that. Bethany never seemed to appreciate she had a family who loved her. Never even appreciated you.'

I gazed at her, as if for the first time. 'I often felt the same way, that she was ungrateful. My parents were dead, but she never valued hers, never realised how lucky she was.'

'Mine too,' Polly admitted, her face lit up by the moon, an indescribable sadness passing over her features. It was like looking at myself.

I nodded, finally feeling as if I understood her. 'I wanted her looks, her brains, her courage.'

Polly stopped talking, taking this in.

'Why me though, Polly? Why did you come back for me? After all these years?'

'Because I know how unhappy you are. It's time to end everything. Do you think it's fair to allow everyone to worry about you all the time? Especially Amy…'

'No,' I said, shaking, tears beginning to stream down my face. 'Of course not.' I thought of my daughter waiting with Paul at the top of the cliff. 'I only ever wanted to be a good mother, but I can't do it. She needs more.'

Polly nodded, she jabbed at the air. 'I want the voices to stop but they keep telling me to do things, you see?'

'If you want to protect Amy, then why did you kidnap her, Polly? Why did you want to make my daughter suffer?'

'Because it was the only way to get you to sit up and listen. The only way you would realise that it's time to let her go. She's not yours to keep any more. She deserves more.'

I felt guilt wringing at my heart. Maybe she was right. I had to let Amy go, be free of all the problems I brought to her innocent life.

Polly threw her head back, looked up at the sky.

'Paul's up there. He's come to help us. To help me get Amy back.'

She looked back at me, annoyed. 'I don't think you're listening to me, Sophie. You need to let Amy go.'

'I will,' I shouted as the wind picked up again. 'I promise. But I have to get her to hospital first.' Something shifted in my stomach, a nervous sensation started to build.

'One last thing. Do you know why Zander employed you?'

'Because I was good at my job, because,' I tried to get some saliva moving around my mouth, 'because I reminded him of Bethany… I was a kind of comfort.' In my heart, I hated to admit that he might have taken me on for that reason alone, nothing to do with my degree or my ability to do law.

She stood up again and moved toward me. As she did so, the end of the ledge fell away, crashing into the rock below. Polly looked at where she had just been sitting – now air – and turned back to me. She wasn't frightened at all, I realised.

'Exactly, that's what your life has become. No parents, no Amy and a job where you remind someone of their dead daughter. Think about it, Sophie. Is that what you want? Does that sound right to you?' She laughed. 'It's quite macabre, don't you think? Keeping your dead daughter's friend on so he never has to really let go. That's all you are. A reminder of a dead person.'

My head was reeling, unable to believe that for twenty years I had been kept on in a job, given a great office, a fantastic salary, practically bought my house, all because I was just that: a dead woman's friend. I drew my hands around me, suddenly feeling exactly how wet and cold I actually was. Like a dark shadow had fallen across my path and I couldn't crawl fast enough to the warmth.

'That's not all,' Polly said. 'I killed Bethany that night, right here on this cliff. Where you're about to die. You were here, and you blacked out. Do you want to know why you blacked out?'

'Why?' I felt sick.

'Because I could see in your eyes, you wanted her dead too.'

'You're crazy.' Anger and hurt rattled through me. 'You are crazy.'

'No, Sophie, crazy is the fact that your friend died right here and a couple of hours later you went out clubbing. That's the definition of crazy. You met Paul that night. The man you would later spend years of your life with and he had no idea that you had been at the cliff where your friend fell hundreds of feet into nothingness.'

I stood frozen to the spot, looking down at the swirling water below. I shook my head. I refused to believe it was true. 'It's isn't true. You are SICK!' I shouted, tears streaming down my face, mingling with the salty air.

'Sophie,' came a voice from behind me.

I whipped around. 'Paul!' I moved toward him and stopped when I saw he was holding his phone up.

'I'm sorry, I've called the police,' he said. 'I had to do it. For everybody's sake.'

The crack of a gun stopped me in my tracks. Paul slumped to the ground. Polly walked toward me now, her face twisted, almost as if she was weeping.

'No!' I screamed, looking at Paul's still body, tears of unspoken regret and hurt streaming down my face.

Then I felt the gun against my own head, and I stood, slowly twisting my body around. Polly brushed the barrel against my stomach.

'Polly, I have a daughter up there who needs me. Do you want her to end up alone?' I looked at her steadily, trying to hold off the panic overwhelming me.

Polly lowered her head, visibly crying now.

'She needs me. Please don't do this.'

Polly pressed her lips together and as the tears subsided, an amazing serenity passed over her face. I dared not move and waited for her decision, my pulse racing. Polly lifted the gun and I closed my eyes, offering a silent prayer to Amy. I couldn't face looking down the barrel, like Bethany had all those year ago. I wasn't as brave as her.

Moments later, I heard the gunshot, but I was still standing. It was only when I heard the thump of Polly's lifeless body hitting the ground that I snapped my eyes open and I looked down. Her head was turned toward Paul's, a bullet between her eyes. Then, I watched in horror as her body slid over the cliff edge and into the churning water below.

EPILOGUE

It wasn't the same interview room. But I was sat opposite DI Ward again. I noticed, too, that this time there was a one-way mirror.

The detective looked worn. She was pacing the room, her fists bunched as though ready for a fight. I could see it was taking every inch of her being to control her anger toward me.

'We want to help you, Sophie,' she said again. 'But you have to help us.'

I snorted, the medication was wearing off: reality was starting to hit.

'We want to help you live with your daughter.' I knew it was a lie.

'Is she OK?' I asked again. 'Is Faye OK? When can I see Amy? I need to make sure she's happy. See her for myself.'

Amy was in Faye's care for the time being.

'Yes, she's fine. They're both fine.' The DI licked some spittle from her lip and sat down.

I nodded, my finger tracing an indent on the desk top. 'There's nothing more to say. I've told you everything.'

'It's just we've checked records, Sophie, and Polly doesn't exist. There was no Polly attending Aberystwyth University whilst you were there.'

'You just need to find the body.'

'Well, there are divers out there but it might be easier if you tell us the truth.'

I gripped the edge of the table, counted to three, and then dropped that and counted to four because counting to three didn't work. 'I am telling you the truth.' My words slurred slightly, the sedative was losing its grip.

She leant down and placed a plastic see-through bag on the table. Inside it had a black coat.

'That's Polly's coat!'

DI Ward smiled. 'It's got your hair on it, your fingerprints. Sophie, it's your coat.'

'No, it's not. It's Polly's.' I sighed deeply, this was taking a long time. The longer I was in here, the less time I was spending with Amy. She needed me.

DI Ward leant back in the chair, puffed out her cheeks and rubbed her forehead. 'It's just that until we find that body, if it exists, you are currently the only person at a murder scene. We need to find the body or even a record of this person that matches what you've told us.'

She brought out another bag, placed it on the table. Inside it were tweezers and gloves, and the now familiar paper that Polly's notes had been formed on.

'You've found evidence then,' I said, relieved. 'There you go, that should help you.'

'Yes,' DI Ward nodded, 'at Shamrock Place. The place is derelict now.' She grimaced, her knuckles turning white as she gripped the bag even tighter. 'I've found a record that you were a patient there as a child. Why didn't you ever tell anyone about your condition, Sophie? Not even Paul?'

Panic clawed at me. 'What condition?' I straightened my back and looked desperately around me. 'Where's Darren? I want to talk to Darren, he's the only one I trust. I want to talk to him alone. He knew about the medication, he knew everything.'

'Darren can't help you now.'

'Why not?' I said, fear rising in my throat.

'He's referring you to a unit where they might be able to help you on a more permanent basis.'

I sensed someone shift behind the mirror and I knew that it was over. Standing up, I shouted and screamed, my own voice echoing around my head. I even clawed at the table whilst two officers tried to restrain me. Someone put a pill on my tongue and pushed a water bottle toward my mouth. I glugged it back, and waited. Waited for my body to grow numb, but it never numbed my mind, and that was where the problem lay.

If you loved *S is for Stranger* then turn the page for an exclusive extract from Louise Stone's chilling new psychological thriller, *Never Out of Sight*.

I would my soul were like the bird
That dares the vastness undeterred.

The Daring One, *Edwin Markham*
The Gates of Paradise and Other Poems (1928)

FIVE MONTHS AGO

The fly buzzed around him, its incessant hum thundering loudly in his ear, but still he dared not move. His eyes wandered momentarily from the woman standing in front of him – her full lips glistening with saliva – to the window. The room was airless. He knew the fly would die. Sensing the hopelessness of the situation, the fly returned to the window – firmly shut – and slammed against the windowpane once more. The April sun shone brightly outside, lighting up the room, warming his office further. He noticed the dust dancing in the stale air, and returned his attention to his captor.

'You need to leave,' he said.

His body had grown sticky, nervous energy emanating from his every pore. He slowly lifted his hand and placed a finger between his shirt collar and bare skin, moved it back and forth; seeking relief from the starchy material.

She smiled knowingly at him. 'You don't want that.'

He dropped his hand, laid it on his thigh and willed his leg to stop shaking. 'This isn't right.'

She reached behind her, felt for the key, and turned it in the lock. Click. Her gaze remained on him. 'You've wanted this for a long time, Gareth.'

He gave a small shake to his head. However, knowing he needed to be clear, he shook his head again, with greater force. 'Rosamund, I have never wanted this. Any of this. You have clearly misinterpreted something I've said.'

He had reverted to the tone he used in lectures. Matter-of-fact.

She walked to the edge of the sofa and sat, crossing her long, shapely legs. He wished she wouldn't sit there. Not like this. Only an hour ago, she had sat in the same position, her knees together, laughing softly at a joke her colleague had made about HenryVIII.

Now, it was different. It was wrong.

She leant back in the cushions and he noticed the way her shorts rode up. He knew he shouldn't look, that it would only make matters worse. He couldn't tear his eyes away as the frayed denim crept up her smooth skin. Forcing himself to swallow, he tried to forget how good her skin had felt. Then, he saw it. He gasped.

A wry smile spread across her face. 'You remember?'

He nodded.

'I knew you'd like it.' Her slender hand rubbed the area where the new tattoo prickled angrily. 'I had it done yesterday. The guy,' she laughed, 'asked me why I wanted it. Told me, he'd done a few Latin quotes before. All the normal ones: "Seize the day" and all that.' She grew serious. 'It's right, isn't it? The Latin, I mean.'

His throat had closed up, his mouth cotton-dry. 'The kiss of death.' He looked away, concentrating on the fly once more. 'It means the kiss of death.' He eyed the glass of water on his desk, yearned to drink from it.

'That's what you said to me. That night. You said kissing me was the kiss of death.'

His breathing had started to quicken, his head reeling. He needed air.

She rose from the sofa and edged toward him, stopping a foot short of his chair. 'Gareth, you called it that because it felt right.'

He gave a sharp shake to his head. 'No, I called it that because my wife was in the next room talking to my colleagues, to your friends, the other students, and...' He stopped, let out a long, shuddering breath. 'If she found out, my marriage would be over.'

She placed her finger under his chin and lifted his face, giving him no option but to stare into her eyes. They were a deep blue. But he already knew that.

'You wanted it as much as I wanted it. I felt it.' She smiled again, her ridiculous youthful excitement shining through. 'I felt you *respond*.' She whispered this last word. He understood, now, what it meant when people claimed that it had only taken one second for their whole world to come crashing down around them.

She was pushing him. Threatening him.

He needed to take control. His voice, however, had given over to fear.

'Do you want to kiss me now?'

He shook his head vehemently. 'No.'

'I know you're fighting your real feelings.' Her words were clipped: a line she had practised, perhaps, to make herself believe it was true. Or was it?

'Rosamund, you need to leave or I will have to call someone in here.' He waited a beat and, when she didn't move, he tried again. 'I'm asking you to leave. This is wrong.'

She dropped her hand and took a step backward, a small whine escaping her lips. 'This is not wrong, Gareth. Wrong is you taking advantage of me, wrong is you wanting me even though I am your student.' She released an abrupt laugh and his eyes snapped toward her. 'In fact, what you did is illegal.'

He stood now, forcing his jelly-like legs to display some sort of fight. 'It wasn't illegal, Rosamund. Unethical, perhaps. Illegal? No.' He realised he may have admitted to something and he stammered. 'Y-you you were very forceful, I didn't intend for anything to happen. You,' he paused, 'consented.'

She narrowed her eyes. 'I'll give you one last chance, *Professor.*' He flinched at her sarcasm. She then giggled: he was amazed at her ability to shift effortlessly from one mood to another. 'I know you want me and I know you don't want to be with your wife any more.' Her hand toyed with her necklace. 'I'm not unethical. I've been brought up a good Christian girl, see?' She lifted the gold chain and a small charm – a cross – swung in the air, catching the sunlight momentarily. 'For me, you're everything that's *right* in the world.'

'You're twenty-one, Rosamund. You've got your whole life ahead of you. I'm almost fifty.'

She laughed; it had the same joyful lightness that he had noticed in September when she first arrived at their weekly seminar.

'You're bored in your marriage. I can understand that. I mean, that's what happens, isn't it? You're probably thinking, why doesn't Sue put any effort in any more? I expect you haven't had sex in years.'

Shame washed over him as he remembered the times he had thought just that. 'Please don't use her name.'

'Why?' Rosamund raised an eyebrow, challenging him. 'Because it makes what you did more real?' She furrowed her brows. 'I mean, what *was* she wearing at the college ball?'

He thought back to Sue's dress: she had had it for years. 'I thought she looked wonderful, she always does.' He spoke vacuously: a well-rehearsed line. He remembered

thinking that the dress no longer fitted her properly. If he
was honest, yes, he had noticed she bulged in places she
hadn't used to.

'I don't believe you. Did she look as good as me?'

'I have no opinion of how you looked.' He dropped his
gaze to the floor, heat creeping up his neck.

'You told me I looked beautiful.' She pouted and
scratched her arm. 'Beautiful. I remember you saying it
and I felt… Do you know what I felt?'

He didn't respond.

'I felt like the happiest, luckiest girl in the world.'

'You need to go.'

She clenched her jaw. 'I'll tell her. I'll tell your wife.'

His chest grew tight and he glanced at the framed photo
of Sue on his desk. 'You can't do that.'

'I can. You led me on.'

'I have done nothing of the sort.' He turned to face her,
his eyes focused on the painting behind her. 'You must stop
this ridiculous, girlish behaviour.'

She watched him steadily, her face twitching with
mounting anger. 'I could make your life hell.'

His mind whirred. Any clarity muddied as soon as she
had shut the door to his office and turned the key in the
lock. 'Why would you want to be with me, anyway? I don't
go out, I don't do the things guys of your age do. And,' he
faltered, 'I don't feel that way about you.' He placed a hand
on the filing cabinet, grateful for the cool of the metal.
'You will find someone who loves you, who's just like you.
I can't give you any of those things.' His words settled in
the still air. He could hear Simon in the corridor. 'There are
people around.' He wasn't sure if he said this to calm his
own jagged nerves or to warn her off.

'I don't care who's around.' She walked calmly to
the window, lifted the lever and pushed it open. The fly,

barely alive, responded to the rush of air and flew drowsily outside.

Perspiration clung to his upper lip as he watched her close the window once more. He rubbed the base of his back with his shirt, stopping a trickle of sweat in its tracks.

'I'll call security,' he eventually said.

She laughed: hollow, disbelieving. 'No, you won't.'

'How can you be so sure?' His voice cracked involuntarily. 'I'm well within my rights to call security, now that I've asked you to leave.'

She curled her lips. 'I'll tell them what you did.'

His heart hammered in his chest. 'I didn't do anything.' He glanced at the necklace, at the cross.

She caught his look and frowned. 'You don't seem to realise what you've done.'

'I shouldn't have allowed anything to happen. I knew it was as much a mistake then, as I do now.'

'Then why do you look at me like that? Even with the others here, I see you looking at me, I can feel your eyes on me.'

Fear pricked his skin; a wave of goose bumps travelled across his arms and the length of his back. She moved toward him and placed a hand at the base of his neck, her fingers softly massaging his hairline.

'Please get off,' he whispered hoarsely, his eyes briefly closing and giving in to her touch. 'Please.'

'Gareth.' She continued to ply his skin with increasing urgency as she shifted forward once more, her breasts grazing his shirt. 'You want me. You want this again.'

His breathing came hard and fast. 'Get off.' He couldn't touch her. He knew he couldn't touch her. 'Get off.'

'Gareth.' She brought her lips toward his and lingered above his mouth, her breath sweet – the smell of cheap candy – enticingly close. 'Gareth.' She brushed her lips against his and he stumbled backward toward the desk, his hand knocking the penholder – a gift from his daughter, made at school – to the ground. He looked desperately at the broken clay shards, back at her.

'No. No. No,' he gasped. 'Get out.'

She didn't move, her face twisted with fury and hate. Any thoughts he'd had of her face reflecting a youthful lightness were tainted forever.

'Get out,' he said again, pleading.

She nodded slightly and moved toward the door. Turning, she looked back at him.

'You will regret this. You'll lose your job. You'll lose everything.' Her hand inadvertently touched the tattoo and she rubbed it: an indelible reminder of their affair. 'You will regret this.'

She turned the key and, pushing her shoulders back, left. The door remained wide open.

He waited, his ragged breath echoing in his ears. Believing he was now safe, he strode to the door and slammed it shut, turning the key once more. He stumbled to the sofa and sat, elbows on his knees, his hands over his face. Warm tears soaked his skin.

He wanted to tell himself that it would blow over, that her words were empty, unthinking. He couldn't. Instead, his mind was racked by an image of her naked body lying on the hotel bed, the smell of coconut on her skin, limbs tangled in damp sheets.

ONE

Truth or dare. That had been the choice.

Keira Sullivan stood halfway up the hill, balancing on tiptoes, her hands gripping the handlebars of her bike. She jerked her head toward the farm, a sixties bungalow nestled in the dip, a few metres away.

'He's there,' she mouthed.

Zoe nodded and smiled conspiratorially at her friend. 'You dare me?'

Keira wasn't sure any more. 'You could just tell the truth.' She glanced at the farmyard again and could make out the figure of a man working outside. A pale-coloured sheepdog ran frenetically around the yard and she glimpsed several other dogs, in kennels, whining noisily off to the right of the house. A small radio sat on the ground where the man worked and, although she couldn't distinguish the tune, she caught the odd note on the wind.

'Ask me again,' Zoe said.

'OK.' Keira hoped her friend would just answer and then they could go home. 'How many times have you –' she began. But, before Keira could finish her sentence, Zoe was off, freewheeling the short distance to the farm gates. Keira jumped up onto her saddle and pedalled quickly to catch up. Keira came to a halt a few feet from Zoe.

Zoe stopped abruptly, in view of the farmer. His name was Jerry Wyre. Keira knew that much and, rumour was, he beat his wife. Keira also knew that, if the rumours were true, then they were playing a very dangerous game. Keira watched, in horror, as Zoe hitched her already short skirt up.

He refused to look in her direction. Instead, he continued to tighten the bolts on a rusting tractor, his eyes never leaving the job in hand. This was not the first time they had ridden by the farm this summer. Most days they headed in the direction of Blackwood Forest and sat at the top of Dyers Hill, looking out over the vale. Having spotted Jerry the first time, it hadn't taken long for him to become an object of fascination. Keira's cheeks grew warm just thinking about some of the sordid conversations they'd had about the man.

Zoe looked at Keira and smiled, before shouting over to Jerry.

'Hi.'

He stopped; his shoulders remained hunched and his eyes stayed with the tractor. Zoe continued to watch him, her hand resting on the top of her thigh. Keira willed her friend to turn away. She wondered, now, if it was easier for Zoe to complete the dare, rather than answer the question, rather than tell her the truth. She couldn't imagine they kept any secrets from one another.

Keira trusted Zoe with her life. Yet, now, she wondered if Zoe was keeping something from her. That thought alone lodged a ball of unease in her stomach. Why couldn't Zoe just answer the question? Keira had asked because it seemed harmless. But Keira had seen the momentary look of fear in Zoe's eyes. It had been fleeting, but she had seen it.

Keira watched Zoe lick her lips, perhaps nervously, though it looked lascivious, and wait for a reaction. Zoe was stubborn; she wouldn't leave easily. Keira should have known this was a stupid dare. Zoe was unlike other girls she knew, unafraid of her sex appeal, and Jerry was undeniably attractive in an older man (she could hear her mother calling him a 'working-man') kind of a way.

Jerry eventually raised his head and stared in her direction. He appeared to look through her, no visible emotion. 'What do you want?'

Keira noticed that his voice was deep, rough with an Irish lilt.

'Mr Wyre,' began Keira. She could hear the sing-song, mocking tone in her friend's words, and grimaced. 'Keira and I were wondering if there were any jobs you'd like us to help you with on the farm?' Zoe looked over at Keira, a smirk on her face.

She had completed the dare.

Keira struggled to keep an evenness to her voice. 'Come on, Zoe. We need to get back.'

'Mr Wyre?' Zoe prompted.

He stared hard at Zoe, his face stony. 'Go away. I've seen you girls passing by here. We don't want any trouble.'

Keira's heart pounded as she silently urged Zoe to give up.

'We just want to help out. We don't mean any harm.' Zoe flashed him a smile and Keira pushed down the pulsing anxiety at the base of her throat.

'Go away.'

'Fine,' Zoe said, a haughty edge to her voice. 'Your loss.' She manoeuvred the bike forty-five degrees so that the handlebars faced Jerry, and placed her right foot on the pedal, rotating it slowly until it reached its full height. Zoe cocked her head to one side. 'You know, it's not very gentlemanly to be looking up a lady's skirt.'

Keira sat back on her bike and wobbled forward. She wanted to grab Zoe by the sleeve of her shirt and drag her away. Jerry remained unmoving, except for the rise and fall of his chest.

A woman appeared at the front door to the bungalow, her fingers kneading the edge of a tea towel.

'Everything OK?' the woman asked in a small voice.

'Just fine,' he replied, his eyes fixed on the girls.

'What do you girls want here? Are you bothering my husband?'

Zoe smiled. 'We're just asking if we can help around the farm.'

'Shouldn't you be at school? How old are you, anyway?' the woman asked.

'Fifteen,' Zoe said. 'School starts in a couple of days. We didn't mean any harm.'

'Eleanor, go inside,' Jerry said to the woman.

She looked momentarily unsure, nodded and returned indoors, leaving the door open.

'Go away. Leave us alone,' he said.

Zoe shrugged, remounted her bike and sped off. Keira rode wordlessly behind her, stopping only once by the sign welcoming visitors to Chilcote village.

'I can't believe you just did that.' Keira shook her head in disbelief. 'I didn't think you would do it.'

Zoe laughed loudly. 'You dared me. You said, "Go and talk to Jerry Wyre", so I did.'

Keira swallowed. 'I also asked you a question. I thought you would take the question.'

Zoe's face hardened. 'No.'

'Right.' Keira was at a loss for words.

'Anyway,' Zoe said, relaxing, 'he's not bad-looking. I was quite enjoying myself.'

'Why won't you answer the question?'

Zoe murmured, 'Because you wouldn't want to know the truth.' She got back on her bike. 'See you, Keira.'

'Zoe,' Keira shouted after her.

Zoe stopped, looked over her shoulder and stared at the ground. 'You know, it's just the one.'

Keira knew she was lying. She had known her friend for long enough to know that much. 'It was just a silly question, Zoe. Let's forget about it, yeah?'

Zoe's face brightened. 'Yeah.'

'Anyway, you completed the dare.' Keira smiled. 'Never thought you'd do it.'

Zoe rode off, shouting, 'Double-dare me to go back?' She waved as she turned the corner.

Keira put her hand up in farewell. They had come up with four rules, sworn on each other's lives never to break.

1. If a dare was completed: they win a packet of cigarettes.

2. Double-dare: the initial dare was completed, they could take the same dare further.

3. If a double-dare was completed: they win five packets of cigarettes or get their homework done by the other for two nights.

4. They would destroy all evidence of truth or dare.

Truth. That's all Keira had wanted. She had been sure of Zoe's answer and, now, she knew Zoe was holding back. She didn't know everything about her best friend and, acknowledging this, hurt twisted in her stomach. Zoe was meant to be the one reliable person in her life, the person who had made the last few months bearable, and now she suddenly felt so alone. What had Zoe meant by 'You wouldn't want to know the truth'? That's exactly what she did want to know. Maybe Zoe had kept it from her because she knew Keira was a virgin. Keira thought this unfair.

She had told Zoe about her crush on Todd, a guy in her year. They had moved into the village in early June, just as the media attention on her family had, thankfully, started to fade away because the girl, Rosamund, her father's student, had dropped the charge. Keira had only spoken to Todd a couple of times, when he had been walking up the hill from school by himself. Otherwise, the couple of times she had seen him with his mother in town, he had ignored her. He probably, like most kids at her school, had been told to avoid the Sullivan family.

'*OK, Zoe, truth: how many times have you had sex?*'

Keira rode home, feeling miserable, realising she hadn't been told the answer after all.

Keira hadn't turned her phone on all evening, or most of the next day. She had wanted to shut herself away from it all. It was easy to hide in her room these days, ever since her parents had stopped having evening meals together. Ever since her father had started drinking more heavily. *Ever since...* Those two words preceded everything in her life now.

It was as if life just changed overnight. One week in April, a sweltering week, unusually hot for spring, it was as if nature had been trying to warn her. Before she had arrived home to the news about her father, she had been in town after school with Zoe. They had picked out a couple of crop-tops from New Look and sat outside Costa Coffee drinking iced coffee (even though she didn't like the taste, but it felt grown-up), and smoking. Bliss. She had spotted Todd in the record store where he worked. Zoe must have caught her looking, because that's when she started the ribbing. Keira didn't mind. Zoe was her best friend and she had always told her everything.

Keira brushed a tear from her cheek, waiting for her phone to ping to life. Two new messages. Zoe had sent her videos. One lasted a minute. The next was four and a half. Keira checked the time. They had been sent an hour ago.

Zoe's face appeared on the screen. 'Hi, Ki-Ki. Look where I am.'

Keira peered more closely as Zoe held the phone away from her face and directed it toward the open space behind her. The farmyard. Keira's pulse quickened as she was hit by the realisation that Zoe had returned to the farm today. Alone.

Zoe's face filled the screen once more. 'OK, here I go.'

The image then darkened and the sound muffled. Keira desperately turned the volume up to its max.

She could hear a woman's voice. It could be Jerry's wife.

Zoe reappeared and she was laughing. 'Already been told off,' she whispered, clearly enjoying herself.

The video stopped.

Keira opened the next one and waited.

Zoe reappeared and Keira felt a heady rush of relief at seeing her friend's smiling face. 'Right, I'm off to find Jerry.' The shot moved up and down with the pounding of Zoe's feet over tarmac, then over a stile and along what looked like the edge of a field.

After a couple of minutes, Zoe spoke into the phone. 'There he is.'

Zoe angled the phone so that Keira could see Jerry sitting up against the front wheel of his tractor; his eyes were shut and his face tilted up to the sunshine. He must have heard Zoe's footsteps and he brought his head up.

'Go away.'

'Is that all you're going to say to me?' Zoe's voice was tinged with sullenness.

'Leave me alone.' He jerked his head toward the phone. 'What are you doing with that thing?'

'It's a phone.'

'Get lost. Girls like you are trouble.'

The image was lost as Keira presumed Zoe had dropped her phone into her pocket. Keira held the phone up to her ear, their conversation inaudible. Then, the video cut out.

Keira started a new message, her hands clammy.

R U OK?

She rose from her bed and waited for Zoe to text back. Keira looked out her bedroom window at the dusky sky, the gentle pitter-patter of rain on the glass.

Keira's phone beeped.

DOUBLE-DARE COMPLETE. Z xx

Keira smiled and deleted the videos. She would buy Zoe her cigarettes tomorrow.

TWO

The weather had turned overnight. Keira's cheeks tingled as the chilly air whipped against her skin. The orange-brown leaves, previously hanging onto the remnants of summer, had started to fall. The thin wheels of Keira's bike skidded over the crunchy layer covering the ground and, minutes later, she was outside the farm buildings. The front yard was empty, the tractor standing alongside the barn. She noticed the dogs were quiet and the sheepdog was nowhere to be seen.

Unsure of herself, she dismounted and leant her bike up against the wall. She looked up toward Charlcombe Manor, the large estate that sat on the outskirts of Chilcote. As her eyes fell away from the large house and focused on the bungalow once more, Keira was sure she saw a curtain twitch. Fearing Mrs Wyre might come out again, Keira made a move to grab her bike.

Zoe's text had read:

Come to the farm.

She wheeled her bike further away from the farmyard and caught sight of the stile Zoe had videoed yesterday. Keira leant her bike up against the stone wall, climbed over the stile and walked up the side of the field. It was surreal following in Zoe's ghostly footsteps. The September sunshine was warm on her face and the only sound, other than the cawing of rooks overhead, was her feet hitting the dry ground.

Wheat lined the field, but it hadn't been harvested yet. It had been an unusually wet summer and many of the local farmers were holding out a bit longer to give it an opportunity to dry in the autumn sunshine. Keira's right hand caressed the tops of the wheat crop as she walked. The husks felt rough to the touch. The browns and yellows of wheat and rape were sewn into the land like a patchwork quilt.

After a mile or so, Keira came across a wooded area and, as she entered, the temperature cooled and the air felt damp. The sun was unable to reach through the canopy of trees and, where it had, the light was dappled. The fallen branches were covered in lichen and moss, the earth softer. Above, the rooks circled the wood. Keira watched them, a shiver running through her. As they called to one another, Keira thought how the noise resembled shrieking children. *Caw. Caw. Caw.*

Keira stopped, wondering where on earth Zoe had got to.

'Hello.'

Keira spun around and came face to face with Jerry.

'I didn't s-s-see you coming.'

'I live and work here. I'm never far away,' said Jerry.

She smiled, nervous chatter building inside her head. 'I'm looking for my friend.'

He cocked his head to one side. 'Why would she be up here?'

Keira's mouth turned dry. 'Not sure, really,' she lied.

'Yes.' He stepped closer. 'Not safe, these woods.' His hooded eyes conveyed no emotion.

She glanced upward. The rooks overhead had grown in number and some sat on the highest boughs of the forest trees. A group of twelve or so circled above the forest's awning.

Jerry pointed at the birds. 'They've found it.'

Keira tensed. 'What have they found?'

'The deer.'

'Deer?'

He focused on her, his eyes steady. 'Shot a sick deer earlier. They'll be tearing it up.'

A sour taste had developed in her mouth, its acridity lingering at the back of her throat. 'I really had better get going.' Keira gulped, urging saliva to travel down her throat. 'Bye,' she squeaked and rushed past Jerry, in the direction she had come. She smelt the stale sweat coming off his clothing, mingled with cigarette smoke. Her stomach lurched and she broke into a run. She made her way past the wheat and rape fields. The sun had disappeared behind the clouds and, now, the rape did not glisten, the wheat did not appear at all idyllic.

She could see the stile and quickened her pace. Her bike remained propped up against the wall and, breathing heavily, her heart thundering, she jumped on and pedalled fast away from the farm.

She stopped on the edge of Chilcote and withdrew her phone from her jacket pocket. The phone rang through to voicemail.

'Zoe, it's me. Ring me when you get this.' Keira forced her breathing to slow. 'I went to the farm, went up the side of the field. I couldn't see you.' She paused and added, 'Please ring me. I'm worried.'

Zoe would laugh at her when she got the message. *Worried?* She would tell Keira no one ever need worry about her. With that thought in mind, Keira headed back home, to Rose Cottage, stopping briefly to buy cigarettes from the small corner shop. The owner, Mr Rees, had no idea how old she was. He had been selling her and Zoe cigarettes for over two years.

Keira stuffed them into her inside pocket and headed home. If Zoe continued to see through double-dares, Keira thought smiling, she would have to rob a bank. No point asking her parents for more pocket money. Ever since her dad had been asked to leave the college, they had halved her pocket money and tightened their purse strings. She would have to do Zoe's homework instead. Hopefully, she thought, Zoe would just tell the truth.

As she rounded the corner, she was surprised to see both her parents' cars outside Rose Cottage. They had all left the house at the same time. It had been early, the sky etched with pinks and greys. Her mother should have been at the library where she worked and, this morning, she had a meeting. Her father was out every day, looking for work – although, from the smell of whiskey on his breath, Keira was sure that he spent his days in the pub. Nevertheless, he had climbed into his beaten-up Volvo this morning and trundled off down the road.

She dropped her bike on the grass and ran inside, barely managing to stop herself colliding with her mother in the hall.

'Keira,' her mother said gravely. 'Have you seen Zoe?'

'Wh-wh-what do you mean?' Keira drew her jacket around her, the cellophane wrapping of the cigarette packets crunching against her T-shirt, her heart quickening.

'Cathy received a text from Zoe last night saying she was staying with us, that she had grabbed some clothes and that she'd come here.' She put a hand on Keira's shoulder. 'Do you know anything about this?'

'I was here all night. You know that.'

Her mother nodded. 'That's what I told her. I told her that we hadn't seen Zoe.' She clutched her throat with her hand. 'Obviously, I wanted to check with you first… Seeing as she might have been here and…'

Keira wanted to finish the sentence off for her mother: *She might have been here and we wouldn't have noticed, because we wouldn't notice if you came back with a nose-piercing. Ever since...*

Her mother shot Keira a look of regret and Keira wished her mother would stop; she didn't want her mother's pity. She fixed her eyes on Keira as if she could see the fag packets under the denim of her jacket.

'Do you have any idea where Zoe might be?'

Keira looked at the floor and thought about rule four: destroy the evidence. The videos... Her mind flitted to Jerry Wyre. He had appeared, suddenly at her side, and there had been something about him that had creeped her out. Keira shook her head.

'I don't know where she is,' she said, her eyes not meeting her mother's, and she went upstairs.

Zoe couldn't be missing. She had texted her:

DOUBLE-DARE COMPLETE. Z xx

She had asked Keira to come to the farm...

Keira was hit by the sudden realisation that Zoe might not have sent the texts. That Zoe might never have completed the double-dare. That Zoe wasn't on the other end of her phone.

ACKNOWLEDGEMENTS

I am enormously grateful to the following people:

Charlotte Mursell, my fantastic editor, for believing in this story and helping make it what it is today.

The rest of the brilliant team at Carina UK.

My incredibly loving and patient family. My brother, Edward, for his brilliant sense of humour and my parents, for believing in me.

Also, my gorgeous son, Finn, who provides me with laughter and love on even the most challenging days.

Last and – as the saying goes – certainly not least, to my partner in crime, Jon, whose unwavering support from the get go has been amazing and who is, quite simply, my rock.